The Things That Grow With Us

Jordan Anderson

If you like what you read, or even if you hate it, please consider reviewing it on Amazon or wherever you purchased it from.
Every review counts.

jordanandersonfiction.com
Contact: jordan@jordanandersonfiction.com

Cover art by Vlad Mel
Cover design by Jelzoo.com

ISBN: 0-9983541-1-2
ISBN-13: 978-0-9983541-1-8

Foreword

Some quick thanks to my writers group (Matt, Katie, Michael, Nathan, Quinn, Nikki, Lindsey, Val and Lily) as well as my mother for her edits and my father for his unrelenting support. Thanks to those who beta-read my stories. The feedback and criticism was invaluable to this process. To everyone I didn't mention, thank you for the encouragement.

Thank you so much, reader, for your interest in these stories. It means more than I can say. Lumped together like this, this collection feels like some sort of offspring I'm letting go of. New stories are calling to me, though. I hope you enjoy your time with these as I did.

Jordan Anderson

"I created the Event Horizon to reach the stars, but she's gone much, much farther than that. She tore a hole in our universe, a gateway to another dimension. A dimension of pure chaos. Pure... evil. When she crossed over, she was just a ship. But when she came back... she was alive. Look at her, Miller. Isn't she beautiful?"

—Dr. Weir, *Event Horizon* (1997)

The Further We Soar Into Madness

"At this horror I sank nearly to the lichened earth, transfixed with a dread not of this or any world, but only of the mad spaces between the stars."
—*The Festival*, H. P. Lovecraft

"Mr. Jamison?"

From one of the three red cushioned chairs in the dimly lit lobby of the Pratt & Rochester building, a young man glanced up toward the voice. The neon blues and oranges of the datapad he held in his lap shined like a kaleidoscope in his piercing eyes. He stood, clicked the datapad to sleep and slid it into the leather bag hanging from his shoulder. He did not respond to the inquiry but simply walked toward its source at the south side of the lobby.

The light on the wall just above the elevators illuminated with an off-hue orange. The young man could see the woman who had spoken his name standing underneath. As he approached, she took a breath before beginning her spiel.

"Mr. Jamison, on behalf of us here—"

"What floor?" he interrupted.

The practiced expression on the woman's face was stunned momentarily. When her expression threatened a sour look, the young man's indifferent gaze did not falter or lose its focus. He simply stared at her.

"Uh, oh, uh, right. Yes. This way, please," she stammered. Her words and her movements were frantic with a type of anxiety that set the young man's irritations on fire by proximity alone. Being near any individual void of real confidence was like listening to a baby scream at the top of its lungs. It was like being near someone sick with a type of infection, like one could smell it on a person if one paid attention. "You'll be meeting with Mr. Rochester, himself. He personally handled your father's estate." She reached for the elevator buttons and the fake smile had returned to her face when she looked back to him. The button labeled '23F' was the only one lit amongst the dormant rows of plastic bulbs. At the bottom of the panel, below B1 and B2, was a button labeled LIBRARY - C12 ACCESS ONLY.

There was a *ding* and the doors opened. The young man followed his escort into the elevator. His expression did not change but the fingers of his right hand extended and contracted at his side and his teeth ground the entire way up. When they reached the top floor, he didn't wait for her but simply stepped out of the elevator and moved toward the large oak door at the end of the hall. The woman followed quickly after.

"Here we are, Mr. Jamison," she said, speaking as if he wasn't already moving toward their destination. "This is Mr. Rochester's office. If I may, can I get you anything to drink or someth—"

The young man reached his hand out, turned the knob and stepped in. He shut the door and the woman's face disappeared along with her voice behind him.

The man in the chair on the other side of the wide oak desk was already watching his guest over glasses that sat low on his nose. He wore a white button up shirt with a dark red tie. In his hands, he held what appeared to be some old parchment, laminated for preservation.

"Ah, Edward," the man said. He removed his glasses and motioned to one of the two leather chairs in front of the desk as he stood. "Please, have a seat."

The young man did not move but remained where he was just inside the door. He regarded the man standing behind the desk with a calculated gaze. After a long moment in which only the air conditioning whir and the patter of rain on the windows was audible, he spoke:

"You must be Rochester."

"That I am, good sir!" The man moved around the desk toward

his guest with his hand extended, gold rings glinting on his middle and ring fingers, accompanied by a wide greasy smile on his face. "Walton Rochester, son of Albert Rochester, the very man who started the original firm over forty—"

"I don't care."

The man stopped in mid-step and went silent, his hand still extended for a brief moment before slowly lowering. His expression was one of surprise, then of irritation. "Now you listen—"

"No, *you* listen to *me*." The young man's eyes were vicious, almost predatory. "I don't give a fuck how many clients your firm has or what font the letters of your name are on the side of the building. A series of phone calls and I could have you on the corner of Welsher Avenue begging for street change by lunch hour. I am here for one reason and one reason only. You know who I am. You know who my father was. Do not waste my *fucking* time."

A tense silence lay between them in the air. Rochester looked stunned. His mouth moved a few times as if he were going to say something else in retaliation, along with his face exhibiting no less than five different expressions. After a long pause, he sighed and nodded with a forced smile. "Yes, Mr. Jamison."

A few moments later, Rochester's assistant left a small safety deposit box on the oak desk as well as three folders of various paperwork and files. Edward Jamison stood behind one of the two leather chairs, staring at the items that had been delivered and laid out before him.

"And I'm sure I don't need to tell you, Mr. Jamison," Rochester said, "but do not hesitate to ask if you need anything and, uh... I'm sorry for your loss." At that, the lawyer cowered out of his own office, gently closing the large door behind him.

The room fell once more into silence and Edward remained still. Behind the ornate desk, wide panoramic windows looked out over the damp sprawling metropolis. Rain flowed in streams down the cold glass. The sky was grey and overcast and the other skyscrapers in view appeared monochromatic in comparison to the warm glow of the wall lamps inside the office. The carpet below the young man's shoes was a deep blue and the walls were painted burgundy, with various achievements and certificates framed and hung on either side of the entrance at his back. He moved around the front of the first leather chair and sat down, eyes still fixated on the grey world outside. For the greater part of a minute, he let the dull overcast light saturate his sight, feeding his stimuli with a cold meditative comfort.

The latch of the deposit box clicked loudly before he pulled open the lid. Laying against the bottom of the container was a manila envelope and on top of that was a data card and an object wrapped in a thin magenta cloth. The piece of fabric was smooth to the touch and practically dripped off of the object when he picked it up, revealing what was actually two items concealed by it: a small stone sculpture of some kind and a large amulet, encased in worn gold and attached to a rusting necklace chain. The gem in the center of the amulet was immaculate, glinting deep emerald green in the low office light. The small stone sculpture was brown in color and the rock it was made of was porous, ancient. The shape roughly resembled that of a human skull except that it was missing the jawbone. Instead of two normal incisors among the few that were etched into the thing, it had a single large one that protruded from the center of the mandible under the nose like some long fang. It was a depiction of a type of deformity or some imaginative dogma. Edward placed both the amulet and the stone effigy onto the table next to the storage box then removed the data card, turning it over in his fingers before placing it on the table as well.

The manila envelope was sealed with a hardened splotch of black candle wax, emblazoned with the relief of his father's ring. He recognized the image of the ram's head from which familiar horns spiraled and the wax crumbled as he ran his finger along the inner flap, falling in bits to the table below. He slipped his hand into the envelope and returned with a stack of handwritten pages bound together with a hard plastic clip. The pages were crisp and the handwriting elegant.

It was his father's handwriting.

He removed the clip and tossed it onto the desk. Before he read the words on the pages, Edward let his fingertips glide over the indentations in the paper from the writing. He glanced back over his shoulder toward the door. There was still no one else in the room, so he turned back to the letter and began reading.

Edward,

I hope that in the twists of my letters and in the slope of my handedness you may see only what I offer: honesty, and a promise of power no other can possibly give you. I admit that I was not the type of father a child needs. Not only was I neglectful, but, frankly, I had things of more importance to do. I didn't claw my way through the grime of this fetid world only to be shackled by the products of my biological faculties. This is a world of chaos and any expectations held upon me are those of a society I do not care to address or be a part of. You may be the fruit of my loins but you have yet to show me your worthiness of the fruit of my labors.

I fear any other type of offspring would've thrown this letter into the trash by now but I know that you will still read on. I have always known you, Edward, even if our time spent together was intermittent. It does not matter that you spent much of your youth in private schools. I threw as much money as required at the best education I could find. Even outside of school, I tried to give you the freedom owed to a son of the Jamison house. Yet, I could always see it in your eyes, that same apathy that I, myself, have felt my entire life.

These petty wars between the East and New West are the games of children's minds in adult bodies, of rats and of squabbling infants with no sense of existential relevance or evolution. This whole world is a stockade, writhing with the piglets of consumerism, victims to their own mammalian greed and animalistic instincts. Money, luxury, sex, status, fame... It means nothing without true power. I know you, Edward, because I know myself and I believe we seek the same thing. We seek an answer to the unanswerable. We seek purpose in a world without it.

What would you say if I told you there were things much older and more cosmically relevant than money or notoriety and that I could show you the Path that leads to a true destiny? Where does one even begin when attempting to explain the unexplainable? How does one describe the color of the void or the smell of the vacuum? Alas, it will be a difficult endeavor, for certain, but an endeavor I will take nonetheless for, if anything were to happen to me, in you rests the immortality of our bloodline.

After founding Dynam Industries those years ago, I have invested my life and sacrificed much to achieve the level of knowledge that I have, to find meaning behind the seemingly mundane subsistence of this life. I have spent endless nights reading sensationalist "accounts" of occult knowledge for any bit of truth. I have poured over antiquated texts and spent a fortune on artifacts that are hundreds, in some cases thousands, of years older than we are.

It has finally paid off and I believe it's time to make you aware of my true work.

My son, I have found our pilgrimage.

*

The airlock that led from the main corridor of the crew quarters into the room labeled LONG SLEEP CABIN hissed as it slid open. Captain Phineas Washington stepped through. The airlock slid closed behind him. Fluorescent lights above shimmered off the obsidian skin of his muscular chest and shoulders as he moved a towel around his body, collecting the sweat generated from an hour on the cardio bikes. It was the same routine he had done every morning for the last couple weeks, once he'd recovered from the atrophy. His tendons and joints had been sore, his bones weak and his head pounding, side effects of the long naps. After a few hours of cardio each day, though, and a couple of painkillers when needed, his body had begun to feel somewhat normal.

His mind on the other hand...

'Phi', as his old Navy mates called him, reached to the panel left of the airlock and clicked the fluorescents off. Except for the blue glow of the StatHUD screens on the front of each vertical cryotube and the cool pink radiance of the embryonic fluid in which the rest of his crew slept, the room dimmed into darkness. The captain stared down the middle of the two rows of bodies in liquid suspension.

It had been almost six months since he'd spoken to any of the crew, five months while he slept in stasis alongside them and three weeks since his own AutoVive process went off. It had also been six months since he'd had a drink... The only communication he'd experienced since having been awake was with Dynam Flight Control back home and even that was only scheduled for once every five days, per their established procedures. Messages took three hours to reach Launch Control from the distance they'd come, which was leaps and bounds ahead of the prior technology, but it still didn't satiate his cravings for what lay back on Earth. He thought the conversation was what he missed but his heart had ached for whiskey. It was the only thing his body desired in order to stave off the inevitable succumbing to whatever it was that seemed to be knocking at his psyche in those first few days after he awoke.

There was a heaviness, too, he hadn't been able to pinpoint, resting somewhere on his heart or in his lungs, a physical manifestation of the unfamiliar life he'd awoken to find himself in. He'd kept a cool head throughout all of it until he left cryosleep this last time around, until he awoke from the mucosal glass tube to a silent ship in the dead of space. He couldn't say that he'd sobered over the long nap. He'd just existed in unconscious numbness. Initially, upon waking, it had felt as if he was animating someone else's body using a mind that still hadn't completely found itself out of the darkness that it had slept in. Sometimes, while performing evaluations or even taking a piss, Phi's mind slipped back into that numb darkness and he knew that void somehow. It was recognizable, something that had left traces of itself inside of him during the cryosleep, maybe even existed from before those months spent dormant. Some days, it crept back into him like a warm death, intoxicating as well as terrifying, creeping along the musculature under his skin and behind his eyes and in the contours of his flesh.

Phi had done the long naps a half a dozen times during the supply running for the military but never for more than a week or two at a time, and only on the extensive trips for the occasional distant delivery. In the black of the vacuum, if a man found himself in confusion, or irrationality, he could regurgitate everything he'd been taught about the universe and space and physics in search of respite, in search of a way to weather the storm of unearthly nothingness and confusion. The truth, however, was that he had no clue as to what influences were truly at work out here and what kind of effects these influences could have on a consciousness suspended in artificial sleep. Though his losing consciousness and regaining it felt to be no different of an experience than those other previous times, in the aftermath of this one he felt something else.

He wasn't only plagued by that which had come with him from Earth. He was sure something else had found him out here.

An hour ago, the alarm went off from the datapad on the stand next to his bunk. It chimed with an alert that today was the day in which the crew was to have their AutoVive procedures initiated. These processes were on an automatic system if manual initiations did not occur. In the *Naval Law and Astro-Maritime Statutes* guidebook, however, the book that all captains were required to practically memorize in the Navy, it was recommended that every step of the AutoVive procedures for the standard crew are both initiated and overseen by the captain for two important reasons. The first was simple: liability. The captain's responsibility is not only to manage the ship and its crew but to maintain the integrity of the operation and the health of the people involved in it. Watching over a process as intricate as a multiple crewmember AutoVive was almost a necessity, no matter the advancements in automated tech. The riskiest step to all of it, Phi knew, was the initiation of the Captain's waking for, if something were to go wrong, no other crew member would be conscious to help.

The second reason for the captain overseeing the process was a bit more complicated. Even with the latest technology, the effects of cryosleep still varied too greatly. Sometimes, the worst of it was mild nausea and having someone already there with a bucket to vomit in was necessary. Other times, it was atrophy or pinched nerves from the involuntary coiling of muscles and tendons over time. There was something else, a secret that the Mil-Tech giants kept hidden from not only the general population but most military personnel. Phi had never witnessed it himself but he'd heard of high level Navy intelligence having documented proof that a small but significant percentage of service members involved in cryosleep were going insane upon waking. The higher-ups in the Navy's space program were well aware of this particular side effect. It had been mentioned in the contract they made the recruits sign upon completion of the academic program prior to employment, except that it was on page one-seventy-four of a three-hundred page packet, with about a thousand places to initial and sign. It was apparent there were things they wanted buried in the intricate trappings of "legalese". Instead of the side effect being labeled as *insanity*, the verbatim text said *increased or altered emotional intensity.*

It had all been a blur when he'd skimmed through his own copy of the contract back when he'd first joined but, frankly, he hadn't given a shit. Whiskey had been in his blood, as it still was now, and his heart cried for it constantly. It had ruined his life or he had ruined his own life and whiskey was simply the vessel. Phi didn't think it mattered which was the truth. Joining the Navy at thirty years old was, at the time, his only idea to get sober.

This wasn't the Navy, though. This was private work. After the shitstorm in Del Santos four years ago, when he'd punched his fleet admiral and received a dishonorable discharge, Phi had gone from being Captain of the cargo runner *NSP Regulus*, moving supplies and trade goods between the three major space stations (the ISS, the ATG, and the 8V out of Norway), to being unemployed, washed out and having nothing to show for it. Military pension would have been stable but they took that away when they kicked him out. The economy was horrendously inflated and had never recovered from the Debt Crash of 2023. The military had become the most stable employment for a citizen but that was no longer an option for him, unless he tried to join the UN Army. Phi had no intention of becoming a lackey for an oil-mongering organization but he also didn't kid himself, that even in the Navy, he knew there were secret motives saturating every mission and private money flowing like rivers behind it all. At some point, a man had to make a decision, though, no matter how late in the game.

The captain returned his gaze to the cryotubes ahead. Their pink glow almost shimmered in the darkness. The only other light came from blinking plastic buttons covering the wall behind the row on the left—stat monitors for the health of the ship, oxygen levels, energy consumption and the controls to maintain them.

There were four cryotubes on each side of the center aisle of the room but only seven of them had been occupied with inhabitants. The first tube on Phi's right had been his own before the AutoVive process woke him. Though his faculties and state of mind seemed to have repaired themselves from the initial side effects, he experienced vivid dream states when he slept each day. He'd awoken from sleep many times these last few weeks, jolted and gasping for breath. His mind's eye displayed a reality in these dreams, one in which he was stuck inside the cryotube without an oxygen mask, the pink liquid watering his vision and suffocating him.

He was the captain. There was no one there to help him.

Phi reached for the StatHUD panel mounted on the right side of the second cryotube. Inside was Natalya Sovikov, the 'Assistant to the Executive', according to her crew profile. Held in amniotic suspension with wires entering and exiting different places on her body, she looked peaceful despite the invasive life-sustaining paraphernalia. Phi punched in the release code and a whirring sound emitted from the base of the tube as the pink fluid began to drain into the grated slots below. It would be approximately three minutes before the tube was empty of the stuff.

He moved down the same row to the next tube and punched in the release code for the Flight and Navigation Specialist, D'Artagnan La Felios, the only crew member Phi had known from before. He'd met the man when he was stationed at the Joint-Spec Naval Base deep in the woods of northeast Canada, before his time on the *Regulus*. La Felios was in Radar back then. He was a goofy French-Canadian with a raunchy humor, a silly way with women and a laugh the captain couldn't get enough of.

The final tube in the row was occupied by the Medical Examiner and Psychologist, Eilah Winthrope. Across the aisle was her husband and Systems Engineer, Jeffrey Winthrope, and next to him, Christoph Lansig, the other Systems Engineer. Phi entered the codes one-by-one to start the AutoVive process on each of them.

Back at the front end of the row, across from where the captain had slept for over five months, was the very man this flight was funded by. Floating unconsciously, with veins visible throughout his lean pale body, was the CEO of Dynam Industries, Harold Jamison. The man had hawk-like features and, even in his sleep, appeared to carry a look of discontentment and irritation. The wrinkles on his face did not indicate years of laughter but decades of irritation and malice.

They didn't bother to tell Phi how they knew so much of his background when they called to offer him this gig. It had been three years since he'd been in the captain's seat of a ship. Dishonorable discharge... Funny thing was, instead of sobering him up, it only made things worse. Instead of realizing that punching the fleet admiral for making a comment about Phi's very real alcoholism was a bad decision, the event seemed to simply occur without his own conscious thought. After being discharged, Phi drank himself out cold each night that he could. The hours they were giving him with the pipe-laying crew had been dwindling and many of those nights were spent with the old man he knew very well, Old Jack Daniels. More often than not, he'd work the entire morning still drunk from the night before. Then he received the call from the recruiter at Dynam.

Even after bringing up some of the less-than-honorable mentions of his past, they wanted to see him and were offering a decent sum of money just for hearing out whatever proposal they had prepared for him, five hundred dollars just to go to the interview. It was that night that Phi poured the rest of his whiskey down the drain, but not before taking one last long swig of the old man to remember him by. Decisions made in order to save himself were just as easy as decisions made to destroy himself, especially when it came to alcohol. Self-destruction was just as much a part of him as self-preservation and the waves of his life seemed defined by spans of time in which he had given in to destroying himself, events that showed truly how lost he could be, how broken he really was. He was moving into his mid-forties now and yet he wasn't sure if he'd ever come to fully accept that aspect of it all, the part that sat hungrily in the deep recesses of his soul like an addict, shaking and slobbering as it waited for the next taste of that sweet burning misery.

Jamison's assistant, Sovikov, had Phi sign packet after packet of paperwork (standard liability contracts and reiteration upon reiteration of the non-disclosure agreements) before beginning to even speak of their proposal. Severe legal action for any misconduct was threatened on a few of the pages he was required to sign. He always thought that he had well established standards for the type of work he would and would not do, the questions he would ask about the morality of the tasks he was given, but it didn't matter the company emblem on the side of the ship or the product in the cargo hold, not anymore at least. Work was work in a time when decent employment was scarce, especially in the non-military sector, and getting to captain another ship was a chance he didn't think he'd get to have again.

The first hour of the interview was spent reviewing his history, just him, Ms. Sovikov and her stack of files. She had a list of talking points ready beforehand, praising him (*eleven years as Captain of the NSP Regulus, certification in all four standard AstrOS architectures, excellent flight aptitude at the age of forty-two, plenty of training and experience in emergency ship handling*). There were others that weren't so flattering (*parents deceased, no kids, divorced, discharged from the navy for assault, alcoholic*). A part of him felt ashamed at the time, especially because 'alcoholic' being the last on the list seemed to make it stick in the air more. It *breathed* more. However, he had simply nodded in agreement and occasionally responded with *Yes, ma'am*. He thought for a moment that she was simply listing the reasons as to why he wasn't what they were looking for and began to prepare himself for a denial. She eventually moved on to the mundane details of his childhood, education, work history outside of the military. And then, right at the end of the hour, the door to the interview room opened. That was when Phi met Harold Jamison for the first time.

Europa... That was their destination.

Phi tapped the code into the keys of Jamison's StatHUD display and the radiant pink amnion drained from the tube in which the tycoon slept.

The mess hall of the *Artorius* was on her port side, imbedded in the aft quarter of the ship. A long window with retracted blast shutters looked out to the dark sea of space. Phi sat at one side of the octagonal table in the center of the room, closest to the Med office doors, and La Felios, Lansig and Jamison sat on the stools to his right. The lone halogen light above the center of the table burned brightly in the dark hall. The airlock hissed and then closed behind Ms. Sovikov as she entered, still drying her hair off in a towel. She sat to Phi's left, between him and Systems Engineer Winthrope. Winthrope and his wife, Eilah, were mumbling low words to each other as they held hands and ate their protein soup.

Not many words were exchanged as the crew filled their stomachs. La Felios mumbled something about the instant coffee he was drinking but each of them kept to themselves for the most part. A few of the crewmembers still looked groggy. It didn't appear to be anything other than the normal fatigue of extended cryosleep but Phi made it a point to keep an eye open. He was reading over the same mission report he'd read many other times throughout the last three weeks and he remembered having read it prior to mission launch but the words had barely registered back then. At the time, the paycheck was what he was concerned with... that, and getting back into a captain's seat where he belonged.

His eyes scanned once again over the document glowing from the datapad's screen.

15:21 08.15.2046

To the crew,

First and foremost, welcome aboard the Artorius. This ship has been part of a project of Dynam Industries and its subsidiary joint operations for over twenty years. It is a labor of love, of passion and, most importantly, of man's continual need for exploration, to throw himself into the unknowns of reality beyond his wildest imaginations for the sake of life, itself, and spreading our conscious experience. She's the second rendition of our Solar-Sail transport prototype, equipped with both launching and re-launching capabilities, due to the thrust-recycling technology onboard. I couldn't be more proud of her or the team that helped build her.

You'll find all of the details attached in separate documents to this message. Twenty-one days after launch, the automated drop-ship will follow us, carrying with it two more members of the Dynam team as well as the supplies we need to set up the secondary excavation dome.

We should count ourselves among the most privileged in all of time, ladies and gentlemen, for we are traveling to the far reaches of our solar system. Our eyes will bear witness to horizons no one else has ever seen. Ours will not be a public fame, though. Only we will know of our travels to Jupiter's moon, Europa, for the immediate future.

Fret not. We will make history. It's simply all about the timing.

Sleep well.

H. R. Jamison

CEO Dynam Industries

Phi sat there with the glow of the datapad pouring into his eyes.

It played with his sight in the dark mess hall as he regarded the crew around him once more, observing the different unique lives and how they intertwined. The gravity of the mission he had signed up for, after all these miles and months of silence and sleep, finally settled into his bones then like hardening plaque. There were questions, unanswered inquiries he had about the inner workings of this whole mission. Sure, he had the ability, just as anyone, to put on some show or simply follow protocol in the face of fear or doubt. And, when he thought about it, Phi was sure he'd still rather be here than back on Earth. Back home, emotional debts came collecting quite frequently in the night and the bottle still waited, goading him into Old Jack's warm embrace. There was something about this mission, though, about all of this that Phi just couldn't place. He'd felt it the moment the interview with Sovikov had come to a close. There was some kind of tension behind every moment of those two following weeks leading up to mission launch and the inevitable cryosleep, like walking toward a guillotine that he had volunteered himself for. That was the problem, that the entire process was effortless and the steps seemed taken *for* him. He knew he was a drunk. What he didn't know was why Jamison had chosen him over any other captain or ex-pilot candidates from the Naval Veteran's Staffing Agency. In fact, he was sure that the Agency shredded the resumes of those who were dishonorably discharged.

Yet, here he was.

After being kicked out, he'd ended up back in southern Mississippi. The lines at the Unemployment Offices had been disheartening. He'd taken work where he could get it near his home town, doing mostly labor and construction. He rented a place in the trailer park near the gravesite where his mother was buried eleven or twelve years ago. Being able to visit her again was one good thing to come out of the whole mess, at least. It had been quite a few years since he'd gotten to come to her grave and talk with her. When he spoke to her in his mind, he said things like *It's alright, Momma. I'll be with you soon enough*, and sometimes he would smile because he could swear she heard her voice respond with *It better not be any time soon, boy.*

He heard her now. *Phineas, if you don't stick up for yourself, them boys at school will never let you be.*

A light chuckle escaped his chest.

"What's so funny?" asked a soft accented voice.

"Hm?" Phi glanced up from the mission report that he'd been staring at, not reading, for the last ten minutes now. Sovikov was eyeing him with something that looked like indiscriminate curiosity. Phi chuckled once more and clicked the datapad off before sitting back in his chair. "Your parents still alive?"

"No."

Her abruptness gave him pause, then he said, "Same. Funny thing, trying to remember them on a daily basis, keeping them in your thoughts and all that. Most of the time, it doesn't work. The memories... fade. But then, out of the blue, you sometimes hear some sort of response to your thoughts, or a memory of something they had told you at some point, more vivid than anything else."

They sat in silence a moment as Phi looked back toward the datapad and clicked it back on.

"Maybe that's just me," he mumbled.

Sovikov was silent for a long moment before her features relaxed a little and she said, "Who did you hear?"

Phi stared at the datapad, the words on the screen burning into his vision but he did not see them. His thoughts were elsewhere. "My mother. She was sassy but wise beyond anything I could imagine. Sometimes I remember what she says, and sometimes I don't. Sometimes I just see her face."

"When did she die?" Sovikov asked.

Phi took a gulp from the lukewarm coffee in the plastic cup in front of him. "A little over ten years ago."

"I was raised by my aunt," she said. "My parents were lost in The Conflict."

"Was your home near the Russia-Kazakhstan border?"

She nodded.

"I'm sorry to hear that," Phi said. And he really was.

There was only one war that people, even in the New West, referred to as *The Conflict*. The New Syrian Conflict had been the result of the Syrian Islamic State resurfacing back in 2026 and 2027 with more power, influence and weapons than any time in the last two centuries. Through a series of monthly, if not weekly, terror events, with casualties in countries like Russia, France, Kazakhstan, Turkey and Armenia, the earth had entered a neo-

Cold War. Since then, Doomsday propaganda poured like bile from all media outlets, as if a great pustule had burst over the whole of everything and the human race had simply lifted their mouths to take their fill of the shit being fed to them.

Yet, how petty the conflicts of the world seemed this far away from it all. There was no propaganda in the dark of space, no law or enforcers of it, and yet strangely it wasn't freedom Phi felt out here. Every inch of the void around them crushed against the outside of the ship and would seep through any crack in the seams to kill them, sucking the oxygen from their lungs with the smallest chance it could get. They were human sardines in a tin can sailing across the ether, trapped among nothingness and death, *real* enemies, not those created by some hive of political rats.

Sovikov cleared her throat. "Well... My aunt's voice is what I hear at times."

Phi's own memories were a tether back to a home that never let go and he thought it might be the same for her. Maybe both of them were still ruled by the memories of the past and the ones they'd lost.

There wasn't much talk amongst the crew after that. Once the carb-loaded protein food had been eaten, they'd disbanded throughout the ship. The digital HUD interface embedded in the front of Phi's work station glared with blue and teal colored text and half a dozen mission files glowed up on the screen. He sat up from the Captain's chair, tapping the HUD closed, and walked toward the thick glass of the front viewport. The shutters had been opened and Jupiter, massive and foreboding, was suspended in the black abyss ahead of them. The ancient Romans had named the planet after the king of the gods. Being so near its massive size, Phi couldn't blame them. If only those ancient astronomers and philosophers could've seen it from this distance, been this close to it. The flowing storms of gas made rows of different colors across the entirety of its surface. Some of the storms were the color of rust, others white or grey or a sickly yellowish hue. The layers appeared like sediment, as if the planet wasn't gaseous but rather some gargantuan sphere of rock, perfectly cut out of billion year old sediment. And then there was the eye, the red-orange spot seemingly placed off-center by some crazed demigod supposedly the size of Earth. Phi tried to imagine himself on the surface of the giant, standing in the center of an Earth-sized storm. Its color was rustic and its ocular shape surreal. He wondered what it would be like to be swallowed by it.

This truly was a place for the gods, out here in darkness. Humans held no dominion in the black of this vacuum and, as Phi looked upon the king, he couldn't help but lose his thoughts. The sight of it vexed him. Standing there, behind the thick glass, he couldn't stop himself from witnessing its power.

*

What does it mean for knowledge to be 'forbidden'? Can there even be such a constraint put on an abstract thing like knowledge?

After having spent much of my fortune and even more of my time into the study of an alternate path of knowing, one that could bring meaning and fulfillment and, more importantly, true power, I discovered something that had exchanged many hands prior to my own and, ultimately, caused the insanity of each who had held it before me.

I have searched through many books of the occult, of rituals and sacrifices, séances and incantations, but all were misleading... until I had found the book in the black Canadian forests. And within the book I had read such wondrous things, my son. The back cover of the tome was a slab of wood an inch thick. Embedded into a diamond shaped profile was an amulet. "The Eye of Blood" is its name, as I found out later. I've left you the sister piece, named "The Eye of War". I will not mention the tasks I endured to obtain this other amulet, so simply understand that both are required for their part in all of this. Sacrifices have been made. Prices have been paid.

Edward's eyes shifted from the pages he held in his hands to the oak table in front of him. The amulet lay on the cloth it had been wrapped in, reflecting the gentle lambency of the wall lamps off of the green stone in the center of the thing. There were ridges carved into the rough gold encasing, as if it had been put through some sort of machine, marring the edges with the scars of an unknown grinding.

Deep within the thick pines of northern Canada, your uncle Brenton and I tracked down the mossy ruins of a cabin, hundreds of years old and swallowed by the forest long ago. It was there that I had found the aforementioned book, hidden in the cellar under stacks of other literature. It was filled with notes a previous owner had written on the matter of the amulet embedded within, possessed by madness if the cadence of the writing was any indication.

In the margins of the pages, there were scribbles of ancient jewel-crafting, of cosmic forces and dark realms of forever shifting unreality. They must have been insane to make such claims of the unknown without connecting the pieces together. However, as I continued to read, I began to understand. I began to see where the ones who came before me had lost their way, where they had treaded upon the grounds of the Cosmic, yet did not truly understand what they sought as I did.

It was then that I realized that it wasn't simply that I had stumbled upon a process that would've occurred, regardless of the man who decided to make it his life's work to seek this energy. This was my destiny. The years of my life, of my experience and conscious will, were the other pieces to this puzzle. I understood then just as I understand now that it had to be me. The nights of reading book after book, translation after translation, the faith I had in my own will, to find the truth of it, served to place me in a position of knowing the True Path. You will come to know, as well, that our bloodline is the vessel to the awakening.

In the book, in the space at the end of a particular chapter, someone had sketched a pattern onto the page. The red ink had bled into the paper, with three lines parallel to each other while one streaked across all of them like the horizon. It was a symbol, the same that was carved into the gold encasing of the amulet in the back of the book—three lines with one crossing diagonally through them.

A man does not inherently become mad from exposure to the amulets or the occult writings. No, the men who held it before me undoubtedly went mad because they lacked the technology to reach the final destinations of the Path, to fit the final pieces of the puzzle together.

A specific scroll I had purchased, antiquated and fragile as a newborn, spoke of the 'resting place of the ritual, at the feet of the Lord's most faithful subject.' All of my research, up until that time, pointed toward the 'Lord' mentioned here referring to Jupiter, the Most High. Yet, Jupiter's most faithful subject was unknown to us. In my research, I studied Jupiter, both the mythological figure as well as the astronomical body. I studied the dozens of natural satellites of the great planet, especially the Galilean moons. Io, Ganymede and Callisto produced nothing of interest. However, I came upon spacecraft fly-by photos of Europa. There were images of the great rust-colored lashes across its iced surface, hundreds of miles long and tens of thousands of years old. I later discovered shots of the lesser photographed side of that moon and then another piece of it all fell into place.

Words cannot describe the feeling that came over me when I saw the pattern of lashes at her Jovian point. They were in the same shape as those drawings in the book, the same as those etched into the gold of the amulet's encasing.

Salvation awaits on Europa, Edward.

Imagine having the very key to immortal power resting in your hands only to see the final step is 365 million miles away... I fear that would drive any man to the brink of insanity and push him right over. The time in which we live, the capabilities of our technology, all point toward the fate of this endeavor being certain.

I am the one who will obtain this power of true cosmic potential.

At the time of our exploration, I had neglected to tell my brother of my discovery of the amulet. I simply removed the backplate and the jewelry before sharing the texts with him. Being as arrogant as always, Brenton took the responsibility upon himself to pursue the only lead he believed we had discovered—the markings and notes scrawled in the books all pointed toward Europa.

As I said, though, each piece of the puzzle has its purpose.

Do you remember when your uncle Brenton left two years ago? Not that you were ever close to him but that was his final trip, Europa his final destination. He took with him the first version of our Solar-Sail transport, a ship called The Acolyte, along with 6 crew members and a vague idea of what he would find there. He thought that scavenging through ancient texts was my job and that the information he received was accurate and detailed. The truth was that I simply chose what information to give him, leaving out bits of data here and there that I thought would aid him too well.

Don't get me wrong, I love my brother. He followed the Path in his own way, just as I did, but true power comes with true sacrifice and nothing will stand in my way, not even my own blood. You would do well to remember that upon my return.

*

The ventilation systems and pipes that ran along the rafters down the central corridor of the ship crooned and whirred with the recycling of oxygen and thruster fuel. The airlock to the Captain's Quarters hissed open and Phi stepped out of the room. His boots clanked against the grated floor with each step. When he reached the bridge, he was still tightening an arm strap on his H.E.T.E. suit.

D'Artagnan La Felios looked up from his monitor. "We're about fifty minutes out from initiating the landing sequence. Trajectory is locked, pressures are stable, and we're looking real good on the ATMUS. I've bounced our signal through the Kaliopi satellite and used its tracking data to establish our main route for descent. She'll land just fine but, while we approach, I'm going to run through the sim once more."

Phi sat down into the captain's chair. "Thank you, Specialist."

The truth was he'd barely heard what La Felios had said. His thoughts were rattled and preoccupied with something he couldn't quite explain, an experience he'd just had while back in his quarters. He'd been changing into the H.E.T.E. suit, had already zipped both legs up, attached the straps from the suspenders to the pants and was sitting on the bed, leaning over his knees and tying his boots up, when one of the buckles of the left suspender broke off from the strap. It flipped and clattered down onto the cold metal floor. Upon seeing this, he stood and moved to a small upper closet, the width of a medicine cabinet and about two feet deep. He knew there to be extra trinkets and clips for a myriad of gear in the storage compartments, so he moved to search through the closest one. The latch to the cubby clicked as it opened and, when he'd drawn the shutter back on the compartment, something flashed in his vision. The small amount of darkness in the overhead compartment vibrantly ebbed back and forth. Phi's faculties had locked in a stasis for a moment that felt like an eon. It wasn't in his physical vision that he saw the thing but in his mind's eye, as if staring into that little darkness opened a portal to the realms of his psyche. He saw the face of his mother, decayed in the box and dress in which they'd buried her. Writhing from the holes in her dead flesh were worms he'd never seen before, grotesque fat white things with strangely human-shaped heads that glistened in a sinister light, some indeterminate glare from deep in the heart of his nightmares.

The captain could still see it in his thoughts. The memory of the experience was still fresh. There was something in the space out here, in the void through which they sailed. His eyes remained cool and collected, staring out at their destination but under his skin was an anxiety, a tension that mounted as Europa and the almighty Jupiter grew within the frame of the viewport.

The airlock from the Maintenance Corridor hissed behind Phi and, when he turned a glance toward it, his eyes caught Harold Jamison's as the man was stepping through the door. Jamison still wore his clothes and around his neck was a thick gold chain with an amulet hanging from it. It had a rough gold encasing in the shape of a diamond, holding a deep red jewel, much larger than any Phi had remembered ever seeing. Held in the man's left hand was the black handle to an aluminum case with the words DYNAM INDUSTRIES printed across the front of it.

Phi stood and extended his hand. “Mr. Jamison, did you need help finding your H.E.T.E. suit, or are you planning on staying aboard the ship after traveling all this way?”

“Captain Washington,” he said, meeting Phi's hand with his own. “I apologize for retiring to my bunk so frequently since we've awoken but it has not been in vain. There is much research yet to be done. I trust your abilities have led us to our destination properly.”

Phi hadn't realized until then that this was the first time he'd seen Jamison out of his bunk in almost three days. Jamison's gaze was determined, almost savage, as he stared behind the captain, out of the viewport to the celestial bodies. When Phi's attention followed, Europa was well within sight. Though so far from the sun, this moon of Jupiter was still lit from its light with a brilliance he couldn't think of how to describe. Great red-brown cracks, hundreds of miles long, crisscrossed over the icy surface in seemingly random patterns. At the bottom right of the moon, from their view, was the Pwyll crater. In Phi's mind, a movie of its origin showed the meteor burning through the atmosphere, billowing mountains of fire rolling off of it before slamming into the great shell of ice. He imagined what that type of event would sound like from the distance they were at now, the cataclysmic eruption undoubtedly deafening all that would hear it.

Jamison's free hand had moved to the amulet dangling from his neck when Sovikov approached from behind and whispered something to him. He nodded and responded with, "Go ahead." She moved back toward the central corridor, typing something into her datapad as she walked out of sight.

"In an email that should arrive momentarily, you will find a letter," Jamison said loudly, still gazing out of the viewport. "I'd like you all to check it. I have done all of this, spent my fortunes on this operation, this ship, and the execution of this flight, but I've intentionally left out some of the details of this mission. It was too important up until this point to prevent the leaking of *any* of this. I'd like to fill you in on the rest of those details now."

"What details, Jamison?" Phi's voice was deep and accusatory.

Jamison retorted with a stern look. "Check... the email."

Phi turned to his station, opened the digital interface and navigated to the email inbox. He didn't like surprises and risking the lives of this many people, including himself, in order to hide the true motives of something as dangerous as a space flight wasn't something he'd agreed to. The last thing he needed was to be caught up in some sort of smuggling or human trafficking ring, or held ransom hundreds of millions of miles away from home.

A new message from *Sovikov, N., on behalf of H. R. Jamison*, with two attachments, glowed in the inbox. The captain expanded the email with a command into the keyboard. The first attachment was a picture of another angle of Europa. It was titled "Europa_sub-jovian_1". Jupiter hung in the darkness behind the moon. In the far distance of the shot, the sun could be seen shining brightly. Otherwise, the picture appeared relatively unremarkable. The second attachment was titled "Europa_sub-jovian_2". This one was the same shot, only it had some sort of thermal imaging filter over it. Everything in the picture was cold and purple, save for the white-orange heat from the distant sun... and a small blip on the surface of Europa, almost exactly on the sub-Jovian point.

"I have sources that were able to gain access to the Kaliopi data storage," Jamison began again, "as well as its onboard camera. We took the infrared capture just before the satellite moved around the other side of Jupiter on its last orbit. *That* is a heat signature of some kind on a world full of ice. It is no coincidence that our landing site is very near this... anomaly."

"What is it?" Engineer Lansig asked.

"Why, it's the entire reason I created Dynam Industries to begin with." Jamison smiled at the crew as if expecting them to understand what he meant. He looked wired and when the team remained silent and staring, the slick-haired benefactor chuckled. "Allow me to explain. The Kaliopi was launched in 2019. After eight months, it reached the orbit of Jupiter and began along its trajectory, collecting information via sonar, radio and telescopic sensors. With this new piece of technology in place, astronomers used it to prove Europa's 'thin-ice' model incorrect. The truth of what it showed was that the ice crust was between 10 and 30 kilometers thick in most places around the moon."

"Most places," repeated Eilah.

"Yes," Jamison said. "Most places, save for one specific area, that bit in the picture, the orange amongst a sea of purple. The ice is only ten meters thick underneath our anomaly, maybe even less. Some pictures and information have been released to the press detailing the composition of the ice around the entire moon, lots of pictures to appease the curious masses, et cetera. However, the public has not been made aware of quite a few things. Sonar readings from the initial scans picked up something underneath the surface during a particular pass-over. There were half-a-kilometer long swaths radiating in the deep oceans. The engineers and scientists at NASA hypothesized that it was either a mineral deposit or a type of waterborne gas. My research, however, denotes it to be something much more. I believe it is an artifact or a structure of some kind, suspended somehow in the cold depths. Not only will we have the opportunity to investigate the anomaly, but at this shallow point in the ice, we will be the first humans to have access to water samples from the subsurface oceans of any celestial body outside of Earth. If water is the key to life, we may be able to discover something wondrous on this journey."

Phi imagined what could lay under the kilometers of ice, the black oceans that had never seen the light of day, that no human eye had ever laid upon. He shook his head and stood from his chair, then moved towards the man, his thoughts clouded by the irritation grating at him. "Jamison. You mean to tell me that you gave us false mission information?"

Jamison's expression sank into a scowl. "And what do you care? You're still getting paid upon arrival back to Earth. I'll even throw in an extra twenty percent to each of your salaries if you return to your station and do the job you were hired to do without bothering me further. Fly the damned ship."

"What?!" The captain's blood boiled with fury. Adrenaline raced through his limbs, snowballing into his anger. "The job we were hired to do was to escort an ice-core sample mission. Now you're telling us we're here to find out what this anomaly is? How ambiguous of a mission statement is that? How are we prepared for this? You've put all of our lives at risk, Jamison, by not including all of these details when we were back at Earth because, you know what? If you would've told me that you wanted me to join you on some nebulous amateur's mission, a goose hunt for something we know almost nothing about, I would've told you to shove that contract up your ass."

Jamison laughed. "Is that so? Why, you'd still be looking for rent money in a sea of government and military employers that wouldn't give you, with your alcoholism, a second glance. I have a deep file on you, *Captain* Washington. How long had you been out of good work before I graced you with employment, hm?"

Phi remained silent, staring down into the man's face.

"You may have done things a certain way in the Navy but, out here, this is *my* operation." Jamison stared right back. "Don't forget who is writing the checks here."

La Felios interrupted. "We need to prepare for landing."

Behind the specialist, the viewport was filled with an iced landscape. Huge swaths of rust were slashed across the surface they descended toward.

The trajectory was turbulent as the ship moved into the thin atmosphere of the frozen moon. Each of the crewmembers were harnessed into their chairs. Jamison was in one of the extra seats behind the Captain's station. When Phi turned back, the man was strapped in but flipping through yellowed pages of an old tome, running his fingers along the texts. His mouth moved silently as he read. Phi looked closely at the cover and saw that it was made of thick black leather. Emblazoned in a gold filigree on the front was a symbol Phi had never seen before, one displaying three parallel lines with another crossing diagonally through them.

Ms. Sovikov was locked into the seat next to Jamison, staring down at her own hands.

Miles upon miles of ice lay below them on their descent toward the landing zone. Jupiter lay massive and foreboding above with its eye hovering just over the horizon line. Phi could feel its weight in his bones and his imagination ran off again, picturing their ship losing its trajectory and being slingshot straight beyond Europa and toward the gaseous titan. Its gravity would pull them in and they'd breach the tempestuous storms, their ship hurling into an iron surface they'd never see coming.

A loud whirring sound filled the cabin as they sunk closer to the frigid crust. The turbulence was stronger now, shaking and rattling buckles and hanging straps around the ship interior.

"Landing thrusters initiating," La Felios called out.

The ship lurched with a sudden speed decrease and Phi leaned forward with the momentum. There was a thud on the grated floor to his right and, when he peeked over his shoulder, he saw the black book sliding across the floor.

"Damnit," Jamison cursed.

Moments later, the ship had slowed its forward propulsion and was now descending vertically to the ice below.

"Thirty feet," La Felios reported. "Landing gear out."

The ship groaned and Phi laid his head back to close his eyes. The descent caused his insides to roil like a cement truck filled with napalm. Even with his eyes shut, he was hit with the sudden feeling in his gut. He always hated this part.

"Ten feet."

The ship vibrated heavily as the thrusters burned and the ice rose to meet them. There was a long slow crunch underneath the ship as the landing gear sunk into the stuff. La Felios clicked over a group of switches in front of his seat and the expulsion of the landing thrusters slowly diminished into a quiet purr.

"What the fuck?" Engineer Winthrope had already unbuckled himself and stood, gazing out the starboard viewport.

Phi unstrapped the harness attached to his seat and rose. He moved to stand next to Winthrope and peered outside.

"Is that another ship?"

*

I remember when I received the recordings from Brenton's helmet camera. Base had lost contact with the Acolyte and, I will admit, a part of me was worried for my only brother. I was sitting in my office, reading through a specific text we had acquired from a seller in Argentina, when Ms. Sovikov informed me of the data acquisition. A ship diagnostic and a forced camera feed copy had been initiated by my command three days earlier. The process took half a week to retrieve the information from the ship's records.

The initial diagnostics had come back clean. The Acolyte was in excellent condition, was equipped with more than enough fuel to re-enter orbit and slingshot back to Earth with some to spare, and the condition of the hull was well within the realm of expectations. Much like the Artorius, the ship I will be using to reach Europa, the individual camera feeds from the H.E.T.E. suit helmets recorded into the ship's black box mechanism, allowing for later retrieval.

When I received these recordings, I was ill-prepared for what I would see.

In the lockbox that contained this letter, you should also find an SD card. I've included the recording from my brother's helmet camera for you to view. The other feed recordings were destroyed with my discretion. There are just some things that shouldn't be seen unless one has the mind to face true oblivion and we both know how the rest of them, the cattle that surround us, frighten easily.

Edward set the pages down onto the oak desk next to the small stone effigy. He slid the datapad off the desk and into his lap and turned the SD card over in his hand. "Dynam Industries" was printed in small text with a serial code. He slid it into the port on the left side of the datapad. Cool blue light emitted from the screen and he tapped into the device manager UI. The SD card held fifty terabytes yet there was only a single file:

09122045-130448ETS_JAMISON_B_CAM04.sub2

The video codex opened up and Edward double-tapped the device to make the video fullscreen. He dragged his finger along the base of the display to max the volume out.

Zzzt.

"—at the size of it. Jesus Christ," a voice cut in as the video started.

A louder voice from within the helmet that the camera was in said, "Ladies and gentlemen... I give you Jupiter, the King of the Gods."

The footage was grainy and, in the top left corner of the screen, there was an overlay of text that said JAMISON, B CAM04 - REC. It had been almost three years since Edward had seen his uncle Brenton, but there was no mistaking the voice. It always reminded him of his father's except without the higher tone of constant cynicism.

His uncle panned the view over toward the ship, to the iced ground beneath them, then shifted the camera up toward the massive planet. Up in the darkness, it clung to the black ectoplasm of the universe, filling a good half of the feed. The planet's great eye was half shadowed and half lit by the sun, staring off into the dark unknown. The great storms roared across the surface in rippled streams.

Zzzt.

The recording cut to a point further in time. Labored breathing could be heard from inside the helmet. His uncle appeared to be walking, stepping over ice chunks, making his way around a pressure ridge. Spikes of ice, twenty feet high, rose up to create walls that they navigated around or through, a natural maze made by the shifting of ice plates or something similar. Occasionally, his uncle would look behind as they walked. Four other crew members followed him. Their helmets had small lights on either side of the faceplates, near the top, and oxygen tubes ran from underneath to packs that were strapped onto the backs of their suits. Two of them carried a long silvery container between them, a tool or machine of some kind.

A minute of radio silence went by and along the same pressure ridge they'd been following, they came upon a break in the wall where it crisscrossed with another of the taller pyres of ice.

“We should be able to get through here,” the muffled camera voice said.

A female voice responded through the in-helmet comms. “Be careful, Brenton. Can we even get over that, or...?”

“Oh yea, we should be fine.” And, with a grunt, Edward's uncle reached ahead and gripped the ice on either side of the break, hoisting himself up. The camera jerked as he about lost his footing but his stance retained and he slid down the other side of the ridge smoothly.

A few minutes passed while Brenton helped the rest of the crew over the slope, at one point grabbing a hold onto a handle of the trunk the team carried.

"Jesus Christ," one of the other crew members complained. "You'd think for three million dollars, they'd make this fucking thing a little lighter."

Brenton chuckled inside the helmet. "Tell me about it."

The crew assembled at the base of the small slope. Brenton's camera turned toward a stand of ice spikes, at least a dozen feet high, protruding only a few paces from them. In its shadow, they stood and checked their gear before he led them out into the sunlight.

The horizon on all sides was littered with countless ridges and individual pressure spikes, crystalline blue and three times the height of any crew member. They were the jagged borders to the alien view of Jupiter, still waiting for them beyond the horizon. Its storms were indifferent yet sinister. Directly in front of them was a flat expanse of ice, some kind of pasture of frost, cleared of any pressure ridges and layered in flat ice, chunks here and there no larger than a football.

Roughly fifty yards ahead of them, almost directly under the ominous planet's eye, something was sticking out from the ice. The recording was grainy but Edward could see the black spike, smaller than any of the ice forms they’d shown so far.

“There it is."

“Oh my god. I can’t believe we made it. I can't believe I'm here.”

A woman’s laugh came over the comms.

Edward's uncle said, “McKinley, start unpacking the drill, if you wouldn’t mind."

“Will do, Mr. Jamison," she said.

“I’m going to go see it.”

The camera bobbed as it turned back out toward the black spike and began moving. Brenton was breathing heavily once more. The space between each breath was filled with moments of immense silence from the planet above and the hulking darkness of the vacuum. The condensation flared on the inner glass of the faceplate only to be removed by the in-helmet fans before the next gulp of air.

The ice crunched under Brenton's feet as he walked, hardly audible beyond the enclosed helmet. The feed was directed toward the black thing sticking out of the ice when he slowed to a stop, thirty feet from it, and looked down to the ice below. It was bluer here, as the water appeared to be much closer to the surface. Edward could see it through the video and wasn't surprised when his uncle took softer steps upon continuing his way toward the unknown monolith. Walking slowly and carefully, it took roughly two minutes for Brenton to reach the thing. As he closed in, the composition and color of it became clearer through the recording. It was not a black spike as it had initially appeared but was a porous dark green stone pillar, about four feet tall. It was crowned by a slanted plate on the top, angled toward the camera. In the plate was a diamond shaped relief. Brenton reached out and traced a gloved finger along the indentations.

Edward’s eyes inspected the amulet on the table, the *Eye of War*, as his father had called it. It was of a similar size.

A massive *crack* erupted from the video. A woman’s scream shrieked over the comms, interrupting Edward’s attention. His eyes returned to the datapad just as his uncle's camera looked back toward the other crew.

One of them was only about twenty feet behind Brenton on the ice. Their H.E.T.E. suit reflected brightly in the light of the distant sun. Three of the other crew members stood a few meters beyond that with the long boxed tools. Somewhere between them, sticking out of the ice and dancing twenty feet into the air, was a black serpentine mass. It writhed itself into coils and extended back and forth, gyrating and wriggling. Before Edward could understand what he was seeing, the thing came down in a whipping motion as fast as a bullet, smashing two of the crew and the drill box that sat between them. The woman's screams were instantly silenced.

Another roaring crack came through the feed. Out of the ice, a second serpent broke through just feet away from the camera, pushing up to tower over Brenton and the crew member nearest him. It had skin like slick rubber and there were things that looked like sores or gashes littered all over it.

"Oh, my g—"

The mass whipped down and shattered the faceplate that the camera was behind.

Zzzt.

The video ended. The REPLAY and CLOSE buttons on the datapad illuminated brightly in the dim office. Edward's eyes simply stared at the paused screen, reflecting and brooding on the very unique feeling he was experiencing.

He watched the last thirty seconds once more and then tapped the screen closed and set the datapad down onto the oak desk. He picked his father's letter back up.

Upon watching the video, you will see my brother, your uncle, dying. You will also see the artifact and my destination. Brenton did not approach this the way that I have, with reverence and piety. He thought it more of an exploration, an adventure, and let his own pride lead him to his doom.

Even if I had shared the amulet with him, he would've found a way to muck it up. He lacked the necessary faith. I have read the true texts of Othuum. My brother had just as much a chance to read them as I did. One must be willing to throw away everything, loved ones and even life itself, to toss one's soul into the eternal unknown in order to gain the true glory of the Old Ones. It is the amulet, the Eye of Blood that I carry, that will protect me from the leviathans of that bizarre abyss. I seek that which man has been evolutionarily bred to fear, the darkness of alien oceans and the black behind the veils of reality.

True power lies there, as you have now witnessed.

It waits for he who is worthy.

*

Phi stared at Harold Jamison, who hurriedly strapped on the rest of his equipment and secured the H.E.T.E. suit he wore. The suitcase and the book were never far from him during this process. He held them squished between his ankles while he put on his gloves, even bending over to check multiple times that the case was securely shut while he did so. His eyes had looked strained since the ship landed on the packed ice, like some furious impatience had arisen within him. His attention appeared to be focused on getting out onto the surface quickly. The crew had already asked their questions regarding the other ship. They were waiting for a response from the man now.

Tension heightened over a few long moments and then he spoke.

"My company sent a ship prior to this one." It was simple and concise. His gaze remained at his boots while he strapped the base of the suit legs in with them.

Phi stood from his chair. "You know, I am gettin' real fucking tired of you withholding information from us about this mission, Jamison. Do you understand how far we are from home? If we're supposed to be successful at doing whatever the fuck it is we are doing here, we need to know the details of the situation, goddamnit!"

Jamison did not respond. He finished the last clasp on the inner padding of the helmet before slipping it under his arm. His assistant, Sovikov, was finishing the preparations of her own suit and pack right next to him, twisting and buckling just as quickly as her employer.

Phi felt the tendons twitch in his forearms and he closed his fist.

"The captain is right, Mr. Jamison," said La Felios. "You are definitely paying us quite well to be here, there's no doubt about that, and there aren't many people who get to take this trip, to see what we are about to see. But shouldn't the safety of the crew be our top priority?"

Jamison stopped and turned to La Felios. His eyes were strange and narrow. When his expression then changed as if by command, he finally said, "You're right... I apologize." He turned toward Phi. "The truth is that I've never done anything like this before. I have my reasons for keeping some things private but this is the first time

I've been to Europa, as well." He walked toward the starboard viewport and looked out of it. "The Acolyte was the first ship my company sent. I was obviously not on board her but had allowed a different team to lead the first mission. It was a lack of confidence on my part... to allow someone other than myself to head the first trip. They landed and then we lost contact with them. We haven't heard from them since."

Engineer Lansig, who had hardly spoken a word since waking from cryosleep, looked up from his own suit adjustments. "Who was on that ship?"

Jamison appeared surprised to hear the man's voice, glancing toward Lansig before returning his stare to the viewport and the frigid horizon without. "A captain, a small trained drilling crew... and my brother."

"Brother?" Dr. Winthrope asked.

"Yes. So now you know why I am here. My brother is missing. I'm here to find him or any of the other crew from the Acolyte and, if time allows it, examine the anomaly."

Sovikov approached the airlock behind Jamison and began punching commands into the door console.

Phi took a step forward. "One last question, Jamison. What's in the case?" Phi pointed down at the briefcase the man was holding. He'd held it on his person like a fetish or crucifix would be held by a holy man.

Jamison stared into Phi's eyes. "Now *that...* is something I will not tell you. It is of no danger or concern to any of you."

The inner door of the main airlock hissed open. Sovikov had already stepped through and Jamison followed quickly after.

"Hold on, let me put on this—" Engineer Lansig began to say, stepping toward them and pulling his second glove on, but the beeps of the airlock control pad UI were followed immediately by the hiss of the door closing. Jamison had begun the depressurization process for himself and his assistant. The doors could not be opened until it was finished.

The rest of the crew stared through the glass at the two.

"What a prick," La Felios snarled.

Lansig affirmed. "No shit."

With the process of pressurization and then depressurization, Phi knew that he and the rest of the team wouldn't be properly outside for another ten minutes. Jamison and Sovikov would be out on the ice before them with plenty of time to begin executing their unknown plans.

By the time Phi set foot on the ice, twenty minutes had passed. The slick icescape was covered in the sheen of the distant sun. Ramparts of frost, packed from enormous displays of natural pressure and shifting, sprouted all over the scene. Jamison and his assistant were nowhere in sight, though Phi could see footprints in the crusted snow below leading off in the direction ahead.

A voice scratched over the intercom. “Testing, testing. This is Jeffrey Winthrope. Testing.”

“Yeah, we got you, dear,” Eilah’s voice came in.

Phi adjusted the comm levels in his helmet using the HUD screen on his left forearm. Lansig and La Felios carried tools down from the open airlock. The things were held in silvery metallic cases, all of which had the same appearance in assorted sizes. When the two had retrieved the collection from the airlock, La Felios punched some keys on the external control panel and the outer door hissed shut.

“Alright, people,” said Phi. “Let’s get a comms check. La Felios.”

“Check.”

“Lansig.”

“Check,” Lansig’s voice cracked through the helmet speakers.

“Jamison.”

There was no response.

Phi repeated himself. “Jamison.”

Nothing.

“Goddamnit,” he cursed. “J. Winthrope?”

“Check. Come on, Jamison. What the fuck?”

“E. Winthrope."

“Check."

“I don’t even think there’s a point but N. Sovikov?”

More radio silence.

“Alright, people,” Phi said. “I don’t know about you but I have no idea what this guy's planning. Truth be told, I don’t want to stick around to find out but I don’t know if I could live with myself after leaving someone, even someone like him, stranded on a moon hundreds of millions of miles from home.”

“Yeah." Lansig stood from the crates. “We have drilling equipment and the sampling tools already unloaded. He may have lied to us, or at least omitted quite a bit of information, but I'd personally still like to see this anomaly. If we still want to grab the ice core samples, I'll need a few hours. It's up to you, Captain."

“Agreed,” Engineer Winthrope said.

“Alright.” Phi turned back ahead, toward the closest of the ice ridges. “You three go find them. Stay on comm channel two and track your locations with the surface maps on your datapads. La Felios and I will be on channel three. Just click over if you need us.”

La Felios was looking up at Jupiter when Phi turned toward him. He didn't move, only stared. The immensity of the planet in the sky above seemed to sink down onto Phi when he looked as well, settling itself into his flesh through the suit. He hadn't experienced the feeling when he'd first exited the *Artorius*. He felt it now, though. The sheer size of the planet was more than intimidating. It was oppressive. It was otherworldly and incomprehensibly alien and what bothered him most was the deep red eye stuck to the planet's gaseous mass, cocked to the side from where they stood.

“La Felios,” Phi said, his gaze still up to the king. “Help me look in the other ship for signs of survivors.”

A moment passed, and then La Felios’ gaze lowered and he turned toward the captain.

“Yeah... Yeah, sure.”

The *Acolyte* was almost an exact copy of the *Artorius*. Its airlock doors were closed when they approached and Phi stepped up the staircase to the control panel to right of the outer door. Each step was hardened over with a coarse layer of sharp ice. To the panel, he entered the same access code he used on the *Artorius*. The outer door hissed and then it opened, exposing the empty interior of the airlock. Phi stepped inside, La Felios followed and, after the pressurization process was initiated, the outer door closed and they stood waiting.

“Leave your helmet on when we get in until I check the O2 levels in the ship’s ATMUS," Phi said. That was, of course, assuming that the reactive software put into the *Artorius* was also put into this ship. ATMUS handled the atmosphere for the

Artorius, maintained carbon and oxygen levels at their most accurate representations of a clean Earth filtration, and also served as a diagnostic repair software for the ship's various stabilization systems. "It's been neglected for over a year. The state of the interior is hard to guess until we get in there. Who knows what will still be operational."

"Aye, Captain."

Five minutes passed and the background humming from the pressurization systems came to a quiet. Phi was surprised to find himself bracing for some sort of encounter and his breath grew shallow as he waited for the inner airlock door of the *Acolyte* to open. Heavy moments crawled by. Neither of the men spoke over the comms. Another hiss sounded and the airlock slid open.

The bridge of the *Acolyte* was dark, save for Jupiter's eerie glow through the frosted viewport. Phi tapped a few keys in his suit's HUD screen and turned his helmet lamps on. Two small bulbs lit like headlights on either side of his perspective and illuminated the rest of the derelict cabin ahead. A moment later, La Felios' own headlamps came to life.

Hoarfrost covered most everything. The stuff glinted like stars in the ebbing shadows, coming to life only by the light of their lamps. The structure of the interior walls and control panels were branded with the angles of human engineering but the sharp frost gave the place an almost ghoulish organic look, as if this place was the lair of some creature that dwelt within the frigidness.

Estimating from the layout of the *Artorius* that he knew, Phi turned toward the walkway leading to the rear of the ship. There was a panel on the wall just to the left of the threshold between the bridge and this corridor. Ice crystals cracked off the plastic cover of the panel when he opened it. He pressed the ACCEPT key and the small LED display embedded in the panel lit up, though the screen was partially obscured by frozen condensation. Lines of digital code glowed blurrily behind the layer of frost, signaling the booting process of the ATMUS.

La Felios passed by and moved down the walkway toward the stern. "I'm gonna check the rest of the ship."

Phi nodded. "Roger. Be careful, D."

"Always am."

As he stood waiting for the ship's systems to fully boot, he watched La Felios disappear into the bowels of the craft. The silence in Phi's helmet seemed to thicken and gain viscosity as the seconds ticked on. His eyes closed. His heartbeat thumped through his veins and, in the darkness of his mind, he saw his mother's face again. It wasn't flashed imagery like last time. This time, she slowly came into view from the void behind his eyes. It materialized from the black, a phantasmal manifestation, and he asked it *Why do I keep seeing you out here, momma?* In response, her face warped and shifted and broke open from its form to spread out over his imagination in waves of undulating tatters. They were wriggling and writhing, the pieces animate of their own accord, like the maggots of some unknown grime from another dimension. Waves of brief but potent nausea unfurled throughout his body, rolling under this skin of his stomach and pelvis.

The bright light of the monitor stole Phi's attention back, and he realized then that he'd opened his eyes again at some point. There was something *here*, something just on the verge of tangibility, teetering on the razor edge of substance and nothingness in a deeply confounding way. It was here because he could feel it, through his suit, in the air or in this space. It wasn't the cold. It was something else, an essence that he sensed. Whatever *it* was had entered him during his sleep, slithered around and left a trail of slime over his soul upon its departure. It was what he'd encountered on the *Artorius* in his bunk, in the storage cabinet, on the way here. It was what he'd seen in his nightmares, in the cryotubes that never let him leave. The thought of never having actually awoken from the long nap, that all of this had been some sort of romp through the misery and stresses of his subconscious, sent chills down his back.

Phi shook his head, breathing deeply, and scraped the rest of the frost from the small screen. The bootup sequence had completed and the program sat at a login window. Phi's intuition about ATMUS being the software on this ship had served him properly. It was the same as on the *Artorius* and so he input his company credentials then hit the ACCEPT key once more.

"Holy fuck!" La Felios cursed over the comms.

Phi shifted to look down the walkway from the panel. "D. What the hell?"

"Captain, you need to come see this. I found one of their crew."

Phi glanced back toward the screen. The red letters of ACCESS DENIED blinked under the username and password boxes.

The walkway was grated steel and Phi's heavy steps echoed in the darkness as he made his way down the tunnel toward the rear of the ship. When he reached the opening into the mess hall, he saw the light from the other headlamps.

La Felios stood next to a body. It was slumped into the corner of some cupboards. As Phi approached, he saw that the man wore a H.E.T.E. suit with no helmet or gloves. There was a pool of dried brown blood coming out from underneath him, hardened to the metal floor plates through time and under the same frost that covered everything else. The man's greyish-bruised skin was cut at the wrists. A small cooking knife lay encrusted in the left hand. The flesh of his face and neck were grotesquely hued and deeply sunken, exposing the shapes of tendons still taut just under the skin. On the floor, stuck to it by the dried blood, was a datapad. Its screen was dark.

La Felios leaned over the corpse. "Thank god we can't smell this." His hand unruffled the front layer of the dead one's H.E.T.E. suit and flattened out the embroidered name on the left side of the chest. "R. Blake," he read aloud.

Phi moved to the other side of the body and crouched down. The datapad was crusted with the old blood, but it came up off the floor easily enough. It left a square relief of hardened coagulate on the metal below. He pushed the power button on side of the device and was expecting to see the one or two second dead-battery symbol appear. Instead, the screen lit up and began its standard boot sequence.

Phi smirked. "Good man, Mr. Blake. Looks like our friend turned it off before he... did that to himself. Maybe we can find something on here, something that can tell us what happened."

"Should we tell the others?"

The captain shook his head. "Not yet. I don't want to cause a panic until we have more information. Let's wait to hear from them about Jamison. We'll mention it then or fill them in when we rendezvous." Phi looked down toward the body while the datapad booted. The man's hair was frozen to the flesh of his forehead, which had lost much of its opacity, appearing almost gelatinous. Defunct veins snaked thin and lifeless under the skin.

The datapad's operating system came to its login screen. The username and password fields were already filled in. Phi tapped the screen to finish the login process and the interface transitioned into the Dynam Industries employee module. The hazy grey-blue background accentuated the teal interface text. In the top corner of the screen, the folder hierarchy was displayed:

INBOX
OUTBOX [1]
DRAFTS
TRASH

La Felios stood and came around to Phi's side. "Get anything with that yet?"

"Yeah. There's one outgoing message."

Phi held the datapad angled to the side so that La Felios could see and they both read the note in silence.

We came all this way in the name of exploration, in the name of human discovery. We talk of our ancestors proudly, claiming them true adventurers. They knew nothing of what lay beyond our world. There are horrors out here. It's one thing to speculate about the stars from the comfort of our own world. It's another to actually be here. We were not meant to be this far from home. I have seen darkness in its truest form out here.

I don't know how to fly the ship off this fucking ice cube. I'm not a pilot. I was just along for the ride to impress Mr. Jamison for my internship in Dynam's Medical R&D. None of that matters now. I won't let this place, those things, swallow me while I still breathe. I think it's better to end this myself, but I'm scared. I'm scared it will hurt.

Hell exists and it's out here. It's under the ice and it waits for my corpse. It took them and it'll come for me soon. I don't want it to have my body when I am gone but I don't think I have a choice. This place is a grave.

"Jesus. That's some cryptic shit," La Felios murmured.

Phi finished and agreed. "Yep." He skimmed through the letter one more time, then handed it to La Felios.

"What do you think it means?," La Felios asked. “What *things* was he talking about?"

Phi exhaled deeply, trying to will more sense into the situation he now found himself in. “I'll be honest, I don't know. I do know, however, that we need to get back to the rest of the crew. My credentials aren't working on this ship's ATMUS login. If we can’t get this ship back online, we’ll need to return to the Acolyte and send the base report ourselves. We've got a body. Who knows how many others there are. Either way, hop over to channel two and let them know we’ll be on our way to get them in just a few minutes. I’m shutting this operation down. We're going home.”

“Aye, Captain,” La Felios nodded. “Also, let me give the ATMUS login a try. I was an employee before the Artorius launched last year. My login may still work.”

“Go for it. I’m going to grab the black box. The information on it might help piece some more of this together.”

"What'll we do about Jamison? You know he's gonna say something."

The captain said, "Fuck him," over his shoulder as he exited the mess hall.

Ice granules crunched under each of Phi's step down the walkway. La Felios followed until breaking off to the control panel once they both re-entered the cabin. Phi moved to the navigation screens in between the pilot’s chair and the main navigation displays, the bulbous screens of which were dead and sheened with hoarfrost. Underneath the displays was a panel. He unlatched and opened it to reveal a bed of identical slick black hard drives. One of these was labeled DIAG-SYS-REC PRIMARY. The mechanism released it from the bay, ejecting it partially when Phi pushed the drive in. He grabbed it and stood, glancing out the viewport once more.

The darkness above—

The distant waning sun—

Jupiter...

“Got it,” La Felios said.

The lights in the cabin flickered above, strobing for a brief moment before illuminating fully, snapping Phi from his gaze. There was a chorus of booting noises for all of the systems in the ship, a collective emission from the air vents in the walls in a mechanical crescendo. The *Acolyte* breathed once more. Buttons lit up on the control panels along the front of the cabin and the overhead display staticked for a moment before resting at a black screen with small text in the bottom corner that said NULL.

“Excellent." Phi turned back toward La Felios. "I’ve got the safety drive with me but I’m going to check for the original files in the ship's computer system now that it's up and running.”

The central navigation screen entered into another startup sequence. Streams of code ran by in the black backdrop before transitioning into a directory menu. Phi entered a few lines of commands into the keyboard under the main status console and found the original copies of the diagnostic recordings for not only the ship’s onboard systems, but the H.E.T.E. suit recorded camera feeds of the *Acolyte's* crew.

“Switching to channel two,” said La Felios.

“Roger.”

Phi could hear La Felios’ mic cut out of the channel. His increasingly feverish thoughts were left to themselves while he searched for logs in the ship’s shared computer drives and listened to his own breathing. His mind kept returning to the planet hanging in the black beyond the cold horizon. His eyes flicked up to the great celestial body and the dead man’s note came back into his thoughts.

Hell exists and it's out here. It’s under the ice and it waits for my corpse.

Phi navigated to the video recordings folder and scrolled through the files separated by crew member name:

JAMISON, B. [1]
CARLIN, D. [1]
PORTER, M.
GILL, H. [1]
COLEMAN, C.
BLAKE, R.

He tapped the keys to enter the JAMISON, B. folder. Inside there was a file titled <NULL>. He hit the ENTER key to select it but was met with a prompt stating FILE CORRUPTED. DO YOU WANT TO DELETE? Y N. He tapped the N key then returned to the file directory.

The captain glanced back. La Felios' mouth moved noiselessly, communicating to the others on a different channel. Through the two helmets they wore, it was impossible for Phi to make out what the pilot was saying.

Inside the CARLIN, D. folder was another file titled <NULL>. Phi was met with the same error message as before, so he backed out and returned to the previous directory. GILL, H. was the only one left with a file. Phi selected it, expecting to see another corrupt video message.

"Captain!" La Felios had switched back over to channel three. "Captain, something's fucking happening!"

"What? What's wrong?"

"Swap to channel two, now!"

La Felios appeared to already be switching back a channel as Phi tapped the screen of his own HUD and followed suit. The temporal silence over the comms was thick and the anticipation was just as heavy in his nerves.

The radio clicked over to channel two.

They were all screaming.

*

It's in our blood, my son... the yearning for power beyond that which we've experienced. This eldritch "anomaly" on the fringe of our solar system will be my lantern in the dark. It is a beacon meant for those who possess the necessary knowledge, artifacts and will to obtain transcendence.

I know not what awaits me, yet I do not fear. The rituals of Old run in our veins and I possess the faith needed, the will to reach beyond. I believe you have that will, too, Edward. All you need is the faith.

I own the Pratt & Rochester building you are undoubtedly reading this from. In the library, at the bottom floor of that building, is all of my work, all of my research, every note I've taken and every book I've had to search for, every item I've killed for. In the lockbox I've left you, you should find a keycard that will let you in. I am leaving all of it to you, to continue my work until I return. No one on the face of the earth has access to that floor now except you. You now also have access to all of my monetary assets and bank accounts and you've been given the rank of Chairman of the Board for the company, so that you may oversee any of the major changes my snaking colleagues will undoubtedly attempt whilst I am gone.

Have faith, my son. Learn faith from all that I have gathered and all that I have pieced together. I am giving you and only you the opportunity to meet the apocalypse with preparation. Should you choose to squander or derail the path I have set before you, that is your choice to make. Just know that my arrival will not be a quiet one and those who are seen lacking will grind under the cosmic wheels of irrevocable change.

Prepare for my second coming, my second birth, and make no mistake, Edward;

I will return.

H. R. Jamison

Edward reread the last few lines of the letter. After he'd finished it once more, he set it back onto the oak table and sat back in the chair, staring out of the large office windows. The sky was still grim and the rain still poured in sheets. It clattered against the glass, made liquid shapes among the grey, and he once again felt himself settling into his vision. His mind came to a slow rhythmic grace as it reflected on the words he'd just read, the words of his father. He allowed only a fractional moment to separate himself from the path that now lay ahead of him, a brief but crucial stasis in which he simply sat and absorbed the dreary light from outside. Then he stood.

He slipped the keycard into the inner pocket of his suit jacket, then took the letter and the small stone effigy and placed them on top of the datapad before grabbing the whole stack and moving toward the door of the office.

As soon as he stepped out into the hallway, the woman from before was at his side.

"Ah, Mr. Jamison. Is there anything I could—"

Edward moved around her.

When he reached the elevators, he hit the down arrow on the panel and, luckily, one of the three was already there. A *ding* signaled the far left one and he moved toward it and into the elevator. He slid the keycard from his pocket and tapped it against the reader on the panel, then hit the bottom button, LIBRARY - C12 ACCESS ONLY, and pushed the CLOSE DOOR button twice.

The waiting woman stood a few feet outside the elevator with an appalled look on her face. The thick metal doors slid closed.

*

The airlock was two minutes into its depressurization process. La Felios assembled his mining pick from the pack he wore, linking the segments of the tool together with a quickness. It was cold oiled steel and reflected the airlock's overhead lights when it was held up. Phi watched and listened to the comm feed of channel two.

The screaming had lasted about thirty seconds. When Phi had first swapped over to the channel, Eilah Winthrope had been hysterical, crying out her husband's name (*Jeffrey! No, no, no, Jeff! Please!*). He heard nothing from Engineer Lansig or Jeffrey Winthrope. Eilah's crying became intense, interrupted only for the intermittent heaving breath of horror, and she'd managed to scream *Oh God, What is that?* before her voice had cut out.

"Eilah!" Phi called into his mic.

There was no response. The airwaves sounded of emptiness, void of any signs of life or consciousness. The moments of silence permeated a type of indescribable weight.

And then there was a quiet sobbing over the channel. Phi thought it was Eilah's voice at first but, behind the cries, the voice started chanting. It was Russian. Her muttering was almost silent, a background noise to the feed, and Phi recognized that it was Sovikov.

"What is that?" La Felios asked. "It sounds like she's saying the same thing over and over."

The eyes of the two men met. Phi said, "I don't speak Russian but it sounds like a prayer to me."

Though his hands moved willfully, prepping his suit and checking the life support stats on the HUD embedded into his forearm, the desperate muttering had sent Phi's mind rolling through old memories of when he was a child back in church, when he was with his mother and two aunts. He watched the choir sing, watched their richly colored robes sway as they moved with the music. Phi was dressed in his Sunday best outfit, singing along with the hymns. His family stood all around him and he remembered being happy, feeling grateful for where he was, who he was with. Then his attention shifted. Hanging against the wall above the pulpit was the bleeding statue of Christ crucified on the wooden cross. Phi had stared up at the bloodied man many times as a kid, burning the image into his thoughts.

The light next to the door changed from red to green and the outer airlock opened. Phi beheld Jupiter sitting on the horizon and stepped down the six retractable steps and out onto the packed ice. He lost sight of the planet in the shadow of the pressure ridge that separated their landing zone from the anomaly and the rest of the crew.

Christ still bled in the space of his imagination.

“Sovikov," Phi said. "What’s the situation where you guys are? What happened to the rest of the crew?”

Sovikov still murmured incomprehensibly but, behind that, someone else was breathing heavily over the comm. Phi hadn’t noticed until this moment.

“Lansig, is that you? What the hell is happening?”

Sovikov's prayers quieted. Phi could now only occasionally hear the sharpness of her whispers, intermittently halted by sobbing.

“Eilah? Jeffrey?”

The unknown breather behind it all inhaled harder now, large breaths sucking in and out. And then, in a raspy choked voice, it spoke:

“*Jamison...*” It was a last curdled word, an accusation of some kind riding on the tail end of a death rattle.

Phi moved away from the ship, jogging parallel to the ice wall. Below his feet, footprints from previous suited boots riddled the snow and marked a trail ahead of him along the base of the ridge.

A slow laugh flowed through the little speaker of the headset in the helmet. It chuckled lightly at first, then built into a hearty sound. “This is it!" Jamison yelled over the comms. "They obey! Ha ha ha! They obey!”

Phi glanced back and saw La Felios jogging in tow, still wielding the ice pick assembled inside the airlock. The shadow of the pressure ridge on their left was over them and Phi picked up his pace. The gravity was much lighter on this ice-crusted satellite but he had trained for this and adjusted quickly.

Jamison's voice came again over the whispers. This time he spoke almost musically in some language Phi could not understand. "*Ehak tlukovik etna sel chikvolis*," the man chanted. "*Atnek sartivin ehak tlukovik...*"

There was a break in the ridge coming up and the footprints led over the lowered portion of the ice wall and to the other side. Phi made no pause before stepping up and through the gap. He slid down to the ice a few feet below and La Felios skidded right behind him. They stood in the shadow of a natural wall of ice spikes. Footsteps led around the base of the formation and Phi led he and his pilot to the other side.

When he stepped out into the sunlight, Phi was once again humbled by the sight of Jupiter in the darkness above. Its immensity commanded his attention, nagging at some deep core of his mammalian mind, something buried in his genes that drove him to stand in awe for the briefest of moments among its presence.

Something nudged Phi's shoulder. His focus returned. La Felios was pointing ahead.

"There he is."

Fifty yards ahead of them, Harold Jamison knelt in his H.E.T.E. suit. He was looking down at the tome he held to his knee and, dangling from his raised free hand, something glinted gold in the distance. Underneath the tycoon, the ice was smeared bloody in large swaths around the vicinity, with a few heaps of dark red piled here and there in the frost. Sat against the base of the pressure ridge behind Jamison was the drill tool box and, up against that, was another crewmember in a H.E.T.E. suit, facing out toward the expanse that opened up before them. The helmet lights were on and the crewmember's head was bobbing slowly. Phi assumed it was Sovikov as she was the only other one he could hear over the comms, still whispering her prayers, but he couldn't be for certain from this distance.

"Jamison, what the hell are you doing?" Phi demanded. "What the fuck is going on?!"

"*Agan'thurak, Agan'thurak!*" Jamison chanted. "*Fil tat Othuum! Agan'thurak, Agan'thurak! Fil tat Othuum!*" His gloved fingers moved along the text in the tome's pages as he sang the words.

Phi closed in, just a few feet away from Jamison, when he was able to make out what the heaps of dark red scattered around the area were. The first one was what was left of Jeffrey Winthrope's face, smashed against the inside of his helmet's faceplate. His legs were gone at the waist. His torso appeared to have been crushed in by some extreme force. The misshapen facial features and disconnected entrails were freezing in the frigid air and the man's blood was already petrified to the ice. Lying next to him was another heap, but the head and arms were missing from the torso. The suit's tag had WINTHROPE, E. embroidered into it.

"What the fuck," La Felios' voice cracked over the whispering and chanting. "What the fuck did you do? What the *fuck*?!"

There was one other heap sprawled onto the shallow ice, out in front of where Jamison knelt. Around the gore were holes in the sheet of ice the size of oil barrels, like something had fallen in or broken through. The black water of the alien ocean underneath pushed up to the surface and shards of ice bobbed against the inside of the circular apertures like children's toys floating in bathtubs.

Phi turned toward the crewmember sitting against the pressure ridge wall and moved cautiously in a wide berth around the back side of Jamison. He reached the tool crate and saw that it was indeed Sovikov sat up against it. Her eyes were hysterically wide. Tears streaked her pale face inside the helmet she wore. Her mouth still moved in quiet whispers.

"Natalya," Phi said, crouched over next to her. The left leg of her suit was completely smashed in, sodden with a deep red from the inside. Phi assessed it momentarily and thought it looked shattered beyond repair. There was a large pool of blood underneath, most of which had already frozen. "Natalya, can you hear me?"

Her lips still whispered. She stared out, beyond Phi and beyond Jamison, to the expanse of shallow ice. Her eyes wouldn't meet his. Phi reached a gloved hand out and set it on her shoulder. She did not seem to notice.

"Sovikov, we need to get you back to the ship and stabilize that leg. You're losing too much blood." Phi was certain she wouldn't last much longer if they didn't stop her bleeding. "I'm going to pick you up and it's probably going to hurt like hell but I need you to be strong, alright?"

She did not respond, her whispers having now devolved completely to barely audible sobbing. Her shoulders racked powerlessly.

Jamison was still distracted by the tome and what he read aloud. The glinting golden item he had dangling in his raised left hand, Phi could now see, was an amulet. It was the one encased in gold with the large red gem inside of it. Jamison had been wearing it earlier. Phi couldn't tell if it was the sun's distant glare or his imagination running off with him but the gem appeared to be producing its own unexplainable light.

"What the fuck did you do to them, *goddamnit*?!" La Felios yelled. Phi turned back to see him standing over the chanting Jamison, his ice axe slightly raised in his right hand. La Felios kicked a heavy boot out and knocked Jamison back onto his rear. The tome slid from the man's knee and its pages smashed into the ice. Jamison's raised left hand faltered to catch his balance and the amulet fell into the slush with it.

There was a rumbling sound, something pushing from below the ice they stood upon. It was underneath their feet, a massive churning in the depths.

Behind La Felios, out of the closest of the large holes in the ice, a black worm slithered slowly out of the water. It's form tapered thicker as it revealed more of itself, appearing as a tendril of slick darkness as it uncoiled into the air. The rubbery skin glistened under Jupiter's illumination.

La Felios was facing Jamison with his back to the alien serpent, seemingly unaware of its presence. "You put all of our lives in danger, for what?!" He stepped even closer to Jamison.

"La Felios!" Phi called out. He still couldn't make out what he was seeing when the thing rose up further into the air, as tall as a tree, behind his friend. Then, like stab wounds, slits opened in the tight skin all over the tentacle. They stretched and gaped open with a horrible tension. Rows upon rows of teeth, drenched in pearlescent slobber, gnashed in each one of the sores. They were mouths and there were dozens of them, chewing and salivating in the cold, sending tufts of alien breath floating into the air with each chomp.

"D!"

The flight specialist looked up toward Phi, who was pointing behind him, then turned around. The wriggling trunk of stretched black flesh slowly danced in front of him like a cobra. The mouths bit and gurgled. "Oh my god..." The ice pick dropped from La Felios' hand to the ground by his feet. "Oh my g—"

The rubbery thing whipped down onto La Felios so quickly that Phi almost didn't see it. The creature had been leaning back and, in the very next moment, it had shifted and then returned to its slow upright dance, moving back and forth, but now there was a splat of blood on the ice where his best friend had been standing and bits and pieces of La Felios' H.E.T.E. suit hung out of one of the mouths. It chewed. Inside, a cud of cloth, plastic and gore rolled around on its grotesquely flayed tongue.

All of the mouths chewed.

The very tip of the tentacle started moving separate from the rest of itself. It peered around, scanning the ice as if it could see with some hidden optical nerve buried within. When it pointed toward Jamison, who was shuffling himself back into the kneeling position after retrieving the tome, the thing rippled and moved into a different dance than it had before. Phi's reality was being turned upside-down. What he thought was real and wasn't real no longer held dominion over the display in front of him. The knots of his consciousness felt to be unraveling and yet, amidst the immediate shock of the deaths of his crew and of his best friend, the captain couldn't help but see it in that moment. He couldn't help but feel something beyond the rage and the nausea...

There was an undeniable beauty in the creature's dance.

The thing appeared about to strike once more, springing itself back again. Jamison raised the amulet into the air. Again, it glowed. The black serpent stopped mid-strike, holding taut for a brief moment. It uncoiled and seemed to relax back into its dance.

"*Agan'Thurak, Agan'thurak!*" Jamison began the ritual once more, reading through the wet pages of the book. "*Fil tat Othuum!*"

The serpent's focus was toward the chanting man, mesmerized by whatever its alien sight beheld from within the amulet.

La Felios... The realization that he'd just watched his best friend mauled by an entity of such otherworldly origin set in at that very moment for Phi. On the tail end of that stream of consciousness came the decomposed face again, the decaying putrefied features of his mother, so detailed that he thought them corporeal, filling his head as well as his reality. And then all the faces of the crew invaded his thoughts. A heavy sob escaped his lips, just one, before he turned back to Sovikov. "Jesus Christ," he murmured. "Jesus Christ..." Tears hung in the corners of his eyes.

Through the faceplate of her suit, Sovikov was quiet and still staring. She shivered and Phi couldn't tell if it was from the cold or what she'd been witness to out here. Her leg was in ruin and her pallid skin made it apparent that she needed to be stabilized and quickly. Phi could hardly think amidst the images that assaulted his psyche now but their shapes, saddening and bizarre, still paled in comparison to what was happening out on the ice.

He grunted as he hoisted Sovikov's body into his arms and stood, tears now running down his cheeks. Above, in the bulk of Jupiter, he saw D'Artagnan's mutilated body fading in and out of the colors, surfacing and submerging in the storms, and he could no longer see the stars that haloed the great planet before. It had all gone black as Death. When he looked back toward the dark serpent, it writhed and disappeared back through the hole in the ice and into the hidden waters below. Jamison appeared to have control of the thing or somehow stayed its murderous tendency with the amulet. Phi had no plans on sticking around to figure out how.

The captain took one soft step, then another, back around to the other side of Jamison and toward the trail of footsteps in the snow that led them here. “Stay with me, Natalya,” he said, picking up the pace. Sovikov's eyes were half closed now. Whether it was the blood loss or the shock that was making her skin so pale, the more porcelain it became, the more the dread in Phi's chest seemed to grow.

He carried her through the opening of the cave-like canopy of ice shards that encompassed the break in the pressure ridge they had come through. Though the slope up to the other side was only about 5 feet long, it was steep. Judging from the angle, Phi realized he would not be able to ascend it without using his hands, which were currently holding a bloodied woman. He was going to have to take a run at it and hope to get enough momentum to reach the top without the use of his hands, or he could tie the straps from the oxygen tank under her arms and crawl up with her attached to his belt. One was fast, the other was safe.

The blood loss was the deciding factor. There wasn't any time.

Jamison still chanted, his voice taking on an almost musical tone. "*Agan'Thurak, Agan'Thurak! Fil tat Othuum!*"

Phi bolted from the slope. He turned in a half-circle that then looped back toward it and sprinted, Sovikov bouncing in his arms. Three long strides with momentum at his back pushed him up over the slope of steep slickness and he landed on the packed frost on the other side of the pressure ridge. With winded breathing heavy against the inner glass of his faceplate, Phi turned toward the ships and did not wait to start moving.

"Natalya, stay with me." He looked down once more and Sovikov's eyes were completely closed, her head leaned in toward his arm and shoulder. She moved occasionally though Phi couldn't tell if that was her own effort or from the rocking of his strides.

"Ha ha!" Jamison's laugh came through the comms. "And it is by *this* gift of my piety as well as this blood that I take from you, my dark Lord, and give unto myself the power of your ageless consciousness, the knowledge of your timeless wisdom!"

The retractable steps of the *Artorius* rattled as Phi ascended each step carrying the weight of two rather than just himself. His arms felt on fire and he could hardly brace Sovikov's body before he set her down next to the outer airlock door. He stood and turned to the access panel. As he punched in the entry code, Jamison's voice continued to sound into his helmet.

"It is with this power that I shall subjugate the rest of these cattle, heralding a birth for you that is worthy of your entrance to Earth. Upon the mounds of bloated bodies, I will construct a throne of flies, a kingdom of anguish that even you, Oh Lord Agan'Thurak, Son of Othuum, would find worthy."

The outer airlock door slid open and Phi crouched and picked Sovikov up once more to move the few feet into the airlock. He set her down against the steel plated wall and punched in the ATMUS commands to the inner control panel, causing the outer door to roll down behind them. The screen displayed that the five minute depressurization process had begun. Breathable oxygen levels would be available inside the airlock in two minutes.

"In the Eye of Blood, inside its core, I see the conflagration that oozes from your eyes, my Lord. In my mind's eye, I can already see your ancient face and, in my bones, I can feel your pull."

Phi crouched down next to Sovikov, trying to better assess the damage to her leg. Blood leaked onto the floor in a slow but steady drip. There was a trail of it, smeared and leading outside the airlock door and onto the steps from where he'd dragged her.

"I have spent my life's gains, made it my life's work, to be here at this very moment. I've killed, coerced, manipulated and done anything and everything I needed to in order to obtain that which was necessary. I even damned my own brother to his death by withholding that which I now... *Ha ha*! That which I hold in front of me! *This* is the symbol of my faith!" Jamison screamed. "*I* am the symbol of my piety! Open your dark eyes to me and give me that which I require, Oh Lord, and I will become the harbinger of your arrival!"

The ATMUS control panel displayed breathable oxygen levels at 98%. Phi continued to stare until it turned to 99% and then until it turned to 100%. His hands moved to the base buckles on his helmet and unlatched them, then turned the entire thing, removing it and exposing his head to the cool temperature of the airlock. After setting the helmet onto the floor next to him, he unlatched Sovikov's and gently removed it, resting a gloved hand behind her head to stop it from hitting limply against the wall. He lowered an ear down next to her nose and mouth and listened.

He couldn't hear anything, nor could he feel any sort of breath coming from her.

"Sovikov," Phi said with tension. He twisted his right glove at the wrist, removing it and tossing it to the floor behind him. He reached two fingers under her jaw, at the jugular, and gently placed them against her skin.

No pulse.

Underneath Sovikov's leg, the pool of blood had grown. The skin of her face and neck was pale, her lips blue. Her eyes had rolled back to half open but there was no life in the slack pupils.

Phi sat back against the inner airlock wall and slid to the floor, poorly bracing himself with his still gloved left hand. His eyes shifted from Sovikov's chilling body to the dense glass of the outer door. He stared out at the other ship, the *Acolyte*, just a few dozen yards out, and then to the black sky above it. Only a sliver of Jupiter was visible from the angle he was facing but it was enough to send his mind sinking further into that darkness that had been overflowing into his existence. This series of events was swallowing him and all he could feel was this misery and a strange type of vertigo, as if he was slipping through those holes out in the ice right now and falling into the depths of the infinite oceans below.

Through the headset speakers of his helmet, buzzing on the steel floor to his left, the barely audible voice of Harold Jamison still spoke. Phi couldn't make out what was being said but the incantatory cadence of the man's words could still be heard.

The control panel light went green. A gentle warning pulsed as the inner airlock door hissed and began to open. Phi moved from it and stood, glancing to Sovikov once more.

She was dead. He was alone.

When the inner airlock had fully opened, he stepped onto the bridge of the *Artorius*. The familiar smell and feel of the place filled his senses, yet the tension in his muscles and the stress in his veins were unhindered by the reunion. He bypassed the captain's chair and moved toward the Navigation panel, toward the station his best friend had held. He looked to the empty seat for a long moment, then typed in the launch codes and flipped a few of the initiation switches. The engines whirred with power. The charging of the ship's vertical lift-off thrusters began, joining the flowing chorus of life support and power systems.

Phi returned to the airlock to grab his helmet, then stepped back to the inner access panel and pressed the CLOSE key. The thick door slid shut. Through the small triangle shaped window, he could see Sovikov's body still sat there against the wall. He was going to leave her in the airlock, separated from himself and the rest of the ship... The body was going to begin rotting at some point on the way back to Earth. He could move her into one of the cryosleep vats, but God knows what six months soaked in that goop would do to a corpse. It also felt wrong entertaining the idea of leaving her body here on this block of ice with those things out there. Even in death, she didn't deserve that. None of them did.

Five of his crew were dead. Phi was sure Jamison would be the sixth.

As he analyzed the different facets of the deaths he'd witnessed, something started happening. From the borders of reality, a buzzing sensation crawled through the aether and wrapped itself around Phi's consciousness. He felt the tendons in his legs twitch and his ankles weaken. Somewhere in the back of his mind or his head, something wavered and eroded his vision over a few microcosmic seconds. Before he could understand what was happening, he'd stumbled over to lean against Le Felios' chair, staring ahead out of the viewport, up to the King of the Gods. Its radiance ebbed like a heartbeat. In his mind and his soul and in the very fibers that made his animus, he felt the power. Something was overtaking him. *Jupiter* was overtaking him.

He fell, then. His paralyzed body slammed against the cold metal floor. Things flashed in his vision, overlaying reality, and he closed his eyes but it did nothing to save him from what he was being shown:

The face of the frozen crewmember they'd found on the *Acolyte*...

D'Artagnan's brutalized expression, worming and rotting in a bed of flowing blackness...

His mother, her dead skin tight against her skull...

A writhing darkness out of which a porcelain face emerges, strange and doll-like, the mouth shifting and biting over and over again...

A radiant display of two galaxies dancing their destructive waltz with each other and a pile of organic blubber, with walls upon walls of endless twitching eyes, floating intently in the vacuum, patiently awaiting its destination within the chaos...

Under black waters and putrid sediment, something unfurling its infinite appendages and ascending, murderously propelling itself upward through the murk...

And then it was gone.

With a sharp breath, Phi opened his eyes. The floor was vertical in front of him. He blinked and felt the cold metal against his cheek, then pushed himself slowly up to a sitting position. "What the fuck..." With every breath he took, the latent tendrils of whatever brief possession had occurred peeled off of his soul like dead skin. The horrendous imagery had subsided from his mind but the fear still had its icy talons lodged into him.

There was vibration under the ship, beneath the ice. He felt it through his palms. It was deep and it was growing. While he could not see whatever it was that shook and moved, he *knew* already, that it was that snaking inhuman thing that had taken the lives of his crew, the abomination that lived in those foreign tenebrous oceans.

Something Phi couldn't pinpoint drove him to witness the horrible serpentine creature again. He had to see. He had to try and make sense of it. Terror and astonishment bled into each other somewhere within the shock, seeming to fill his entire body, buzzing as the psychic episode did just moments before and electrifying in his fingertips. Logic and reason were postponed while his mind reflected on the horror and the events that led to this very moment.

He needed to see again.

Phi stood and moved to the navigation panel and stared out of the viewport. He couldn't see Jamison's ritual from here, blocked by the tall pressure ridge, but the grotesque serpent that danced out of the ice was seared into his memory. His heart pounded maddeningly in his ears. There were so many mouths, of which the teeth were chipped and always gritting and gnashing and grinding...

The captain returned to La Felios' chair and turned on the camera feed's monitoring software. The screen lit up and, in the main directory that the system logged into, there was a list of all active feeds. WINTHROPE, E. and WINTHROPE, J. were both black, cameras destroyed, as was LA FELIOS, D. SOVIKOV, N. was still active, but it faced a corner in the darkness of the airlock, with nothing to see but steel panel meeting steel panel. He typed in the fullscreen command on the one labeled JAMISON, H. The audio enabled in the speakers on either side of the monitor and the screen staticked as it connected to the live feed.

Jamison's camera was directed toward the book on his knee. Phi couldn't make out the text and wasn't sure whether it was because of the writing's strange origins or the graininess of the video feed. The text had pictures drawn into the margins. They, too, were obscured by the low quality of the video feed though they appeared to be drawings of faces, squid-like and vaguely humanoid.

Ancient-looking symbols were sketched in old ink in the top and bottom margins of the page and notes were scribbled in the spaces between paragraphs. Through its strangely innate illumination, the amulet that Jamison dangled created red prisms that projected down onto the pages of the tome. The alien markings appeared to come alive under the bizarre glare. Jamison spoke the eldritch language out loud as he read. It sounded ancient and almost unnatural for the human tongue.

Phi's eyes surveyed the console at his right.

Launch initiation was at 29%.

Jamison's chanting grew more intense. Deep underneath the *Artorius*, a dull crack echoed through leagues of ice and black ocean. The vibration from before had grown into tremors that rippled under the landing gear. Buckles, straps and loose knobs around the bridge jingled in unison with the throbbing, as did Phi's adrenaline, pulsing heavily in tandem.

Through the feed, there was a crash of ice. Jamison's voice quieted to a silence as the camera slowly panned upward.

The amulet swung gently back and forth in the center of the screen, radiating its vibrant ruby light. Beyond the amulet, coiling out of the ice, were more of those slithering black horrors. Their dances of ascension were mesmerizing and terrifying, beautiful and abominable. They totaled six, waving back and forth in unison, side-to-side, with their countless mouths slowly opening and closing, appearing almost to speak to each other.

It was a monstrous procession, one of strange haunting symmetry.

Phi shuddered, putting his fist up to his mouth. His stomach heaved. His anxiety flared. Never had he felt so vulnerable, so completely out of the realm of situations that he could possibly control. They had come to a place at the edge of the solar system, a place where humans did not belong, with a climate unfit for our lungs, entities unfit for our sanity. Coming here was a mistake. This was too far beyond the veil that, up until this point, had protected him from the uncompassionate creations of the universal machine.

In the feed, Jamison stood to his feet, the amulet still held out in front of him. He waited there a moment, silent inside the helmet. Then he took a step toward the tentacles, and then another.

The black things danced slowly, their infinite orifices jibbering and chomping. Jamison's breaths were slow but tense as he moved forward. One of the swaying things passed by on the left side of the camera. Putrid amniotic fluid dripped from the slick swollen lips of the various mouths. Jamison had moved past three of them, then walked around the fourth, when the camera panned down toward the ice. Underneath the thin layer that he stood upon, maybe three feet separating him from the abyss below, a wriggling nightmarish mass squashed and turned and fluttered against the ice from below. There were hundreds of these mouthed eel-like things, furling and waiting just below. Phi's heart sank in his chest at the horrific scene. He didn't know how he knew, or why, but the knowledge of what truly waited below came to him, then. Each of those things was part of one giant entity. They weren't separate creatures but tentacles of a thing that waited below, an all-encompassing organism. He knew it like he knew the inevitability of Death.

This thing *was* Death.

It took a moment for Phi to pry his eyes from Jamison's feed. Launch thrusters were at 58%. Once they engaged, he would set the *Artorius* to go. They would use the gravitational pull of Europa to slingshot the ship outside of Jupiter's grasp and back toward Earth, toward a place not so horrific as this.

Jamison's camera returned ahead to the dangling amulet and the final two dancing serpents. The light from the sun had diminished drastically and the video feed was getting darker as Europa moved into the shadow of its patriarch. The amulet continued to shine brightly on its own. Just beyond the two tentacles, sticking out of the thin ice, was the anomaly, appearing as a tapered black spike over the grainy video. Jamison maintained his slow careful steps toward it. When he passed the last pair of tendrils, gyrating in slow motion, the tycoon let go of a deep breath and Phi felt himself do the same thing.

Jamison reached the anomaly. The details of it became clearer through the monitor and Phi could see that it was a stone pedestal of some kind, sticking three or four feet out of the frozen crust. The sustaining red light of the amulet gave truth to its form. There were engravings carved up and down the sides of it, tapestries of dogmatic depictions and unearthly fables. Phi thought he saw one that resembled those inhuman faces, from the book Jamison had been reading before, but the shadows warped with the quality of the camera and he couldn't be certain.

The relief on the very top of the artifact, embedded into the upward facing plate, was a diamond shape with a thin crevice ascending to the peak and down the backside of it. Jamison ran a gloved finger along the form and then lowered the brightening jewel toward it. The amulet fit perfectly into the slot. He draped the chain over the top and behind and it fell into the thin crevice as if it were made for it. He stood breathing, waiting.

Phi's eyes flicked to the navigation panel. Launch thrusters were at 74%.

The pedestal appeared to drink the light coming from the amulet. Some plasma form of the same red glow then oozed from each crack and indentation on the artifact, setting to life the depictions carved into the alien stone.

There was a twinge of something, then. Phi felt it behind one of his eyes first, like the tickle of an oncoming headache. It started as a pulse but became much more within seconds. External of his body was a tectonic grinding of some sort, planetary in scale, its reverberations so massive that it seemed that reality itself was somehow breaking apart. The ship groaned against the movement and alarms started complaining off of screens on the port side of the bridge.

It was more than the physical world being shaken and tossed. Phi's sight warbled unnaturally. His thoughts melted into one another. His focus was caught by some extradimensional attribute to the quake. The possession was trying to take hold of him once more, that same intent that had shown him those atrocious images when it paralyzed him to the floor a few minutes earlier. The force pushed Phi back into the chair. His tight knuckled hands gripped the armrests savagely as the will that now besieged him cracked from the nothingness beyond into his mind, something sinister. Amidst the mental battle for will and for his soul, Phi saw it in the video feed:

The amulet's radiance beamed from its spot in the relief at the top of the artifact. A pillar of light ascended to the sky like a beacon. The camera panned back toward the way in which Jamison had come. In the growing shadow of Jupiter above, the tentacles moved in unison, rippling and twisting and coiling and uncoiling as if being swept by some unseen current, flowing beyond the visible spectrum of the human eye. The mouths were all shut, the lips invisible in rubbery blackness.

A bright glow shone over the ritual from somewhere off-camera. When Jamison turned back, a rectangle of light had pulled open just beyond the artifact. It was a canvas of illumination, hovering a foot or so off the ground. Its brightness burned to look upon, even through the video. The images that possessed Phi's mind, clawing at his consciousness, melded with what he saw in reality. Twitching eyes manifested on and out of every surface of the control shelf, fluttering open out of the cold metal. Illusion became truth and the truth became obscured.

Overlaid by the haze of the nightmarish mental assault, the green digits on the screen next to the feed showed the launch thrusters at 96%. Phi screamed in his throat to move his hand over to the strap buckle on his left. Pain surged through his neck and ears and eyes and, finally, after stretching himself against the searing electricity that filled him, he was able to secure the belt around himself.

Through the din of the psychic attack and the thousands of eyes surrounding him, Phi could hear Jamison began to laugh over the speakers. It was maniacal and triumphant.

"Ha ha ha! Oh Master, you *will* be my transformation. You *will* be my enlightenment. You *will* be my salvation!"

When the Nav panel showed thrusters tick over to 100%, Phi screamed as loud as he could, gurgling out of the deepest parts of his soul. His muscles burned and the nerves in his flesh were firing, being played with by some unknown force of this place, something from the void that darkly blanketed the distance in all directions. It took all of his effort to move his hand to the panel of switches for launch initiation, every last bit of exactable will spent to push it just the final inch or two further. Finally, he was able to flip them and so he did, then slapped the fat blue button next to them labeled INIT.

The launch sequence initiated. The ship rattled and groaned as it thrusted off the ground. Phi grimaced at the psychic bombardment that peaked behind his eyes. His thoughts were ravaged and clouded and he breathed viciously from the efforts to regain some sort of control. The struggle to hold dominion over his own mind was a battle that cracked the very foundations of his consciousness and, through these cracks, simulacra of the dead peered eerily—D, his mother, Sovikov—and he saw tentacles twisting and creeping through their decayed eyes.

"*Ha ha ha!*" Jamison's laugh grew louder over the comms. The eyes that made up reality blinked and twitched in unison with each hackle and Phi was drowning further and further into them. In the feed, Jamison move toward the gate of light, still laughing hysterically. Its brilliance had consumed the entire camera view. As the ship rose, Phi could see the shine of the doorway of light shimmering out over the pressure ridge outside the viewport.

Jamison took the last few steps to stand directly in front of the rectangle of light, then looked down, directing the camera toward his feet, to the godlike thing that pushed under the ice beneath him. He laughed and sobbed all at once, crying out in a shrill exaltation. "*HA HA HA HA!*" And then he stepped into the light.

Zzzt.

JAMISON, H. -OFFLINE- displayed in the bottom corner of the screen. The comms were silent. Outside, the red light over the pressure ridge had evaporated.

The eyes in the panels, saturating Phi's reality, were gone. He blinked, swallowed and breathed deeply. His body and will were his own again. The rigid fingers of neural paralysis had left him, leaving in their path a cold sweat on his brow, an ache in his temples and a feeling of incomprehensible violation.

The ship continued to rise. Phi watched the dark planet hanging in the abyss and the halo of sunlight over its horizon. In his mind, he saw the cluster of holes punched in the ice, small windows into the black oceans below. He couldn't help but wonder if the things still danced in the darkness like they did in his imagination, or if they'd retreated back into the deep waters. Somewhere inside himself, he still saw the writhing mass moving under the ice. His mind raced through the things he'd seen, both through Jamison's camera feed and in the flesh, the monstrosities and horror that claimed the lives of his crewmembers and more than likely those of the *Acolyte*. Sovikov's body was still in the airlock. So many had died. He knew D'Artagnan La Felios, as well as the rest of the crew of the *Artorius*, would haunt him forever.

The captain sank back into the chair. With the ship shaking around him and the celestial titan suspended in the cold void outside of the viewport, he closed his eyes and rode the turbulence through the atmosphere of Europa and through that which burned in the darkness of his mind.

*

TWO YEARS LATER

Edward Jamison opened his eyes.

His pillow was soaked in sweat. The alarm clock on the night stand read 3:07 AM in dim blue digits and the glow of the moon poured through the skylight above. The night was clear, looking cosmically stellar beyond the glass.

He pulled the blanket off of himself and rolled into a sitting position, rubbing the sweat from his eyes and coughing into his fist before standing. His bare feet smacked against the hardwood floor and his ankles cracked as he rounded the base of the bed and moved into the hallway toward the bathroom. The office was the first room on the left, the door of which was slightly ajar and, as Edward walked past it, revealed nothing but darkness inside.

He stepped into the bathroom and mumbled, "On." The lamp above came to life. The matching marble countertops and bathtub glistened in the moody light. Edward took the glass from the countertop and positioned it under the faucet and the sensors detected it, automatically pouring water.

"Off," he said as he walked back out into the hallway. His throat was dry. The taste of sweat was in his mouth. The water felt good against his lips as he sipped from the glass, moving past the office door.

He stopped.

Light rippled from within the room.

Edward turned back toward the door, lowering the glass from his lips. Bright green flickered out onto the hallway floor. He stepped closer and reached his hand out. His fingertips grazed the smooth curves in the door's ornate carvings. He hesitated for a brief moment, then pushed.

Light pulsed from the north corner of the office. It glowed off of the stacks of loose books surrounding the cherrywood desk in the center of the room. Bookshelves of tomes, glasses and trinkets came to life in the eeriness. The luminescence came from a drawer in one of the bookshelves, beaming out of the cracks in the wood.

Edward approached. As he closed in on the bookshelf, there was an audible purr and a subtle vibration in the floor accompanying each pulse of the light. He reached out to the knob of the drawer and pulled it open. In the middle of the drawer space, half-hidden under a few printed documents, was the source. Swirls of some kind of smoke or mist, a microcosm of roiling elements, moved in brilliant torrents and radiated like an infernal heartbeat. It was the amulet, the one his father had left him, the one that he had called the *sister stone* to that which had accompanied the man to Europa.

The floor shook and the bookshelves and hanging lights rattled in the increasing vibration. Edward's gaze moved from the drawer to the thousands of eyes that were opening out of the walls and floor and from the curtains that covered the large window to his left. They twitched and shook, furious and emanating horrid gazes. They burrowed into his mind, slicing into it with the sharp focus they directed at him. They spoke into him of suffering to come, of a cosmic process set in motion.

The glass of water slipped from Edward's hand and shattered against the hardwood floor. Shards and droplets glinted in the green light as it exploded. The eyes beneath him blinked the glass into themselves and they stared with shredded corneas up at him.

Edward's heel sunk into one of the eyes as he moved to the window curtains and swung them open.

The light of technicolor fire rolled over his skin like the reflections of waves. His eyes grew wide at that which waited in the night sky. Immediate and overwhelming reverie on a level of which he could've never imagined swelled within him, some feeling unfathomable and unexplainable. His knees trembled and bent to it. He had read the letter a thousand times since he'd found it in the lockbox that day. He'd memorized it, every word of every line, and now his father's words seared within his mind's eye:

And make no mistake, Edward;
I will return.

The Tides of Oblivion

The murmurs of greasy unwashed men hummed in the muggy air of the tavern. Fat red candles dripped wax from their pedestals on the walls to the old wood floor and there was a haze floating just under the ceiling from lit pipes and smoke from the fireplace. The low din was occasionally interrupted by a patron's grunt or the fire's crackling wood. The light from the flames danced off of the polished glass and bottles of spirits behind the bar. Dark oaken casks, with crude spigots dripping foam and black iron bands taut around their warped wood, were sat on the back counter behind the bellied barkeep. Thieves, cutthroats and sellswords huddled low in splintered chairs around ale-stained wooden tables. They discussed murderous business in shallow tones, some occasionally giving gestures to each other from across the room, unspoken messages between killers and rapists through the flicker of an eye or the twitch of a hand. Outside the single diamond-paned window next to the door, the night was frostbitten and fog crept along the glass while the snow fell thickly in the darkness beyond.

The heavy oak door swung open, groaning on its ill-greased hinges and opening a portal into the night. The wood of rotting docks and moored ships moaned from the depths of the freezing black like a chorus of old ghosts. A thin but chilling breeze skewered the damp heat of the criminal's den, a gift from the nearby waters of the tumultuous Black Sea. Out of the darkness and snowfall, a figure manifested into the doorway, its face obscured in shadow under a thick hood. It stood average height, seemed of a thinner build and was followed by a few rogue gusts of sea breeze, sending snowflakes in to land and melt on the warm wooden floor. The big door groaned again as it closed. Some of the murmuring quieted. Eyes stared from the dancing shadows in the smoky corners of the room.

The stranger wore a roughspun robe, horribly ragged and stained with unknown greases and fluids down the front of it. Hanging around the neck, however, was a thick gold cord with an immaculate amulet dangling from its vertex. More conversations at the tables quieted as the stranger walked toward the bar, trailed by greedy glances gazing at a gem of that size.

There was a whistle of wind outside just beyond the fogged window and the fire cracked loudly.

The pudgy mountain of a man behind the bar stood at least a foot taller than the newcomer and stared with bagged eyes and a low brow that were indicative of a suspicion built over many hard years as the keeper of this place. Where the barkeep was round and trunk-like, the newcomer was thin under the robe. The unknown patron came to stand directly in front of the bar, pulling back the rough hood and exposing their face.

His skin was pale, his face gaunt and his dark eyes bloodshot. Vulnerability was immediately visible, the trauma of some unknown experience burned into his features like a brand. After a lengthy stare between him and the barkeep, the newcomer slipped his hand out from a pocket and slid two fat gold coins onto the worn wood of the bar. The firelight licked at the currency as well as illuminated the black coiling vines tattooed onto the tops of the stranger's hand and fingers.

"Ale." The newcomer's voice was coarse and it quavered on the verge of cracking. He was young... and scared.

The barkeep's eyes flicked down to the young man's hand, regarding the black markings with scrutiny, then returned his gaze to the newcomer's eyes, staring differently now, filled with an irritation rather than caution.

"Do you know where you are... *boy*?"

The stranger stared back intensely. He gave no answer other than, "*Ale*," then wiped at his eyes and turned and moved toward the back corner of the bar, leaving the two coins without waiting for a response. The barkeep simply stared.

Just beyond the grasp of the sight of the flames, the newcomer found a cracked wooden chair and sat in it with his back to the corner. The shadows kept his features hidden but the light from the lapping fire occasionally hit the amulet hanging from his neck. Slick gold encased a large red jewel that, in its center, reflected the fire's light, glinting prisms off the young man's soaked face and teary eyes as he stared down at it. His breathing was labored and anxious. Drops of water dripped from his long hair to the planks below.

The thugs could sense the fear and distress on the young man like sharks could smell blood in the water. Three men stood from one of the front tables in a synchronous motion and moved like the shadows around them, smoothly and quietly. Each of the three brandished a weapon that glinted in the firelight. The old wood floor creaked under their soft steps as they closed in, driven by a shared avarice.

The assassins were almost within striking distance but, as the first raised his hooked dagger in preparation for the execution, a booming shout came from behind the bar.

"NO!"

The murderers froze mid-stride. They loomed over the young newcomer. One of them looked back at the barkeep with a razor sharp gaze. The moment was held in stasis and then their knives were sheathed but they did not move from where they stood. The rest of the patrons in the tavern went silent. Two more men stood from their tables near the entrance, unable to satiate their curiosity from their seats.

The barkeep's slow steps thudded heavily as he crossed the room. The anger was plain on his face when he arrived in front of the newcomer, drying an ale horn with a rag.

The young man looked up from his hands. More tattooed vines were visible on his neck and throat. The four men stood just feet from him. Other carnivorous eyes stared from the background, glistening in the orange light throughout the den.

"I know those marks on your hands," the barkeep began, a curt tone sharpening his words. "And I've seen those amulets before. You're one of the hill tribe, aren't you?"

The young man did not answer. He simply returned his gaze

below to the amulet still hanging from his neck.

"The *Sovereignty* Decree... Fucking city's never been the same since with all these *things* walking among us. And now, a moondrinker... In *my* bar, a fucking moondrinker."

The young man's eyes returned to the barkeep who, in return, spit onto the floor at his feet.

"The empire may have decreed your ilk a free people but don't you think for a second that means shit to anyone in here, *especially* me. I run this place and I know of the rituals your people perform up in those hills, the dark spells and enchantments your kin whisper to each other whilst you dance around black fires in infernal worship. I know of your people's desires to manipulate and mutate away from the body the gods gave you, turning yourselves into *abominations*! Oh yes, I know all about you heretics of humanity.

"What's more, tonight is the first full moon of this cycle and yet here you are, brandishing a piece of jewelry only given to those who have completed the ritual soul-branding. You're clearly still human, therefore you're clearly a thief. It wouldn't surprise me in the least if you stole that amulet from one of your own kind, you filthy *fucking* moondrinker."

The young stranger stood from his seat, hands shaking as he contracted them into fists. His eyes were wide with intimidation. "It's *mine*," he said in response. The fear was growing in his voice and it was apparent to more than just himself.

There was a long moment of silence. Nobody made a sound until the barkeep broke the quiet, speaking once more with a look of new satisfaction. "Yours, huh? Your ceremony was tonight, wasn't it? That must be it. You've not the spine for committing theft, weak and small like a virgin bitch, and that amulet looks freshly forged. You gave your soul to those black gods this very night, didn't you?" The man sniffed at the dank air. "I can still smell the pungent smoke of the ritual on you, and those stains on your tattered garb..." He shook his head disappointingly, then smiled gently and said, "Tell me, what did you use?"

The young man felt clouded by confusion amidst his anger. "Wh-what do you mean?" he stuttered.

"What *animal* did you use? A bear? A wolf? I'll have your canine head clean off before you can swipe one of your abominable paws at me, demon." The barkeep moved closer and the three assassins inched nearer as well.

"I... It was supposed to be a jest," the young man responded, tears rolling into the fine stubble on his jaw. "Gods forgive me." A heavy sob came on the tail end of a searing pain in his lower stomach, sending aftershocks rippling through his nerve endings. He grimaced but his aggressors didn't seem to notice.

"The Gods have no watch over you anymore, *filth*! Your people don't belong in the city. We leave you to your piney slopes in the northern hills so that you can stay away and out of the lives of the common man." The barkeep, growing more aggressive with each word, reached out and pulled the sobbing newcomer to his feet, gripping the collar of his robe in a tight fist. "You see, *things* like you are bad for business and, around here, anything that's bad for business gets dealt with accordingly. Now, what did you *use*, you spineless little cunt?! What did you *join* with so that we know the easiest way to strip you of your dark gifts?"

There was another long pause. The young man sniffed the pain away momentarily and mumbled something under his breath.

The barkeep moved his snarling face closer. "What was that?"

The young man repeated something in a meager defeated voice, barely above a whisper.

The barkeep's eyes went wide as if a knife had just slid between a couple of his ribs, looking almost terrified, before he melted into a loud hackling. "A *salmon*?!"

And at that, the entire tavern erupted into laughter. Boots were stomping and horns were clanging while mouths hooted from all corners. Two of the assassins that stood next to the barkeep walked back toward their table, chuckling and shaking their heads along the way.

"Oh, bless the gods above *and* below for this day! I think I may laugh myself to death at that one," the barkeep said with a beet-red face. He still held the young man by the collar, chuckling, and, when he'd caught his breath, pointed a fat finger toward a man sitting alone in the corner opposite them, on the other side of the room. "See that one over there, stranger?"

The table stood out from the rest for some indiscernible reason. The surface in front of the shadowed man was empty save for a crossbow, oiled rosewood with a black drawstring.

"That one there's one of the most ruthless bounty hunters in these lands. I've personally seen him dispatch three of your fucking kin after they'd turned. I'm sure he's got their mangy rotting heads hanging somewhere."

The man sitting alone at the table nodded once, a single eye glinting in the shadow under the brim of his hat. "Yeah, I got one of 'em mid-transition," he growled with a rough northern drawl. "Salmon, huh? If I believed you, I'd gut you and fry you myself." He stood to his feet and unslung a pack from his back, unraveling it onto the table next to the crossbow. "I'm gonna guess a wolf or an elk..." A row of weapons and trinkets were pinned to the cloth by knots of leather-string, different types of arrows and knives, crucifixes, stakes and rough glass ampoules filled with colored fluids. "Elk are more popular in the northwest... Either way, this kind of thing is... my *specialty*, you could say." A slick smile revealed a row of dark iron teeth. "We'll get the truth from you yet."

The young man let out a sob and his head lowered, wet hair dangling once more in front of his face. Desperation had brought him to this shithole on the outskirts of the city only to be met by a pack of human wolves looking to strip him of his adornments and his mortality. Pain coursed through his veins as he began to lose hold of himself. The humanity in his vulnerability faded like a shore fog being swept away by the wind and in its place was the vessel in which an irrevocable transformation had now begun...

The barkeep had the newcomer still pinned up against the wall. His grip had loosened a bit while the northern hunter spoke and, when he looked back to the one he held by the collar, his eyes narrowed. "What the fuck has happened to your face, moondrinker?"

In the shifting firelight, the young man's eyes pushed at their lids, bulging from their sockets. A strange eerie groan crept from his open mouth. His teeth had sunken into his now swollen gums, appearing like tiny nubs. The shock of such an alien sight sent chills down the spines of a few observers, even in a tavern such as this.

"Ohhh," The barkeep said. He extended his free hand back behind him. "You're gonna start changing now, are you?" The remaining assassin slipped the handle of a curved dagger into his palm. “No matter. We’ll take care of this nice and quick. I know a few men who’d pay some coin for a head like yours.”

Flames shined off the blade as it rose to the young man’s throat. The mutating skin reflected the light off of the rainbow prism scales that rapidly had begun to grow on his neck and jaw. The barkeep had a sadistic grin on his face as he leaned in close. The curved oiled blade rested onto the young man’s jugular and the big man snarled. “I’m gonna take your head off, moondrinker, and then I’m gonna let my friends fuck your thin little corpse. *Gyah*!” he shouted and ripped the blade at the young man’s neck. When he looked to the dagger after the killing move, it still rested on the skin of his victim. The flesh had not broken. He pushed and tugged at the knife, small strikes at the young man’s jugular, but it never gave. The blade wouldn’t cut through and, right in front of the struggling barkeep's eyes, the skin hardened over with even more thick diamond-like scales.

The young man’s face was directed up to the low ceiling above them. His mouth slowly opened and closed as if he was drowning in the air yet one large black eye stared down as it swelled in the mutation.

Anger flashed across the barkeep’s face. He drew the blade back, still holding the young man up by the shirt. “Alright. You’re not gonna make this easy, are—”

A webbed humanoid hand rose up and smacked against the big man's face. It gripped with scaled fingers. Veined membrane stretched and wriggled between each digit. The remnants of the tattooed vines had disappeared under the chitinous growth of scales now formed over the tops of the fingers and knuckles. The barkeep’s head shook for a brief moment before the hand collapsed into a fist. His heavy body fell to the floor below, sputtering fluids onto the worn wooden planks from its obliterated cranium.

Men stood from all tables. Some shouted while others unsheathed oiled steel from their ready scabbards.

Brains dripped from the newcomer’s webbed twitching hand. He gazed with bulbous eyes towards the other men standing around the tables. The corners of his mouth were already beginning to extend back on his face as the shape of his skull beveled and narrow into something grotesquely inhuman.

A few men retreated toward the entrance but then the barkeep’s headless body was flying through the air, tossed by a quick move of the moondrinker's arm. It slammed against the heavy door. The thick corpse blocked it from opening for only a brief few seconds as the men tried to move it out of the way.

That was all the time the creature needed.

The thing was at the door in microseconds, swiping its webbed hands at the men in a blur of shining scales and a mist of blood. Within moments, the retreating men were reduced to a mound of gore. The amulet still hung from the creature's neck, bloody and glazed in the light of the flames.

Men shouted and screamed as the slaughter began. An attacker rushed from the right, swinging a twin-headed axe at the beast. The moondrinker, seeming to anticipate the attack perfectly, sidestepped and retaliated with an upward thrust of its right webbed hand, claws as fast as lightning, ripping the jaw off of the attacker and sending him to the floor in a panic of gurgling blood. The creature screamed a shrill cry that sang of transformative agony and a heavy bloodlust. Men came at it from all sides with swords, daggers and heavy objects like chairs and candelabras only to be struck down in quick messy deaths. The fireplace flared. The bed of entrails grew underneath the charging feet of attackers while the beast punched holes into rib cages and swiped limbs off at the joints.

A hissing sound came out of the din as a black bolt zinged through the air. It sunk into a section on the creature's back that hadn't grown scales over the discolored flesh yet. In the far corner of the tavern, the hunter was reloading a second bolt from the quiver on his hip. He pulled the waxed cord back to the spring clip and slid the slender projectile into its place.

The creature made a blasphemous sound when it attempted to reach the bolt lodged into its back, its range of motion restricted by its continual transformation. When its initial strain couldn't reach, a grinding knuckled sound curdled out from under the flesh of its shoulder. The joints separated and twisted and turned and then its webbed hand got a hold on the bolt. Just as it ripped from the blood-slicked flesh, there was another hiss as a second bolt pierced through the air. In a flash, the beast sidestepped and dodged the second bolt, its large unblinking eyes fixated into the corner now. Its mouth still moved open and shut, open and shut. A man with a large dagger rushed and the creature jabbed the first arrow through the attacker's temple. It turned its attention back toward the far table. The hunter was reloading yet another bolt from his quiver but, before the string could fully draw, the monster bounded across the tavern in a flash of rainbow reflection. A decapitated body crumpled to the floor a brief moment later and the beast stood holding the hunter's still blinking head.

Other patrons continued their aggression. The creature thrashed this way and that, claws ripping through meat and bone, Death glazing the eyes of corpse after corpse. Blood spilled across steel and skin and scales alike. In a short but chaotic battle, the throng had been reduced to a mess and the abomination stood on its throne of gore.

None had escaped its wrath.

A subtle whimpering came from behind one of the fallen tables near the fireplace. The beast could smell fear in the air just as well as it could smell the exposed intestines that leaked shit and the blood smeared across the floor around it. The miasma of horror and excrement was intoxicating to its mutated senses.

From behind the overturned table, a man stood. He gasped when he saw the creature staring at him with those huge black eyes and fell back into the shadowed corner against the wall. His cries were horrified and his hands trembled violently.

The beast slowly stepped towards the man. When it could smell his fresh piss in the air, its webbed fingers contracted and extended in anticipation of the kill. The young man from the hills was gone, his mind and body replaced with something nightmarish and inhuman, nourished by the ecstasy of evisceration and slaughter.

"No, no, no! *Please*, no!" the man begged. "Please! Oh, Gods!"

A few strides from the crying human, the moondrinker dropped suddenly, keeling over as if struck in its core by an invisible force. Its neck was widening rapidly now. Its head sunk into its shoulders. The amulet's chain snapped and the jewelry was lost into the gore below. The creature's body had begun to elongate with the legs shrinking into its torso now and a spined dorsal protruding from its back. It cried out as it turned from its prey in the corner to crawl back toward the exit. The frightened man stared at the thing, motionless due to shock.

Guts and bodies squished under the mutation's heavy grasp.

When it reached the door, it grabbed the crude handle and tore it open. The bodies and entrails on the floor practically slid on their own in the face of such inhuman strength. The transition had almost completed. The beast's legs had fully retracted into its body, as with one of its arms, the other of which was still melting into its scales. The biting night air once again pierced the muggy blood-tinged haze in the tavern. Snowflakes floated in from the cold dark outside. The creature wagged its membraned tail up and down as it flopped out into the night toward the groaning docks and the black shore.

Sand and Wine

The old lock on the door rebelled against the key for a brief moment before it gave. The deadbolt retracted shortly after. A wisp of the shore's salted breeze floated in as the door opened, bringing with it bits of sand that rattled like microscopic beads against the wooden floor of the entryway. Two sets of feet entered before the door shut behind, one wearing a pair of heels and a much smaller set wearing a pair of flats with little elephants all over them.

"You remember this place, sweetie?" the one wearing heels said. Her voice was croaky and tired.

Dani, the one wearing flats, nodded her head. It made her stomach upset to talk sometimes with this new medication. This was one of those times. Truthfully, she only remembered small bits of the place, like a specific stone in the cobbled path leading up from the driveway to the front door that was a different darker shade than the rest, and the shape of the bent gutters that rimmed the house. Dani's mind even struggled with those memories. They were like taffy, melting and morphing in her recollections, never fully taking shape.

The living room of the place her mother called the *summer house* was small. It felt cluttered with two couches, a rocking chair and an old banister that took up most of an entire wall. On top of it sat an old fat television with a bulbous screen and antennae sprouting from it like rabbit ears. The air smelled stale and unlived in. Dani could taste the dust in her throat as she breathed.

"Why don't you go explore, doll." Her mother patted her on the middle of the back. "Go on."

Dani moved toward the kitchen. The aged linoleum creaked under her steps as she walked to the big yellow fridge. The cupboards were a matching yellow with paint chipping at their corners, exposing the brown old wood underneath. The appliances looked old, too. She turned around and crossed the dining area toward the back sliding door. Big brown curtains draped across, thick and wooly, and she parted them like Moses parted the Red Sea and looked outside.

The view was grey with blotches of darker stuff amidst the blanket of a dead sky. The ocean was a dirty blue on the verge of black underneath the overcast and its wave breaks foamed like discolored soda on the shore. The sand was also grey and the little wooden steps embedded in it leading from the house down to the beach were white from the passage of time. The scattered patches of grass were like sprouts of dark hair. Driftwood protruded from the sand like broken bones.

Everything was a shade of grey, as if the wind outside had drained the color from the world. Dani's hands pressed against the glass and her palms seemed to drink the coldness, cooling her blood and sending goosebumps up her arms. The greyness outside reminded her of the way she felt these days and a large part of her wanted to stay here, just like this, forever.

Pop!

A cork tumbled over itself on the linoleum. Dani knew that sound. It happened at least once a night. She turned from the sliding glass door and moved quietly toward the living room. Over at the table, a stream of bloody wine chugged out of a bottle and into the glass her mother held underneath it.

The hallway leading down the length of the small house was dark. Dani flipped the light switch on the right wall and the shadows receded, though the single bulb above wasn't enough to push them completely away. Hanging on the walls were collections of pictures in large frames. She recognized a few younger versions of her uncles and her aunts from the largest picture in the middle. The extended family sat around an outdoor table smiling and a feast of barbequed food was displayed as the centerpiece of the table. There were portraits of her cousins and grandparents during fishing trips and swimming in lakes, and there were many older pictures of other people she did not recognize, posing inanimately in the dim light.

The first door on the left side of the hall was open though Dani couldn't see very far into the dark bathroom. Half of the mirror above the sink was visible, reflecting a bit of the hallway light, and the cupboards just underneath it could be seen. There was a thick dusky rug splayed out on the floor and it looked like some kind of beastly fur in the indistinct gloom.

At the end of the hall, the last door on the left was closed. The one on the right, however, was wide open.

There was a single long window in the wall opposite the door. An old burnt-orange curtain dangled across the entirety of it and, through the thin cloth, the light of the overcast day was luminescent but muted. The bed was made and the mismatched pillows were silent in their perpetual stances leaning up against each other. Brown closet doors stood half open on the right side of the room. There weren't any garments hanging inside but a few quilts and blankets were stacked on the floor near the water heater tucked into the corner.

From out in the living room, television static blared for a brief moment before the signal cleared and a man's voice could be heard. Dani listened to her mother's voice mumble something before a giggle but she couldn't make out the words. For a moment, Dani thought of her father and even allowed a brief wonder as to if that was his voice speaking on the television, but she knew better than that. *He's gone for good*, her mother had said. *I've got all the love you need, sweetheart, right here*.

Trinkets and collectibles were scattered around the surfaces of the room, accompanied by long forgotten pictures in silver frames. Leaning up against the wall, near the foot of the bed, was a mirror almost as tall as she was. Dani's eyes weren't caught by the height of the thing but instead by the frame in which it was encased. Ornate carvings wound up the sides of the gold-painted wood and, as she stepped closer, images of an eternal jungle came into focus. The heads of maned lions poked through perpetually parted shrubs, twig-like legs of cranes held their bodies above never-moving water, and great elephants blew their trumpets silently upward to the trees that remained motionless in the frame above them.

It was something in the way the shadows played with the finish or in the intricacies of the carving but, before she could decide otherwise, Dani's small hands were out in front of her, probing and running along the contours of the animals in the wooden frame. She followed the curves down and she sat herself on the carpet in front of mirror. She was seeing the carved creatures through her normal eyes but, in her mind, she imagined them in the jungle. She felt them through the tips of her fingers and, with the strange aromas of the derelict atmosphere in the room, could almost smell them in her nostrils. She had never been in a jungle before but Dani was certain that what she smelled now was from there, deep in the richly soiled underbrush. They were smells wafting from the mossy branches that hugged from all over, bound by ageless vines that sprouted bright flowers from their skin. The smell of fur and trees and dirt and pollen filled her lungs, bewitching her in the loveliest way.

She could hear the roar of the lion and wild calls of the monkeys, though it was not through her normal ears. It felt as if she could hear them through *other* ears, an extra set somewhere inside of her. Touching the wood seemed to connect her to a realm in which these animals still roamed freely and she could see the rich greens and browns and pinks of the wild in the space behind her eyes. Her imagination blossomed like the majestic flowers she saw, opening inside of her in congruence with her inner eye.

The elephants in the frame were halfway down on either side of it. Elephants had always been her favorite animals. They were big and dopey and sweet. Dani met them on both sides with her hands and drifted her fingers over their trunks. The palms of her hands wrapped around them and she drank the scene like the cold from the sliding glass door in the kitchen. She wished she could be there with them. She wanted to ride on their backs and be in the jungle, away from the pungent smell of her mother's drink, away from the sterile sourness of the daily hospital visits. She wanted to hold the elephant in real life. She didn't know why but she felt like she wouldn't be sick if she was with the elephants...

She didn't think that was going to happen. That wasn't real life, she knew. She'd only ever seen elephants on television, not in real life, and that's the way it was going to stay. Her mother's words replayed over the sounds of the jungle in her mind.

He's gone for good.

A heavy feeling sank over Dani then. It started from the top of her head, trickling down her scalp and the sides of her face, then into her eyes through her temples. She saw her father's smile, loving and playful, and then she saw her parents fighting in their old living room. She remembered the slamming doors. She remembered the screaming. Then she saw the lion again, parting through the darkness between their shouting mouths, and she could smell its breath as it roared. With her real eyes, she saw that her hands still held the frame but her grip felt like it was slipping. There was nothing to hold onto in the jungle that backdropped her yelling parents. Their faces shifted into the faces of monkeys and then into snakes that began to coil around and around. Dani's mind mutated and rippled like water and the forms she saw swirled into each other. Something like a drain had been unplugged in the pool of her thoughts and she watched while they drifted away from her. As her mind emptied, her body became heavier. In the mirror, her reflection wavered and so did the walls behind her. Through her uncertain gaze, Dani saw what appeared to be slits opening on the backs of her hands, yet she felt nothing of pain or even sensation there. And from those slits, the wooden trunks of the elephants protruded and waved up at her.

Dani pulled at the gold-painted frame as her body sank back. Her fingers slipped on one side of it and broke something on the other. The connection to the animals and the jungle, with all its smells and colors and sounds, and to the room around her, dusty and dim, was pulverized and carried off by nothingness.

*

In the abyss, there was a sound. It was over just as suddenly as it had come.

Dani's eyes opened. She was lying on the brown carpet with her face smushed into it. The old smell of it filled her nostrils and stuck to her skin when she sat up. Hazily, her mind gathered itself back into her senses, as if dragging something with it from her sleep. The dreamworld tugged at her consciousness, though its influence drifted away with each groggy breath, hurried by the rotations of her palms rubbing her eyes.

The light from outside the window had grown brighter and more orange than grey. She couldn't tell if that was from the color of the curtains or the color of the sun. She swallowed then breathed deeply and found that her stomach no longer felt upset. Where a sinking boiling ache had been for the longest time, deep in the pit of her bowels, only a gentle warmth existed now, a comfortable nothingness. She observed the still room surrounding. Her eyes met the frame of the mirror and the carved scene caught her attention once more.

The animals had been *alive*.

On the frame, where one of the elephants should've been, a scar of broken wood now existed. She remembered grabbing both elephants before things went dark. On the carpet, somewhat buried in the fibers, was a small chip of gold-finished wood. When she picked it up, Dani could see the segmented engravings of the elephant's trunk and the spiked end where it had broken off from the whole. It was feather light in her fingers. Lining up the splinters with the part on the frame where it had broken off from, she pushed the piece back into place as best as she could. It wasn't perfect but, after a few moments and a couple adjustments, Dani thought it would do. As she stood and took a step back to see how the reattached trunk looked compared to the rest, the sound came again, the same sound that awoke her.

She *knew* that sound.

Though the light in the room had grown slightly brighter, the hallway was still dusky. The bulb above had been turned off. Beyond the threshold into the small living room, her mother's arm was draped over the couch, hanging limply with a wine glass lying on its side on the rug below. The television was silent. The bright static flared like a spotlight over her mother's sleeping body. Dani crept toward the kitchen, imagining herself a cat in the dark. The linoleum creaked once again under her flats and she glanced back, making sure it wasn't heard. The uninterrupted snoring from her mother's slack face informed her of all she needed to know.

The sunlight barely shone through the thick brown curtains in the kitchen but, when Dani peered her head around to the glass, the glare overtook her.

The hue of grey had receded from the world. The evening light had broken through the cloud cover in the far west and it now shone uninhibited. The ocean appeared like a liquid mirror. It reflected the sun's orange light and the horizon shimmered like a million waning jewels, glinting as distant stars do.

And then the sound came again.

After she'd slipped outside and closed the sliding glass door gently behind her, Dani stepped down the half-buried wooden planks and moved toward the beach. Swirls of sand rode the breeze between her steps. The wind was cool against her face, smelled of salt, and the foamy sound of the tide played music in her ears.

Something was out on the beach, moving around in the shallow surf.

In the bright haze, Dani saw a large shape. When the elephant lifted its trunk, with the orange backdrop of the sun behind it, she saw that it was slightly misshapen, like the one from the mirror frame. But then she heard the trumpeting sound and heard that it was perfect. The warmth of joy tingled in her limbs and she smiled with all that her young soul would allow.

The radiance of the setting sun was brilliant and the reflections off of the waves of the ocean made the figures on the beach waver in and out of reality. If Dani's mother had awoken then and looked outside, the light would've played with her eyes, tricked them with the rays of the sun. If she looked closed enough, however, she might've seen, rippling amongst the warm reflections, the whispers of a silhouette, the shadow of a little girl reaching her hand out to the trunk of an animal she never thought she would get to see.

The Gore Hole

The second of the end-of-day bells was just finishing its call and students were already fleeing the school property in every direction. Their distant shouts and laughter heralded their much anticipated dispersion.

Sam Benton didn't rush but stared down at his feet as he walked. The cold autumn chill swirled invisible around him, nipping at his nostrils and earlobes. The track that surrounded the soccer field of the elementary school was made of small bits of red gravel. It crunched under his shoes with each step. Every half minute or so, he wiped the condensation from the thick glasses he wore. His own hot breath and the warm body-heat emitting from the neck of his puffy jacket caused the lenses to fog as he walked. He didn't mind. Seeing the ground pass under him behind the small misty windows made him think of Silent Hill and he loved that game. The cold and the fog were his favorite things about Fall.

The track curved north to continue its loop around the soccer field but Sam didn't follow it. He broke off from the curve and moved up the small grassy incline toward the school's chain-link property fence and the exit to 131st Street. The dew in the grass soaked the bottoms of his pant legs and he could feel his socks getting wet through his shoes.

Someone called his name from behind.

Sam turned to see a chubby blond kid rushing up the grassy embankment after him. It was Ronny Williams, a fourth-grader as sarcastic as they come, a gossiper who always hung around the guys from the neighborhood. His house was somewhere beyond the Mormon church in the Northwest Hills block. Sam was pretty sure Ronny didn't spend a lot of time in his own neighborhood, or even at his own home. There were rumors he'd heard a couple years ago that Ronny's father hit him. Sam never brought it up.

"Sammy! Wait up!"

Ronny approached, breathing heavily by the time he'd gotten halfway up the incline. The cold sun hung somewhere above the clouds. It was still bright outside, even though the sky was obscured behind a grey blanket of overcast.

"Hey Ronny," Sam greeted.

"Sammy," Ronny started, gulping air by the lungful. He reached out for the chain-link and leaned heavily against it, panting like a dog. "Sammy, did you hear about Timmy Jacobson?"

It had felt like forever since Sam had heard that name spoken but he'd thought about it almost every day since last summer, since that day with Isabelle's stomach open and the spiders and the house amidst the trees.

"No, what happened?"

"Oh, man! He went *crazy*, Sammy. He went *crazy*! He took the clown car to the looney bin!" Ronny was always saying things Sam didn't understand. He didn't understand what a clown car had to do with going crazy and figured they were adult phrases that only boring grandparents used.

"Crazy how? What do you mean crazy?" Sam asked.

"Well, Tina Hendricks said that he wasn't in class today or yesterday, and that he was talking about going to see something called the *gore* hole a couple days ago." Ronny emphasized the word *gore* with wide-eyes, like the librarian at school did when she read stories from picture books to the class on Thursdays. "Supposedly he saw it and went *crazy*. Insane! You ever heard such a thing?"

Sam shook his head. "Huh-uh." He tried to imagine what something called a *gore hole* could be and what it would look like but came up blank. In some of the video games he played, there was a Gore setting that could be shifted. *What did blood and guts have to do with Timmy?* was the question he wanted to ask but before he was able to, Ronny continued.

"Me either, until today. Anyway, Joey Campen and his cousin

said they supposedly know where it is and are gonna meet us later, if you wanna come with. There'll be a bunch of other kids there, too." Ronny, still breathing heavily from his pursuit, let go of the fence and clapped Sam on the shoulder, smiling a wide grin. "You're not scared, are you dude?"

The problem was that Ronny was a talker, a rumor-spreader, and Sam knew that if he denied him in this, word would spread of how much of a *pussy* Sam was (Jacob Santos, the Latino kid that sat next to him in class, had revealed the 'proper' use of the word pussy to him, Ronny and four other wide-eyed fifth graders during recess a few weeks after the start of the year). He was confused about what this gore hole was and hesitant to see something that supposedly made his old best friend go crazy.

"Nah, I'm not scared," Sam said. He knew he'd never hear the end of it if he didn't show up. "What time? And where?"

"Meet us at the bus stop at six."

*

Sam had lived on 131st Street his entire life and knew there was only one bus stop Ronny could have been referring to. Though Bridgeton Elementary was within walking distance of home, there was a single bus stop on the loop that went around his neighborhood for the schools across town. It was at the three-way intersection where 131st Street was bisected by Shaw Road.

He arrived home fifteen minutes later, pulling the key out of his backpack and sliding it into the lock of the front door of the house. His mother, being the worrier that she was, had tied the key to the inside pouch of the backpack with red yarn for fear of his losing it and being locked out. Sam thought it extra-dorky and had a habit of looking over his shoulder before pulling out the leashed key, but he didn't think she deserved the hassle, especially with everything else going on, so he never mentioned it to her.

The door shut behind him and he unslung his backpack, tossing it onto the couch. He took his shoes off, made some microwave macaroni-n-cheese and watched an episode of X-Files (the one with the yellow-eyed guy that could stretch through vents and small holes and made nests out of newspaper and bile), all the while being unable to get his mind off of the words Ronny had said back at the elementary school track.

He went crazy, Sammy.

The brown leather chair near the kitchen had chunks missing from one of the arm rests. Sam sat there, the television muted, picking at the frayed white fabric under the leather. His mind simultaneously picked through the events of last summer as it had so many countless times since. He wanted to find out the truth, but not from the shitty kids of the neighborhood. After starting a few math problems from his homework, it became apparent that his thoughts weren't going to cooperate, not until he was on the way to the bus stop, not until he was on the way to finding out the answer to the question that had been burning inside of him:

What happened to Timmy?

Many times throughout the last year, Sam had spent entire evenings debating whether to call Timmy's house or not. When Timmy wouldn't answer his calls during the first few weeks after the day at the black house, Sam had given up. It had been a year now. He still had the phone number to Timmy's house memorized. By force of habit, it still repeated itself with clarity in his mind as a type of jingle or mantra (*eight-four-seven seven-nine-eight-two, eight-four-seven seven-nine-eight-two*). Sam reasoned to himself that he wouldn't have been so compelled to make the call now if he knew that Timmy was still doing alright, maybe making new friends and living his life. He'd even be happy for him. He wouldn't blame Timmy for finding new friends that could be trusted, ones that wouldn't run away. Sam didn't know the truth. That was what ate at him. Yeah, Ronny embellished stories like the best of them, but he usually said what was what when it came down to it.

He went crazy, Sammy!

There'd been no real opportunity to speak to Timmy since that horrible day, at least any that weren't only briefly seeing each other in the hallways. Despite this, Sam still considered Timmy his best friend, if anyone were to ever ask. Inside, Sam felt some hole left unfilled. He didn't think people could just drop friendships like the one they had. It took something horrible and it *was* something horrible that destroyed them. Sam was pretty sure Timmy didn't feel that same desire for friendship, not after how Sam had run away like a scared baby, not bothering to save him.

Something could be wrong, though. Something could be very wrong with his friend, his used-to-be best friend, and Sam wanted to know the truth. He *needed* to know it. Maybe he could help if he understood, if he heard what was wrong, and maybe he could get his friend back and earn their friendship once again, to prove that he wasn't a scared little kid.

Maybe Timmy could forgive him.

Sam didn't recall standing from the leather chair. He approached the house phone and picked it up, dialing the numbers like he had so many times last year and the year before (*seven-nine-eight-two*) and then put the phone to his ear. He listened anxiously as it began to ring.

After four long rings, a woman's coarse voice answered the line. “Hello?”

Sam recognized the voice of Timmy’s mother. “Hi, Mrs. Jacobson. This is Sammy Benton.”

“Oh, Sammy! Oh, it’s good to hear from you. It’s been a while.” Her voice took on a slightly lighter quality. Just the few sentences she'd spoken were already sending Sam’s mind into a nostalgic trip, back to when he'd visit Timmy’s big house and Mrs. Jacobson would make food, asking *what do you boys want for dinner* or *how’s your mother doing, Sammy*, as they sat around the dining room table in the summer sunlight. It wasn’t until this moment that he realized just how much he missed those days.

“Yeah,” Sam said, unsure of what else to reply with. A long pause held on the line between the two of them and then he asked, “I was wondering if Timmy was there?”

There was another long pause and then she answered. “I’m sorry, Sammy. Timmy can’t come to the phone. He’s very sick at the moment and we’re just trying to do everything we can to get him better.”

“Oh." What little hope Sam may have had faded then. "Well... Could you tell him I—”

The call was interrupted by a muffled groaning in the background. The sound was quiet at first but increased in volume. It was someone’s voice, *Timmy’s* voice, broken up by heavy sobs. Sam wanted to ask what was wrong but there was commotion on the other end of the line, with only a briefly audible phrase, “...oh god, the whispers, mommy, oh god oh god...”, before loud crying made it unintelligible. He could hear Timmy's mother gently singing and then the phone clicked and the call was ended.

*

The clouds had begun to clear in the west, exposing the small flare of evening sun that sank below the horizon, but the sky was still overcast above and had grown dark by the time Sam arrived to the bus stop. In the shadow of dusk, porch lights of neighborhood homes had come to life. Dull orange light glowed from beyond the curtained windows of the house directly behind the bus stop. The squeak of a bat came from somewhere above, although Sam could not spot it when he briefly searched. He leaned himself against the street sign-post and glanced down at his Power Rangers digital watch, pressing the nubbed plastic button on the side that switched on the dim little bulb in the display:

5:49 PM

A sigh eased quietly from his lips.

We're just trying to do everything we can to get him better.

He went crazy, Sammy!

Even during the day, the blacktop of Shaw Road seemed to soak up the light of the sun in unnatural ways. Now, in the late evening, Sam could swear he was staring down a river of shadow. They'd paved this entire half of the neighborhood with that dark new concrete and the freshly painted lines running down the center appeared now like white worms. They slowly squirmed in the uncertain light but went nowhere, remaining in perpetuity. Identical gabled roof tops lined both sides of the street as it tapered off into the distance and blue television light radiated from the living rooms of a few of them. Some of the houses had windows that glowed dimly from their second stories like eyes. Tall evergreens cluttered in between the homes and in backyards. There were deep forests on either side of the street, beyond their properties. Towering pines stood like giants along the horizon, black and jagged in the growing dark.

Sam hadn't been down Shaw Road since the worst day of his life. His mother knew about what happened, from what he'd told her after she'd retrieved Isabelle's corpse, and had decided it best they avoid the road any time they were in the car. He'd been grateful for that during this last year since it happened, the day he lost both of his best friends.

He knew that a house, *the* house, the one where his nightmares brought him back to, sat off of a cul-de-sac at the end of Shaw Road, before the big curve that led out of the neighborhood. Now, staring down the long black strip, his mind once again churned through the memories he wished he could forget.

*

There was nothing different about the air that day last summer, nor the smells or the wind or passage of time, nor the sunlight, appearing as bright as it ever had. There were only a few weeks left of vacation and Timmy had invited Sam outside to go exploring around the neighborhood, as was their usual plan each morning. The sky was clear and the air was warm, as if Summer had pushed herself to her very boundaries in order to give the two a bright day to enjoy the last bit of freedom under.

Sam brought Isabelle with him, his fat chocolate lab. She had droopy eyes, a voracious appetite and a walk that was a little funny from her bulk. She was huge but had a quiet raspy bark and she had been Sam's best friend, his confidant and the perfect pillow to fall asleep on for a long time. She hadn't been able to move very fast but she was always just as playful as she was as a puppy and Sam had loved her to death for it.

The three of them—Sam, Timmy and Isabelle—made their way around the neighborhood loop and took the turn at the bus stop to head down Shaw Road. Back then, the blacktop had not yet been applied to the cracked concrete and Sam remembered the bulges in the road from thick tree roots growing underneath. Timmy whipped a stick at the reeds that grew out of the ditch on the left side of the road. The plants cracked loudly against each of his swings. A few minutes of this passed, then he moved along a larger crack, out into the middle of the street and across to the other side. Sam followed, glancing behind to see Isabelle's tongue lolling out of her big doggy smile as she trailed them.

He couldn't remember what they'd talked about on their way. His memories of the walk down Shaw Road were hazy until the point in which they'd reached the cul-de-sac, about a quarter mile before the end. It was when the smell in the air changed from the piney warm fragrance of late summer to... something else. Strangely pungent, the smell that assaulted Sam's nostrils was like rotten food in a garbage can mixed with something electric. Even Isabelle was sniffing at the air as if something were strange about this place. The cul-de-sac was empty, no buildings or discernible property lines. Only old evergreens leaned into each other along its rim. He'd almost missed the gravel drive off to the right as his vision of the area to which it led was obscured from where they stood out on the road. Sam could see a black structure of some kind a bit further in, barely visible through the thick pines.

"I've never been in here," Timmy said. He moved from the road into the cul-de-sac. "Have you?"

Sam's eyes moved through the trees. The cold grip of the previous night may have been all but gone to the warmth of the morning but something was... *off* with how this place made his skin feel. It felt dry and tingles crept down his back. He knew that he wasn't noticing something he ought to be, like someone was staring at him from a place out in the open but he simply couldn't find the eyes to meet with his own.

"Earth to Underpants McGee."

"Huh?" Sam shook from his gaze. "No, I've never been here either. Do you smell that?"

At this, Timmy sniffed the air like a dog. Sam could tell he was more focused on the impression than actually smelling the air, glancing down occasionally to check his own act against how Isabelle was sniffing at the sky, attempting to mimic her perfectly.

"Timmy, do you smell that or..."

Then, a whisper played with Sam's ear.

At first, he wasn't sure he'd heard anything. Birds were chirping to each other from high branches and the engine of a car not too far away faded as it left the neighborhood. Then he heard it again. He couldn't tell what it was saying. What was audible weren't the words spoken but the raspiness of the voice, the clicks of consonants. It shrieked in the quiet sunlight, whispering loudly and chanting something Sam couldn't quite make out.

Timmy gave him a weird look. "Is that someone talking?"

The quiet voice was coming from the direction of the black structure, or from the surrounding pines it was nestled in. Slight relief came to Sam knowing he wasn't the only one hearing it but, before he could respond to Timmy, Isabelle yelped her raspy bark and shuffled off into the evergreens toward the noise, rustling bushes with her bulk as she went.

"Isabelle, come on," Sam called. "Isabelle!"

She was gone into the undergrowth on her way toward the house. Sam moved to follow her path but halted abruptly when he noticed sunlight glinting off of something in his vision, a spider web spread across the shrub in front of him. And then he noticed *all* of the webs strung through branches, under bushes, between trees that nearly hugged each other, everywhere, more than he'd ever seen in one place. Each web held in its center the fat brown arachnid of the northwest forests, with their bunched hairy legs and the milky kaleidoscopic patterns on their huge butts. He imagined the feel of the web on his face and skin and the crawling sensations all over him had he not noticed the disgusting things before diving in after Isabelle.

"Jesus!" Timmy shouted. "Look at all those!"

Sam shivered and turned, moving toward the gravel driveway. Timmy followed, whipping spiders from their webs with the stick he still held. Walls of arachnid infested flora passed through Sam's peripheral. He tried to keep up with the rustling of leaves and the wheezing breaths of Isabelle as she maintained her path through the underbrush toward the black house. "Isabelle!" he called again. A hundred feet down the drive, with gravel crunching under every one of his hastening steps, Sam saw that his dog was outpacing him by a long shot. He heard her break through the wall of foliage as he closed in on the front lawn of the place and watched the dog bolt, covered head-to-toe in thick webs, through the overgrown grass to the back of the building. Sam couldn't remember the last time he'd seen her move so quickly.

The smell of rot and electricity stung in the air, growing more acrid the closer they came to the place. Sam slowed as he approached the front of the dark structure, his eyes feeling a slight burning from the haze. Timmy closed in from behind but Sam's gaze was caught by what was in front of them.

It was a house and the first thing he noticed was the tree growing out of the roof. After blinking a few extra times to be sure, Sam stared up at the tall sentinel that rose from the center of the gambrel roof top. Its needled canopy was spread open like a tarp above the place. Its trunk was wide and had grown through a hole in the shingles. Broken bits of old carpentry had melded to the aperture with time and moss. Something wasn't right about the feel of the thing, combined with the smell in the air. This notion twisted in Sam as if some invisible entity was gripping and pulling at his insides.

Timmy approached. "What the hell?"

Sam's eyes followed along the contours in the bark. The grotesquely colored sap gave it an unnatural glaze. "I don't know."

A few fragile brown leaves were spread across the worn wooden deck that skirted the front of the house, otherwise it was covered in a thin layer of dead pine needles. The house's windows were gleaming in the sunlight but barren of any visible form or shape from the interior, no curtains, no lights. Only thick darkness met the other side of the glass.

It was then that Sam noticed the deafening silence.

The whispers had stopped.

An eerie quiet lay over the forest surrounding the black house, the air still heavy with that smell. Sam remembered a similar electrical odor outside of his Aunt Julie's place, which had been built under huge power lines. When it would rain, the smell was like burnt water. Sam's eyes searched above for anything resembling cables or lines but saw none.

Timmy was already on the deck when he said, "I don't hear that voice anymore". He analyzed the front door, probing some of the moss and needles along the base of the door frame with his foot.

Sam nodded, whether or not Timmy could see it, and slowly moved toward the side of the house where Isabelle had disappeared.

There was rustling in the overgrowth beyond.

"Timmy, toss me your stick," Sam said. He turned just in time to catch it as it wobbled through the air, then turned back and moved along the length of the deck.

As he approached the corner, the sound grew louder.

And then Isabelle appeared from around the other side. Relief washed over Sam as he called her to him, but then he saw that her pace was much slower than before. Something was wrong. A dark substance dripped down her hind legs and into the grass as she moved. It was blood and something else dragged along the ground underneath her. Sam's eyes brimmed with tears. He knelt down to her, unsure of what had happened and uncertain of what he was looking at. He could hear Isabelle whining and her breaths becoming wheezy as she stumbled onto her side on the deck in front of him. The blood slicked tubes that dangled from her exposed stomach appeared almost white against the dark brown of her fur and the earthy colors of the needled crust beneath them. It was a skein of worms that glistened grotesquely in the morning light. Sam had never seen anything like it.

Then Isabelle stopped moving.

Sam had cried out then, unsure of what else to do, what else to feel. Then he heard other crying and, through watery eyes, glanced back toward the front of the house. Timmy stood in front of the window next to the door, his face no further than a foot from the glass. He was sobbing hysterically but continued to stare into the black beyond the threshold. His jeans were soaked between the legs and he was saying something behind his cries that Sam couldn't make out.

In the shadows on the other side of the glass, there was thick darkness and in this darkness, a shape stirred.

Sam didn't know why he did it, why he ran without grabbing Timmy. Fear and sorrow filled him to the brim, pouring over and out in an adrenaline-fueled sprint down the gravel drive, out of the empty cul-de-sac, along the white lines of Shaw Road and finally back to his home in what felt like a blurred rush of time, a surreal dream that he would wake from as soon as he got into his own house and under the covers of his own bed. When he'd entered the safety of his home, though, he did not wake from a dream.

He'd left his only two friends back at the black house.

Sam told his mother about the spiders and the forest. He told her about the tree in the roof of the house and the stuff dangling from Isabelle's stomach. He told her about the whispers, but his mother didn't seem sure of how to respond to that part of the story and simply *shushed* him and held him close.

After Sam had cried his heart out, the next-door neighbor, Arland, agreed to help Sam's mother in collecting Isabelle's body. The three of them drove in her car to the cul-de-sac Sam quietly pointed out. When they arrived, Timmy was sitting in the gravel on the side of the road opposite the inlet, sobbing into his knees. Sam's mother offered Timmy a ride home and, when he quietly sat into the backseat next to Sam, the smell of piss filled the air inside the car. Neither spoke to each other, even as they dropped Timmy off at his house. He never came over to hang out again after that.

Sam couldn't blame him.

They buried Isabelle in the backyard. He cried for hours. His mother had said, with tears in her sympathetic bloodshot eyes, that maybe Isabelle had gotten herself caught on some old wire or fencing or a stray nail. She said that animals don't typically have the patience to wait in a situation like that and will move about, trying to escape, often causing more damage to themselves. Sam knew that she was trying to be helpful but the idea sent his mind into images of his dog ripping along barbed wire, thrashing back and forth. He had imagined it so many times since then and could still imagine it to this day, as if it was an actual event that he'd seen, as if it was a real memory.

Even now, a year later, Sam couldn't remember what he'd seen within the darkness of that house beyond the window, what had sent him running. As an aside to the fear and the sorrow, Sam learned something important that terrible summer morning:

Hell existed. It was a house near the end of Shaw Road.

*

Sam still thought of Isabelle these days and he could do it without getting all teary-eyed like he used to. He still remembered the grey under her chin and her big tongue and her happy eyes and he had learned to try and appreciate the memories of her that he actually enjoyed: all those summers out to his grandfather's cabin in some town called *Cle Elum*, with Isabelle following behind him as they explored the woods around the old man's property, and those countless times with her by his side while they spent cold winter evenings playing Flashlight Tag with the neighborhood kids. Whether it was her raspy bark, her big wagging behind or her heavy breathing after even short distances of movement, she always gave his position away but he didn't care. He had loved her as much as anyone could love a best friend. Sam felt grateful for those memories but, behind all of it, there was a lingering sourness he could not identify, implacable in its definitive existence.

Sam's thoughts of the past returned to the present when two kids approached from the north, Jacob Santos and Ronny Williams. He greeted them and Jacob Santos, of course, found a way to use the f-word in the first few words he spoke. Jacob cussed all the time, sure, but he never picked on Sam or anything and could even be pretty funny sometimes. While they waited for the rest of the kids to show up, Sam listened to Jacob talking to Ronny about the gore hole, the reason why they were out here in the first place. Within moments, the topic had moved to Timmy. Sam had no desire to be a part of the conversation but he also had no desire to walk out into the dark on his own, so he stood there listening and watching Jacob's animated face speak in the dying evening gloom.

"Yeah, I heard it fucked him up *real* good," Jacob said. "My brother said that his mom found him just wandering around old Ashley Hills, not knowing where he was or *who* the hell he was." Ashley Hills was a housing development that had begun construction about three years prior, off to the southeast of their neighborhood. After funding had been lost, the entire project was deserted for 'Future Development Continuation', according to the fine print on the NO TRESPASSING sign that guarded the abandoned homes. Sam had hung out with Jacob and his cousin there a few times during the winter, playing flashlight tag or throwing rocks at some of the derelict construction equipment but, without anyone else there, it was a lonely place to be.

Three more students approached out of the dark of the loop coming from the same direction Sam had. It was Collin Chambers and two other kids from a different class than Sam. He thought the one to Collin's right was named Jeremy but he wasn't sure. Jacob greeted Collin with a punch to the shoulder and they play wrestled for an aggressive moment, bringing each other down to the grass of the yard behind the bus stop, laughing and grunting as they tried to overpower one another.

As one last kid, Matt Foblieski, arrived at the bus stop, the clouds of the east had already darkened to black while the western horizon still glowed with the pale yellow-blue of the setting sun. Jacob Santos had Collin in a headlock. He laughed as his opponent squirmed.

“I give, I give!” Collin managed.

Dusk fell upon the group.

“What’s this thing called again?” the kid Sam thought was named Jeremy asked.

Collin smiled widely. “The *gore* hole.”

"Huh."

"Weird name."

Collin pushed Jacob again as they stood, then wiped the blades of grass and dirt from his knees. “We ready to go?”

Sam looked down at his Power Ranger watch and pressed the rubber nub once more.

6:09 PM.

Collin used his best Arnold Schwarzenegger voice with a big chest and wide eyes. "Come with me if you want to live!"

The group began to move, though not in the direction Sam had anticipated. Of the three routes to take from the bus stop, two of them led further back into the neighborhood around the loop, toward the entrance to Ashley Hills, except Collin wasn’t leading the group down either of them. Collin was headed the only direction Sam didn’t want to go, especially as night approached.

“Hey, Collin,” Sam said. He nodded to his right, toward the road leading further down the loop. “Ashley Hills is this way.”

“It’s not at Ashley Hills,” Collin responded, looking back over his shoulder.

“What? Jacob said that’s where they found Timmy... in Ashley Hills.”

Collin stopped and the rest of group bumped into each other doing the same. “Yeah, that’s where they *found* him but the gore hole is *this* way,” he said, nodding down the road that led to the place Sam did everything he could to avoid, that his mother would intentionally circumvent, that ran toward the all but dead sunlight and to wounds that he now realized were still fresh, opening up once more like new cuts in his skin.

Sam could almost feel what Collin was going to say before the words came.

“It’s near the end of Shaw Road.”

*

Fifteen minutes passed with Collin leading the group down the dark road, its white lines wavering and the blacktop as dark as the night that swelled around them. Sam's thoughts ran madly. He stared into the big windows of each house that bordered the black road, seeing images flash on a television inside one and even saw a family sitting at a dining room table in another, eating and enveloped in a dim warm light from a fireplace he couldn't see. He wanted to be in there, or be at home with his own warmth and the safety of his own house and his own family (which consisted of just his mother). Yet all he saw in his mind's eye was the dark place with the tree growing out of it that glistened with the thick sap, the house that Isabelle ran behind and returned from only to die. Recollections of the worm-like tubes dragging from her stomach overpowered his attempts to keep his thoughts at bay, to stave off the nightmares he'd tried to forget over the last year. Even the conversation from the other kids, loud and rambunctious shouts echoing off into the woods behind the houses, Sam could barely hear, a light din compared to the beat of his heart and the fire of anxiety burning in his nerves.

He wanted to run home. He didn't know how close they were to this gore hole but he hadn't been this far down Shaw Road since that day last summer. He wanted to stop and let his friends continue while he simply turned and made his way back to his house. They would hound him and jibe him for months for being such a *chicken-shit*, as Jacob Santos would undoubtedly say and, for the most part, it would be true. He remembered how they treated the foreign-exchange student earlier this year when the kid wouldn't stay at Collin's house to finish *The Blair Witch Project* because it was too scary. Sam couldn't recall his name but he did remember his teacher saying the kid was *Swedish* and he remembered how much the kid cried that week after he bailed on the movie when Collin and the rest of the group berated him at school. Jacob Santos used the term *chicken-shit* to describe the kid as he told the story to everyone in class during lunch the following Monday.

The truth was that *The Blair Witch Project*, just like many other movies, had given Sam nightmares for weeks, something he would never admit to the rest of the group. It took weeks for those dreams to die off and for Sam to stop crying in the middle of the night from fright. The only thing that would've made those nights worse, he imagined, would've been if he'd gone to school the next day and had to face ridicule for the fear he could not control, for the nightmares that seemed to control him instead. Sam hadn't said anything then to stop his friends from ridiculing the scared kid. Sam ran from that like he'd run from Isabelle and Timmy. And now the same feelings of fight-or-flight were pulsing in his tendons. He felt the same desire to run away from what was unfolding and he was ashamed of this all too familiar fear.

The others still laughed and joked with one another. Ronny bounced from one side of the road to the other, picking up rocks and throwing them at garbage cans while Jacob was picking up rocks and throwing them at Ronny. Sam allowed himself the smallest sliver of hope that they would simply walk by the entrance to the cul-de-sac, shouting and messing with each other without even noticing. Maybe the destination was beyond that place. Sam hoped that his own reaction would not give him away, that he would not give any sign of how terrified he was to pass by that cul-de-sac and that black house again. If they could simply continue down to the turnpike at the end of the road, maybe he wouldn't have anything to be afraid of.

The night around them had grown vacuous. The anticipation in Sam thickened along with the darkness. His hands shivered in his pockets.

And it was only a few moments later, as the group crested a small rise in the road, that Sam saw it. There were many cul-de-sacs in the neighborhood with the same type of concrete and the same type of side-street entrance that ultimately led to a dead end. Yet, even in the obscure evening, Sam knew by some unidentifiable marker that he was looking at the entrance to a very specific cul-de-sac. The hairs on the back of his neck stood on end. His mind ran through the memories once more, the scenes both in his head and in front of him matching each other in shape. The trees, the speed bump into the inlet, Isabelle, Timmy...

"Nah, dude," Ronny Williams said. "Sub-Zero could take Scorpion *any* day. What does Scorpion have? A rope that comes out of his hand? Sub-Zero can *freeze* things."

"Bullshit!" Jacob retorted. "Scorpion is *undead*. He's got a skull for a head!"

"So what? Sub-Zero would just freeze him and then shatter him like that guy in the movie." Ronny shrugged like that should win the argument they had been having for the last ten minutes.

"Dude," Jacob began again. "Scorpion blows fire out of his head. He would just melt the ice. Fuckin' simple. Boom. Plus, you can't kill the undead. They're already dead, dummy!"

Sam winced at the aggressive pronunciation of *dummy.* His nerves felt on fire or the air around him did. The cold air stroked at his cheeks and caused his eyes to water.

"Then how do you explain what happens when I kill you in the game whenever we play, huh?" Ronny's irritation was beginning to show. "How many times have I done the snowball fatality on you?"

"That's in the *game*, not real life, *dummy*!"

The group was just a few strides from the entrance into the cul-de-sac. Sam's eyes analyzed the steps of his friends, specifically Collin who led the group, trying to verify from their movement whether or not they were going to simply pass right by the place. In his mind's eye, Sam already saw it happening, the group simply walking past and him following behind. He wouldn't even need to look. He wouldn't even glance toward the empty cul-de-sac, the woods around it or the direction of the black house hidden in the trees. He wouldn't acknowledge the place, pushing his fears down into a hole they couldn't overtake him from, a hole where they belonged. The prediction was so potent, of the group being loud and just continuing down the road, that Sam already felt the stress begin to ease out of him like the air from a balloon, deflating the anxiety in his breath.

Collin spoke over his shoulder. "You guys are retarded. Reptile beats both of them."

Sam hardly heard this. Collin laughed at his own comment, then began to veer to the right, away from the center of the road, away from the safe idea held in Sam's mind. He was moving toward the entrance to the cul-de-sac, toward the dark trees that had held the whispers and the black house, where the nightmares lived. The balloon in Sam's chest inflated once more, filling with an anticipation that flared behind his ears and in his lungs as his breathing hastened.

Jeremy had joined in on the conversation but his voice, like the voices of the others, was distant amidst the roaring anxiety careening through Sam's veins like a freight train, producing a sound like a thousand hammers smashing into a thousand drums. "Wh-where..." A whisper was all Sam could muster from his jittering lips, a combination of the growing night chill and the adrenaline flowing through him, shocking his blood. His heart thumped loudly yet his feet still propelled him along with the group, moving from the blacktop of Shaw Road to the old concrete of the cul-de-sac.

"Smoke can teleport *and* he's got Scorpion's rope thing," Jeremy said. "Best of all worlds, plus he's badass."

They moved along the circumference of the concrete circle. Sam gazed with cruel nostalgia upon the dark bushes and pines that stood guard at the front of the woods. They'd been home to many spiders and their webs the last time he'd been here. It was too dark for him to discern if any were still there but, with the way the night caused the leaves to appear to shift and wobble, he imagined a fat hairy eight-legged thing waiting under each leaf, behind every branch or twig, with thick webs draped just over the endless needles that crusted the dirt underneath.

Collin was the first to step over the threshold from the cul-de-sac to the gravel caked dirt of the drive. A cold sweat dampened Sam's forehead as he followed, afraid of what lay ahead but terrified of staying back in the dark by himself. The walls of shrubs loomed on both sides and the little voice inside of him that spoke his fears aloud said that the foliage was undoubtedly home to countless observing eyes.

There were other voices, real voices. Sam heard them. Then he saw glowing balls crawling over the trees like spectres. Beams of light were coming from down the gravel drive, from the direction of where the house had been.

The group rounded the final curve in the drive.

Where Sam's memories of this grave place told him the house would still be, with the tree growing out of the old roof and the windows sitting empty and cold, a large vacant square of strange grass now lay. The stuff was short and pale rather than dark and overgrown like the flora that surrounded it. In the grasp of night's shade, the grass almost appeared luminescent, with a glow barely visible to the naked eye and almost perfectly shaped to the foundation of the house that once existed there. The structure was gone. In the center of the empty space, a massive stump jutted out of the ground. Blackened splinters stuck out from the top like clusters of kitchen knives. It appeared as if, instead of being cut down, it had been felled by some brute force. Its knobbed roots snaked rigidly into the soil below like boney ghoulish fingers. Not so much as a single two-by-four or stray brick lay in the vicinity to indicate the house's previous existence…

Except for that bizarre grass.

More light crawled through the trees in Sam's peripheral. He noticed, then, that they weren't ghosts or aliens but the beams of flashlights held by a couple of the eight or nine kids that stood in a line, single file, leading up to the back of the big stump, the side Sam could not see from where he and the group approached from. Collin removed his own flashlight from the backpack slung over his shoulder and flared it to the group, exposing the stump in a spotlight for a moment. The bark appeared burnt, scorched by an unknown fire, but it glistened with some kind of substance that drained from under the coarse ridges like blood, too thin and watery to be sap. Sam's eyes searched the clearing and the surrounding bushes for any signs of a downed tree, the one that once existed here. If the tree had fallen over, there would be a massive trunk still decaying somewhere nearby, burnt by flames or soggy from rain. Only a year would've passed since it had been standing, maybe less.

There was no sign of the rest of the tree. Something else, however, caught his attention.

Behind the group waiting in line at the stump, off near the edge of the tree line, was a kid he couldn't identify from here, murmuring and consoling another that stood facing the trunk of a tall pine. As Sam's eyes tried adjusting to the dark with the beams from the flashlights occasionally making a swipe through the forest, he realized that the kid was not the only one. Standing in the woods along the forest line, scattered about, were at least a dozen other dim profiles. They were motionless forms of shadow, save for one or two of them swaying back and forth, but all were quiet, staring off in their own directions into the woods.

"Whoa, look at the grass." Jacob motioned for Collin to hand him the flashlight. Once in his hand, he clicked it on and crouched to pluck some of the pale plant out of the ground. He rotated it between his fingers and held the light up to it as he analyzed the stuff. In the beam of the flashlight, Sam saw a powder flaking off of the bit of plant and floating in the air in front of Jacob's face. Where the wind had been cold and consistent earlier in the day, here, in the night within the walls of the surrounding evergreens, the air was stagnant and the dust swirled slowly in the cold stillness. Sam remembered seeing a similar type of dust once waft out of the dry mushrooms that grew near the garbage bins at the rear of the elementary school. This grass didn't look like mushrooms, though.

"Be careful of that stuff," Sam warned.

"Yeah, or what?" Jacob responded pompously. He glanced up from his fingers and directed his flashlight toward the line of kids, specifically to the boy standing closest to the stump. "Joey, you piece of shit." Jacob laughed as he stood and moved around the back side of the stump, shoving the kid in line. "You dillweed! You said you were going to... You said you... were..."

Jacob's voice trailed off as he coughed, wiping his nose and mouth with the back of his hand. He stood there, swallowing heavily, looking at the kid named Joey but appearing to not really be looking. His eyes seemed cloudy, hypnotized by the kid Joey's face or something in the woods beyond that Sam could not see from the angle at which he stood. The kid Joey remained silent as well, never moving his eyes from the black trunk, as with the rest of them in line.

They were all silent. All stared ahead to the stump.

"Let's see it! Where's the gore hole?!" Collin asked loudly as he, too, started walking around to the back side of the line.

Jacob's voice was making a mumbling noise as he pointed limply toward the stump. Collin coughed once as well and, within a few moments, his eyes appeared to fog over, too.

"Guys, what's wrong? What is it?" Sam asked. The house was no longer here. The fear of encountering it once more had depleted only to be replaced by an eerie chill from the scene he now looked upon, the two loudest of his friends silenced by what they were witnessing on the other side of the hulking stump, and a bunch of kids standing hypnotized in a line with many more silent throughout the tree line.

It's okay to run, sweetie, his mother's voice spoke in his mind. He wanted to run. He desperately wanted to run. He didn't want to see what was on the other side of the stump and he didn't want to know why all those kids were standing in the woods in the back. This place was scary and there was a wrongness to it all that Sam could swear was reaching for him out here, like a boiled grey hand emerging from the dark. He knew why he wanted to run and had decided then that he was going to, yet something deep inside prevented him from doing so.

It was then that he could taste the powder in the air and on his tongue, spores of the pale glowing grass. That's when he felt the tingling pin-pricking sensation in his sinuses and in his mouth, over his eyes and in his nose. And there was something invisible and thin, like a line of spider's web that he could not see, tugging at his chest, at his insides, forcing him to move forward. It urged him toward the other side of the stump with slow steps executed outside of his command. The world of night took on a strange hue, then. The small slivers of star light above seemed to bob up and down, waver in and out. Geometric patterns glowed out from the black around him.

Sam Benton turned and faced the other side of the stump, the side that everyone else was staring at, through eyes that he'd lost hold of, and only then did he see it: bored into the black leaking bark of the scorched tree trunk was a hole the size of a basketball. A boy was knelt down in front of it with his head sunk into it to his shoulders. Sam's gaze, directed by something unknown to him, moved along the contours of the barked aperture and watched the boy's knuckles as they went white in the passing beam of a flashlight, holding the sides of the stump rigidly. The boy's body relaxed and tensed and relaxed again. Sam could hear a muffled sound coming from deep within the stump. It sounded like a scream, distant and hardly audible. He wanted to know why the boy was kneeling there, why he would submit his head to the stump's maw, but words would not come from his own throat. His voice and his body had relinquished themselves to a force beyond the realm of the world he knew. And as he watched himself, *felt* himself, moving to the back of the line, with Jacob and Collin moving behind him just as witlessly, Sam began to hear the whispers. Sharp words licked in the dark around him. It was the whispers from trees, the same ones he'd heard the day Isabelle died. He couldn't understand what was being said at first but, as it repeated itself again and again, inside and outside his hexed perspective, he was able to make the words out, even if he tried desperately not to hear them.

It's almost your turn, Sammy.

It's almost your turn, Sammy.

It's almost your turn, Sammy.

In Sam's peripheral, the dark wall of the forest loomed maddeningly. From the corner of his eye, he saw the shapes of the other kids standing amongst the trees as unidentifiable shadows. He wanted to escape. Sam's eyes, fixated on the black stump, could almost pierce through the bark to sense the evil that waited for him within. Its wretched fingers had somehow leaked from within the rotten wood and were reaching out invisibly, leading him to where it wanted him.

It's almost your turn, Sammy.

It's almost your turn, Sammy.

The line had shortened while the whispers spoke into his mind with what sounded like oiled tongues. The kid kneeling in front of the stump stood and left. The next in line took his place. Tears of anxiety ran down Sam's cheeks. He thought of his mother sitting at home, waiting for him to return, and tried to scream again, tried to scream for her, but nothing came out except for a barely audible moan.

The line, including Sam, shuffled forward and the child directly in front of him knelt down to the stump, placing his hands on the bark on either side of the deep black opening. The boy's head sunk into the hole and Sam could feel his own chest quivering with sobs that couldn't escape. It was waiting for him. He could feel its anticipation like static along the hairs of his arms. In his lungs and in his mind, he felt the *thing* that waited for him. He felt the eternity it had spent preparing for his turn at the gore hole.

It's almost your turn, Sammy.

It's almost your turn, Sammy.

Sammy. Sammy. Sammy.

The boy's head slid out from the stump, covered in a placenta-like substance, steaming in the cold autumn air of the night. His skin was pale, drained, and his eyes were wide and completely vacant in the dark. A low moan emitted from his slimed lips and in Sam's peripheral, he saw the boy stumble off toward the trees beyond the clearing.

SAMMY! SAMMY! SAMMY! WE'VE BEEN WAITING FOR YOU!

Everything he had ever been and ever would be pushed against the force that moved his legs forward to the stump. His insides burned with wasted effort, useless against the powers that now controlled him. His limbs were being animated like some rigid puppet and, as his body knelt down in front of the stump, Sam screamed as hard as he could in the face of the hole, producing only a breath that fitfully wheezed out of his lips.

SAMMY! SAMMY! SAMMY! WE'VE BEEN WAITING FOR YOU!

The harsh whispers repeated his name and that phrase like a song, some incantatory tune he might hear kids singing in the schoolyard during recess. The voices came from the tall pines that surrounded as well as from within the bowels of the black maw directly in front of him, thousands of whispering mouths, slick with saliva, licking and lapping and chanting.

His hands tingled with possession. They reached up to either side of the aperture and the echoes called for him from within the window to the abyss. The dark consumed his fixated vision and the coarse bark scraped along his glasses and against the skin of his ears as he submitted his head to the hole. There was an almost palpable sense of pleasure, of a long game finally coming to a close, washing over Sam and creeping into his bones. In the blackness, something had been waiting for him. *I can't move! Guys, I can't move!* he wanted to yell but these were only thoughts playing silently in a small place at the bottom of his own mind while his throat and mouth betrayed his command. The aperture cinched closer around his neck.

SAMMY! SAMMY! SAMMY!

And as his body relinquished its straining, with his head and neck encased fully in the tight darkness, the whispers reached a crescendo in a bizarre climax. In a shrill moment of violence, everything went silent and the world outside of the hole was eaten by the void.

*

The blackness was heavy.

Sam couldn't tell if his eyes were still open.

The inner walls of the trunk felt like wet rubber and slickly moved over the sides of his glasses and his nose and lips. The confines fluttered against his cheeks, undulating like the throat of some inhuman beast. The horror cleaving through him shined at the edges of his darkened vision like mirrored glass and he tried to push himself out of the black but his arms didn't move. He tried to move his legs but they made no response either, tranquilized by the oppressing gullet swallowing him.

And then he felt the walls begin to tighten, sucking at him wretchedly. As the throat in which Sam dwelled closed in, air no longer filled his lungs. It was going to suffocate him. Panic grew in the depths of his being as he struggled to breathe. His ears popped and his sight was speckled with the small bursting lights of anoxia. The rubber constricted around his neck and on his face, crushing the frames of his glasses into his eyebrows. He tried to cry but had no breath to do so.

He knew then that this was how he was going to die.

And when he thought that he could take it no longer, when his throat felt on fire from deprivation, the oily walls of darkness fell back and opened up, ballooning out far away from his head. He gasped for the air, no matter its source. His lungs ached ferociously. The tendons of his jaw were no longer clenched shut, no longer silenced by possession, and so he cried into the nothingness ahead of him. After whole seconds, his sobs echoed off of distant walls he could not see, coming back to him like someone else's voice, mocking his lamentations. He no longer felt his hands on the bark of the stump, no longer felt the damp ground soaking the knees of his jeans or the gnarled rim of the aperture against the base of his neck. He could only feel the black around him, only the heartbeat thumping in his throat from a heart he could no longer place.

Sam whimpered, floating bodiless in the void.

From some part of the dark ahead and below him, the sounds of an unseen ocean broke against a shore. The crashing floated up to him along with a mist of pulverized waves, invisible, speckling his face. The mist smelled like dirt and something else, something he recognized. Wet fur… Wet *dog's* fur...

Isabelle.

New tears crept from Sam's eyes as he sobbed, joining with the mist that came up to him from out of the abyss. The insides of his throat and chest were thick with the anguish of old memories being pried out of the sad fingers of his soul. His heart cried out to hold his dog again in that moment and the darkness fed off of it, intensifying the scent with each crashing wave below, each spray of the unseen waters. It smelled of home for Sam, of days lounging in the sunlight with Isabelle, but there was a sourness to it as the sensation grew more intense, a hint of something like rot or decay. The miasma spewed up at him and it burned in his nostrils, causing his eyes to water even more. It was everywhere and, in his thoughts, he saw Isabelle lying in his lap with the white worms hanging out of her. The darkness was toying with him. In his mind's eye, he saw her breaths become labored, or the nothingness was showing him this horrid simulation like a slide on a projector screen. He couldn't tell where his mind ended and the vivid dark began.

"Isabelle!"

And as if reacting to Sam's call, the smell faded then, almost instantaneously. The memories of Isabelle were being siphoned from his mind, leaking across his inner eye as they were extracted from his reality. He felt himself forgetting her, forgetting his best friend, as the surrounding darkness mocked and gorged itself on the sorrow it wrought in him.

Sam felt himself breaking. It was taking her from him.

The place opened up further, then. In the null distance, something caught Sam's eye. The eerie glow of a white fog had birthed, floating along massive cavernous walls far ahead and around him. His eyes sought out the light, consuming it like sustenance in the black as the entire scene slowly came into view. Squinting, he could barely make out the scale of the dark space he floated in. It wasn't a room or nook, small and confined within the hollows of the burnt bleeding tree trunk.

It was a space much larger.

The turmoil of the black waters below sounded like waves of a vast ocean but the body of oil was very much encased in the caverns, Sam could now see. It was a roiling underground lake that he floated above, the waves of which crashed against a shore of dark sand. Tendrils of fog slithered along the water's edge, emboldened by the mists of shattered swells. Further into the cavern, a dim luminescence came into existence out of the nothingness beyond the shore. An old lamp dangled from a rotten wooden post buried in the dark sand. Its light glowed a deep red through its stained glass over a small portion of the distant beach, swinging in the black breeze and tinting the creeping proximal fog a menacing color. Just inside the red glow and barely visible against the surrounding shadows were several dark masses. Their silhouettes were illuminated by the sinister light. They appeared as upside-down teardrops that balanced on the very tips of their shapes. They swayed back and forth in the black sand to the rhythm of the crashing waves and swinging lamp and Sam's heart pounded violently, threatening to break open and out of his ribcage to the very same beat. And then he felt himself losing altitude.

Sam's perspective floated slowly downward through the dark toward the uncertain waters below. Panic consumed him. He screamed again into the massive cavern, his cries echoing in the distance and then back at him in that tone unlike his own. His eyes searched throughout the vast underground for anything other than those *things* on the shore dancing in that red light, someone to help him, anything to give him sanctuary from this nightmare. He shouted for Collin and for Jacob to pull him from the stump, to save him from the grasp of the gore hole, yet he felt no response from the other side. He simply continued to sink down, further and further.

In the distance off to Sam's right, seemingly built into the rock wall of the cavern, a cluster of structures had come into view, their contours outlined by the writhing pale fog. It was a castle, appearing black, cold and silent. At the top of one of the warped stone towers, a small window glowed a warm orange light.

"Help!" Sam didn't know who was in there but he didn't care. "Help me! Somebody, please! Hey, help!" His squealing voice was swallowed by the distance between he and the light and he drifted down closer to the water. More screams burst from his throat.

It happened slowly or it happened instantly, Sam could not tell either way, but at some point, he felt his body once again, its presence, starting with the pressure of a surface underneath his knees. It was not the wet grass outside the stump he felt but something softer.

The black waters had calmed completely save for the ripples coming out from under the object he now floated on. The surface beneath him was not made of wood or metal, but of cotton, a blanket, with hardness underneath it. It was a bed, his *own* bed, and he was kneeling on it while it floated as his only salvation in this lake of gurgling unknown. The same light blue blanket he'd used since he was a toddler was draped over it and the sheets were dampening at the edges, soaking up the ink of the black lake. It was thick and syrupy, like tar, now that he was close enough to see its viscosity.

A deep groan rumbled out from the murky abyss below, like a horn, massive and undoubtedly ear-shattering if not for the depths that muffled it. Something moved under the surface of the lake, sloshing the water below with unearthly strength. The petulant liquid burbled around the sides of the bed. Fetid ripples broke on the surface. Sam's lungs felt frozen with hyperventilation.

Directly ahead of him, the oil of the lake seemed to dip briefly and then it belled up, swelling for a moment that stretched impossibly. Then, it broke open. A titanic sphere breached the surface, rising slowly out of the waters. When it was half-emerged, it went still. Sam's eyes locked onto the massive black bubble in horror. As the streams of oil poured down its sides into the lake, the texture of the thing came into view. It was wrinkled and warted like the skin of a boar, with musculature twitching underneath its bulged surface. The rough mass peeled back then, unsheathing a layer of itself. Sam's heart sank and the terror locked around his throat, suffocating him with a roaring panic. When the thing was fully opened, it revealed a smooth glassy surface, dripping and glistening with the dim red light that emanated from the shore.

The sphere shifted toward him.

In the failing red light, Sam saw that it was an eye. In its center was a fiery orange iris with a cross-shaped pupil like a goat's, white with cataracts. It stared directly at him. He tried to scream, but his body was once again unresponsive, no longer under his own will. The possession had crept back into his bones through his pores or his mouth. It didn't matter. All he could do was stare right back.

The sheets and blanket underneath him had become fully soaked with the black liquid and the bed was beginning to sink. Sam felt its buoyancy diminishing but could not take his eyes off of the ocular mass in front of him, could not attempt to swim away. The staring eye held his gaze like a moth's to a light and, as he felt his knees submerging, a cry of terror hardly escaped his lips. All control of his body was relinquished to the nightmare. The only thing keeping him afloat was sinking underneath him, drifting down into the abyss and he was following it in.

The cold fluid was at his thighs, then his groin. Sam's genitals shriveled, violated by the ink seeping into his clothing and into his skin. The freezing oil reached his stomach. Again he tried to scream, again nothing came of it. Somehow he knew that the water itself was part of this creature, like a massive liquid mouth slowly eating him. He *knew* it as the truth. He was going to be its food. Then the stuff was at his chest. He could smell the stink now, a thick garbage smell with that same burnt electric quality to it, the stuff he smelled last summer. His chin submerged and then his mouth.

The titanic eye followed him as he sank, watching blindly.

Sam didn't want to see what was under the surface. He wanted nothing more in the entirety of his existence than to avoid seeing what was in the dark below. He wanted to shut his eyes away from it and he tried, squeezing as hard as he could, a last ditch effort to fight back against the entity, but his eyelids remained wide open, held apart by a force unknown, the force that mastered his body.

And in the brief moment that Sam had become fully submerged, when he tried once more to yell for his mother, his eyes were open. Even in the blackness of the ink in which he sank, he could see the thing down there where he did not want to look yet was forced to. It was everything he had ever feared. It writhed and took its shape from Sam's nightmares, each and every one of them. Its form was gigantic and horrid. It extended into the unfathomable depths like a black glacier, with its bulbous tendrils gyrating in the cloudy water and its pale alien face floating in and out of the murk. It shapeshifted and appeared in one moment like a wall of human teeth and in another as a mound of haggard breasts, rotten to the nipple. Massive eyeballs floated individually in the darkness, each tethered to the entity by slithering appendages. Sam knew, with what little consciousness he held onto, that this thing was responsible for the slit down Isabelle's stomach that day. He knew what he looked upon was the thing that had waited for him, waited for such a long time. It had goaded him with the destruction of his best friend and the whispers in the trees around the black house and counted on him to return one day.

And he did return.

As Sam sank further into the cold black and into the heart of that decrepit mass, speckles like points of light flooded his vision. His mind turned blank and thoughtless, surrendering over completely to the madness of witnessing indescribable and inescapable horror.

*

The clouds had broken and moonlight illuminated the clearing of pale grass around the fetid stump. The cold still clutched at the kids standing in line, who watched as Sam Benton gently pulled away from the tree trunk. He rose slowly to his feet. His hands were covered in the dark sap though he did not appear to notice. His eyes were wide and watery but unblinking. His face was slick. His mouth was slightly ajar but no sound escaped.

Tufts of spores swirled in the chilled air around his feet as he turned and ambled toward the edge of the clearing. Behind him, Collin knelt to his knees to take his spot in front of the stump.

Sam walked without conscious thought. His shuffling feet breached the forest line where the others were, the ones who'd seen into the gore hole and witnessed their own terrors before him. They stood like scattered statues but Sam did not see them. Instead, he saw only darkness as he gazed further into the forest and the darkness was alive gazing back at him. Damp branches bent and cracked under his steps as he moved autonomously through the underbrush, possessed by his own trauma, to take his place amongst the pines.

Burials: The Speaking Dead

The last of the desert sun radiated from behind the mountains in the distant west, beyond the hundred leagues of salt flats that separated their dark peaks from the searing sands of the *Red Scar*. The ornery groan of a camel echoed out of the labyrinth of the *Scar*'s dunes into the purple evening sky, where distant stars were beginning to twinkle into existence.

An old man sat atop the camel as it strode around a bend in a wide trail winding through the dunes. *The Prophet's Road*, the indigenous people called it. It was the dried cracked bed of an old river from a time long gone, from before the last cataclysm. The old man had heard the stories as a child and, in his old age, had even told them to his own children and grandchildren, young and awestruck and sat around a campfire, anxious for stories of an apocalypse they could only see in their dreams, the horrors of which they could never really know. That was a long time ago. The days of children happily shoulder-to-shoulder listening to stories were gone. There was no place for fables any longer. The days had grown grim and the present was saturated with an almost suffocating morbidity.

The ancient river had supposedly run all the way through to the wetlands, leagues beyond the desert. The old man had never seen the wetlands, himself, having spent his entire life in the southwest regions of the flats. He'd heard stories as a youngster about the foul things that lurked in those swamps, what those lands could do to a man. His destination was not beyond these dunes towards those unknown bogs and marshes, however. His destination lay at the very heart of the *Scar*'s burnt wastes.

The red dunes grew closer as the riverbed tapered into a thin path, an arm's width wide. The old man rode for most of an hour with the evening shroud dampening the air around him while the trail coiled this way and that like the burrowed tunnel of some ancient serpent. And when it seemed as if the path were thinning into a dead end, and the last sunlight would be completely blotted out from the claustrophobic walls of old sediment, the way opened up to a wide and barren lake bed.

The sky was vacuous and immense above. The spread of the remaining sunset shined dimly from behind while the east darkened with the coming night. At the far end of the old dry bed was a platform, stone as black as coal, with a large obsidian crescent rising from the back of it. The crescent's points were directed upward like a devil's horns and the old man shuddered when he looked upon its blatant ungodliness. It appeared like some sort of shrine, eldritch in nature, an homage to cosmic forces he had never known. In the air, the old man could feel it, that many unholy sacraments had come to fruition in this place. His own would not be the first, nor would it be the last.

The lake bed was surrounded on all sides by towering ridges and dunes of sand. Beyond the black platform at the far end ascended a giant dune that stood mountainous over the others by half at least. The top portion of the great mound was still lit by the setting sun. The lake bed below, however, grew dark with shade. Night would be upon the world soon.

The camel shuffled, exhausted and salivating, over the cracked hexagons of dirt toward the platform. As they came within a few feet of the black monolith, the old man slid off of the mat of worn leather. The dirt crunched under his crude sandals and the camel groaned once more.

Mismatched trinkets and bags hung from hempen rope strung to the saddle. Some hanging iron mugs clanged against each other while the old man tugged at one of the leather packs. He unbelted the strap and sunk his hands into it, gently maneuvering his grip around something inside. He held his breath tightly. His hands emerged with a lumped wad of rags, easing it from the pack as if it might turn to dust at any moment. Tears pooled in the corners of his eyes and his hands trembled. A faint sob escaped his broken lips, chapped from prolonged exposure to the grainy winds that had whipped at him throughout the glaring day. He held the lump of rags to his chest and rocked back and forth next to the camel, grimacing with the weight of a growing misery and of desperation heavy within him. After a few long breaths to regain what composure he had left, the old man wiped his eyes on the ragged shawl he wore and moved toward the platform and the crescent rising from it.

In the shadows of the evening, the lurid blackness of the platform seemed to soak up any potential light falling upon it from the western sky. It appeared as if its shape had been cut out of the very fabric of reality, revealing the dark of the void beyond the spectrum of the physical. No light reflected off of its smoothed beveled edges nor had the dry sands of the desert winds fallen upon it. Not even dust dared to settle onto this monolith of fiendish rituals.

Standing in front of a platform of such unearthly craftsmanship, the old man's instincts were crackling. His red eyes strained as they searched the lake bed, shifting from dune to dune, half-expecting to see some spectre or the devilish architect of the platform, gazing down upon him. There was a presence beyond the sight of his teary eyes, somewhere, observing his movements though he could not pinpoint its location.

It didn't matter. His soul was too exhausted. He was here for a reason, a last resort for light in a world that had grown so cold with decay.

The old man returned his attention to the platform. He crouched to gently place the bundle of rags onto the slab. His shaking hand pulled away a layer of the wrapping to reveal the emaciated unmoving body of an infant. Its lips were grey and its flesh lifeless, and the man's cries could no longer be stifled upon seeing it once again. He fell to his knees in front of the platform and wept toward the heavens.

The sky had turned from orange-purple to a deep purple-black and the shade in the lake bed had grown thick as midnight. Sunlight could no longer be seen on any of the dunes, including the giant beyond the platform, but the wisps of hazy sand at the top of the massive thing still reflected the sun's dwindled rays from the far west, appearing like fire above, dancing as they floated off into the high winds.

The old man's tears left dark trails behind them in the dirt caked on his face. Dust had hardened in the lines around his forehead and mouth and the whites of his eyes had gone yellow from hard years and harder memories. And yet he rose and staggered back toward the camel, his aged bones leaden with sadness.

A year ago, the dark corruption, a plague of unknown origin, had swept through his people's village. He could still see the goats, their bodies scattered about, decrepit and roiling with maggots, the morning he discovered the terror. The entire herd, seemingly overnight, had been obliterated by an unknown rot. The livestock had been the first victims, followed soon after by the children and old folk, who perished within days, eradicated by the same plague that took the animals. It was in the water and in the wind. His family and his people were left lifeless and feasted upon by hordes of flies in the wake of the destruction. Only a handful of souls from his village had survived the fetid corruption, seeming to be immune altogether. Of his once large family, consisting of dozens of nieces and nephews and grandchildren, only the daughter of his own daughter had remained alive to keep him company.

How grim the color of the world had turned when, a year after the catastrophe that left him almost empty and void of emotion, his granddaughter had succumbed to Death in the form of black veins and shallow labored breath. The remaining survivors of the plague had also fallen ill and died, one by one. The old man's own arms were tainted with charcoaled veins now. He knew that Death was approaching him swiftly. He felt the ache in his belly and in his thews. The hope of survival had been false and Death rode upon its ghoulish steed somewhere, howling with satisfaction at the game it had played with him and his loved ones. They had not been spared, only saved for later via the lingering sickness biding its own time within their very blood.

He would not have it, not while desperate measures could still be taken and not while eldritch favor could still be called upon to stay Death's embrace. His own life did not matter but the child's was all that was left of the fulfillment he once knew, all that was left to remind him of his own happiness. If she could survive, not all was lost. In her, his own daughter and the bloodline of his people carried on.

When the old man returned to the camel, he slipped his hands into the other pack attached to the saddle. Before removing the object, he probed it with his fingertips, the aged wrinkled leather and the symbol carved into it like flayed skin, the worn page corners and the sticky substance congealed on the binding. His aged hands emerged with a black tome that, despite having been wrapped in cloth and saturated by the desert heat for most of the day, felt cold to his touch. It was unlike any book he'd ever seen, with shreds of pages protruding from it as if entire sections had been torn out and reattached in mismatched positions. Many of the pages were scrawled with handwritten scribbles, some of which were legible and others in foreign languages he had never seen before. The substance stuck to the leather along the binding felt like a pitch or sap of some kind. It looked to be slowly oozing from the book like black blood.

Along with the tome, the old man removed a small glass phial from the front pouch of the pack, plugged with a cork and filled with a milky yellow fluid. He held it in front of his face and swirled it, watching the liquid roll around, then turned and made his way back to the platform. Once more, he wiped the tears from the dirt-crusted bags under his eyes.

As he reached the black altar, he knelt down in front of it and leaned his face in, inches from the wad of cloth and the lifeless head of the infant. Black veins ran like coiled roots under the pale skin of her little cheeks and chest. The old man kissed her forehead twice, then sat back on his calves and opened the strange book in his lap, turning to a specific page toward the middle which was marked with a shred of tattered cloth. The exiled witchdoctor from whom he'd obtained the book had marked the page. The old man could only hope that what he would find within the texts would be instructions for some sort of miracle, something to break through the bleakness that vexed him and his reality. He glided his fingertips along the ornate text, barely lit from the stars above, before he began chanting the first passage under his breath.

All was silent in the heart of the *Red Scar*, save for the heavy whispers of a man who'd lost everything.

After finishing the passage, the old man set the book on his knees and popped the cork from the phial. He poured the milky liquid over his granddaughter's corpse and watched the infant's cloth wrappings darken as the fluid soaked through. The empty phial shattered in a sprinkle of glass when the old man tossed it. He picked up the book and wondered once more if the answer to his misery lay within the texts, within the prayers he'd made, whispering to whatever entities listened in this unholy place.

A tear streamed down the bridge of his nose and dropped onto the open page. In the uncertain dimness of the birthing night, the text almost appeared to absorb the single tear without leaving as much as a mark or damp spot. The old man did dwell on it. His eyes returned to his granddaughter and there they stayed while he sat in silence. The witchdoctor's words repeated in his mind, words regarding the door to true awakening and those who dare to step through it. Long minutes passed as the growing cold began to sink into the old man's fingers. He watched the infant's immobile state and waited agonizingly for something, *anything*. What little he held onto, the desperation aching in the recesses of his soul, was curdling into hopelessness as each moment crept by.

The pages of the book fluttered when he threw it to the dirt beside the platform, enraged and broken all at once. He cried, burying his face into his calloused palms, and cursed the crazed witch's false sorcery for giving him even a glimmer of hope.

There was no hope.

All was truly lost.

The bulk of the universe seemed to weigh on him then, the weight of mortality and defeat, crushing the life and will from him with its indifference to his suffering...

And then, out of the surrounding dark, a sound interrupted his lamentations.

The old man's eyes darted up toward the source of the noise, back behind the horned platform and high above. The giant dune was a juggernaut, black against the purple night sky. In the center of the front face of the dune, swaths of sand shifted in the shadows and poured down. The old man's sobs quieted. His eyes narrowed as he peered up through the dark.

Something emerged from the sand.

A curdled coughing sound echoed out into the night from somewhere within the morphing shroud of sand and darkness. The old man stood and slowly moved forward, transfixed by what was happening and possessed by a curiosity he had never imagined. As he stepped closer, the features of the thing poking out of the dust came into fearful focus.

It looked like a head, a *child's* head.

The thing retched and choked and shouted out over him to the expansive lake bed. Its face was warped and covered in a layer of sand. Its eyes were hollowed black holes. In the starlight, the old man looked upon its mouth, gaped wide as it screamed, *too* wide, as if the jaw were broken and hanging or elongated somehow. Its neck bent into unnatural angles, whipping back and forth while it cried out. The child's shoulders emerged, then, as yet another head surfaced from the sand next to it. This one, too, called out into the desolate night. It was a woman's head, her hair matted with some coagulate and covered in sand. She was screaming obscenities and harshly gagged on the dirt that filled her crippled mouth. There was a hole where her nose ought to have been, bored into the center of her face in some kind of bizarre torture.

The old man stood still, paralyzed with dread, his breath caught in his throat. Beneath his feet, the ground began to shake. The vibration quickly grew in intensity. Pebbles rattled and jumped around his sandals. Runes that had been invisible in the shadows, carved into the black horns rising from the platform on which his granddaughter lay, began to glow a smoky green. They were engraved in a jagged sort of language, unearthly and indecipherable, yet he thought they looked similar to the scrawled notes found in the tome from which he had read.

The sand from the great dune continued to tumble down the front and sides. Dust rose into the sky, making the dune appear to be threatening some kind of volcanic eruption. The camel scrambled off in the direction that they had come, the contents of the saddle-packs jangling as it fled.

Another screaming voice joined the other two from a third head that appeared out of the shifting sands.

Then a fourth head.

Then a fifth.

Within moments, dozens of bodies and heads protruded from the front of the dune, all cursing and yelling from their rotted mouths.

The old man stepped back away from the platform. He covered his mouth, stifling a cry of terror with his shaking hand, and stared up at the animated bodies of what he could only assume were the dead. Their infernal appearances made him certain that they belonged in deeply buried graves, to no longer be a part of the realm of the living but to exist only in the cold frigid wastes of the land of the dead. The heads and limbs squirmed and jerked but none fell from the mound in which they had emerged, stuck to each other by a binding mortar of ectoplasm or some other force. And then the old man could see it, that the mass of rotting bodies and grotesquery were held together in the shape of a humanoid face, enormous with deep shadowed pits for eyes. The tremendous simulacrum fully surfaced, extending across the entirety of the dune.

The old man looked in horror upon the form, incomprehensible and nightmarish, as the suffering screams of the damned grew louder with each moment that passed. It was a chorus of agony, a wretched song of Hell.

A dull *crack* broke from deep within the dune, a shift of earth beneath its bedrock, and the ground's vibration diminished. The bodies up on the mound went still and the heads and their mouths silenced.

Fear melded the old man's feet to the ground beneath him and gripped his throat with rusted fingers. His mind screamed to run but his body did nothing but stand still, grasping for any sense in the madness he now witnessed.

From the dark of the giant face, two small green orbs blinked into life, lit from the bulging nose area of the giant visage. The orbs glowed out of the hollow sockets of the child that had been the first to emerge from the sands. Two more orbs appeared in the darkness, glowing like little balls of light, then another pair. In a few short moments, every rotted head stared with emotionless glowing observation, like a hundred green stars peering down at him through the demented nightscape.

The old man hadn't realized he'd begun to back away until his foot caught a rock and he fell onto his rear. He gasped as he hit the ground, trembling and encompassed by a vast horror.

The collective face slowly began to shift. A line ripped open from between two bodies toward the lower part of the mound. The rotted heads remained silent, still staring with emerald eyes as the maw stretched further. One of the bodies at the corner of the opening mouth split from the groin to the center of its chest and another separated at the waist, its torso pulled from its legs. Old dusty entrails tumbled out into the sand below. The remaining intestines hanging from the body appeared like ragged teeth against the black of the stretching mouth. The collective remained quiet. Fright kept the old man staring upon the terrible miscreation.

From beyond the precipice of the aphotic mouth, a rumbling came to life. It began as a low subterraneous thudding, then seemed to increase in volume, gaining a force or momentum from deep within its monstrosity. Out of the depths of darkness...

BWAAAAAAAAAHHH!

The old man pressed his hands to his ears when the horn-like sound blurted out. Though the horrible sound stopped almost as quickly as it had started, it reverberated off of the surrounding dunes and echoed out into the desert for leagues into the night.

A crystalline emerald light now beamed from the giant face down upon the old man and his ritual. It radiated out of the sunken eye sockets and the great mouth was stretched and glowing, too, appearing like some cosmic gate to an otherworldly dimension.

The wad of cloth on the platform below stirred.

The old man let out a breath he'd been holding for what felt an eternity, allowing his hands to fall from his ears. He stood slowly and, with careful steps, approached the black monolith once again.

The head of the infant lolled back and the emerald light from the visage above reflected in her eyes, open and wandering like the day she was born. The old man cried out, not in pain but with a joy he had left for dead. He fell to his knees in front of the platform and smiled richly, forgetting altogether the face up in the sand, as he watched the infant's fragile chest rise and fall with renewed breath. Laughter mixed with sobs as he nuzzled his face into her baby hair, which smelled of dirt and the liquid from the phial. Death would have to wait for another day to take his granddaughter from him, he knew. The ritual had worked.

The old man gently stroked the infant's cheek and cried in elation as a wave of humility washed through him. He'd dismissed the witchdoctor's rituals too soon and now he was beyond grateful to have been wrong. It amazed him how, even in a time of such terrible sorrow and soul-aching depravity, and after all these years of his life, the potential for beauty and surprise was still alive.

Hope could still be found.

The old man looked up to the massive simulacrum in the sand. The cold necrotic light still beamed but he felt gracious, not threatened, and his heart was shining just as brightly as the dead were in that moment. The glowing eyes of the bodies stared from behind the rays of emerald. Were they looking down at him and his granddaughter, boiling in some silent suffering? Or were they at peace with the miracle they had been a part of? He hoped that, in this resurrection, the souls these things once were had found some sort of peace in purpose. He hoped, where they had come from, they would return to and rest for the deed they'd done for him. He nodded with reverence and returned his attention to his granddaughter.

Her eyes had rolled back into her head. Only the whites were showing now. The old man leaned in close to hear, placing one hand on the infant's stomach and the other cupped behind her small soft head. The infant's breath was labored and wheezy. The lungs were filled with something, and there was an odd dull grinding, like knuckles cracking, coming from inside her mouth and down her throat.

Then her body began to spasm.

The old man choked on his own breath. The elation he felt from the resurrection was quickly replaced with sudden shock. At first he thought she might be cold, as if he hadn't wrapped her enough. The temperature within the steep walls had dropped significantly after the sun had completely gone. Then the spasms turned into a violent shaking. Beneath the palm resting on her torso, he could feel something rolling under the skin and he noticed, then, the flesh of his granddaughter's stomach stretching to a membrane, thin and bulbous. There was a watery ripping sound from underneath her body and the old man removed his hands. The infant rolled onto her side, propelled by something now protruding from her back. Cradled in the bowl of soaked cloth, the little body convulsed as short black stubs emerged from the skin over her spine and reflected the emerald glow of the visage above.

The old man screamed and fell back, scooting against crusted ground, and then everything disappeared.

The visage above had gone dark. The old man's eyes struggled to acclimate to the shadowed lake bed around him as terror ripped into his constitution. The unfolding joints popped and crackled on the platform in front of him. The infant and her rags were a mere haze of rippling shadow in the darkness. A sour sulfurous miasma permeated the air and assaulted his lungs, smelling heavily of decay.

And then everything was lit in emerald brilliance once more. The mound of bodies above beamed its crystalline light, the stretched maw and hollowed eyes glowing once more. The light, however, flickered now, strobing like a dying torch—light, dark, light, dark. And in between each glimmer, the old man witnessed the infant's continual transformation. The cloths he had wrapped his granddaughter in unraveled to the platform as her body rose, now suspended in the air by the strange crustaceous legs that quivered beneath her. Eight crab-like appendages had unfolded out of themselves, black as the stone platform, dripping with a rotten amniotic fluid. Her belly was swollen and undulating skyward. Her head curled back in a horridly unnatural way.

The old man called out to his granddaughter, yelling her name in anguish and confusion. Whatever was left of her had ceased to exist, replaced by this sinister imitation, corrupted and transmuted by forces unknown.

A garbled inhuman scream erupted from the infant's hanging head. Its face grimaced and its mouth spattered putrid vomit onto the platform below it.

She had deserved more than this. The old man would've given his soul in that moment for a chance to undo what he'd done, to create a different reality, an existence in which he had left his granddaughter to her deathly peace. The horror that had grown so quickly in his chest was overtaken by a regret that filled him to the brim. He did not sob, though. Instead, as tears flowed down his face once more, he stared silently, overtaken by the scene that seemed about to swallow him whole.

In the distance behind him, heavy hooves thudded against the ground, echoing off the interior of the lake bed. The old man's eyes did not move, though, for the creature that was once his granddaughter was now descending the cursed platform toward him.

*

Parallel trails of dust rose into the evening sky. Two riders rode atop a set of horses, carving their way over the crust of the salt flats toward the wall of sand dunes that bordered the wastes of the *Red Scar* ahead. The sun was setting behind the mountains far behind them and the spurs on their boots glinted in the last of the low orange light, jingling as they rode. The horses heaved, saliva streaming from the corners of their mouths, and their muscled flanks rippled with each stride.

The front rider was a grizzled highwayman in a blackened, worn duster and wide-brimmed hat. Scars crisscrossed the skin of his right cheek and jaw, cutting pink paths into his graying whiskers. A loosely fit leather belt held a six-shooter on either hip, but the holster on his right was more worn, indicative of his favored side. The guns shined with oil-slicked iron and bounced with each heavy gallop of the horse underneath him.

The other rider, who wore an almost identical duster and hat, save for the pale color of the leather, rode the right flank. The polished wooden stock of a long rifle bounced behind her, sheathed in a leather holster strapped to an ammo belt that was wrapped over her shoulder. A black sash covered the pale rider's entire face below her grey eyes, and the excess fabric floated behind, rippling in the dusty wake of her passage like a rogue banner.

The riders met the wide old river bed leading from the flats into the *Scar*'s wastes. They moved into the shadow of the first dune, losing what little sunlight was left, then swooped right into a long turn in the trail that, as it straightened out, tapered down to a width of two paces wide. The horses did not slow.

"*Hyah!*" the highwayman yelled, fueling the exertion of the beast he rode. The pale rider was silent next to him but her horse kept up in pace without additional instruction. The walls of sand that lined the old river bed closed in around them and the pale rider fell in behind from the flank.

The highwayman's hand disappeared into his duster and emerged with a small crude device. It was cylindrical and mechanical, with little iron gears and pulleys making up its inner structure. He clicked the device on and the gears began to spin, turning along each other's teeth with a slight whirring sound, hardly audible over the hooves below. A small bulb near the top of the thing came to life, glowing a muted golden light.

They were close.

The highwayman shoved the device back into the inner pocket of his duster, then whipped on the reins of his steed as they reached the twisting narrow path. They rode like Hell, shifting momentum this way and that with the winding of the trail. The horses were well disciplined and, after half an hour, the highwayman slowed them to a stop with a "*Whoa!*" as they broke through to the ancient lake bed, wide and empty. Crusted stone ridges and hills of sand surrounded them on all sides and, in the distance, a monumental dune rose to the cloudless dusk sky. Only the very top of the dune was still exposed to the western sunset behind them and the red sand glistened under distant stars that were just beginning to come into view. The rest of the lake bed was drenched in shade and the highwayman's eyes narrowed, peering far into the evening dimness to the bottom of the great dune.

The pale rider trotted up next to him and unholstered her long rifle, holding it in firing position, and gazed through the worn scope. At the base of the monolithic dune, black horns rose from a black platform and someone was knelt on the ground in front of it. There was a smooth leathery sound as the rifle returned to the holster. The pale rider's grey eyes glanced to the highwayman.

"Yeah…" he responded under his breath. "It's there." The highwayman's knuckles tightened around the reins and he let out a "*Hyah*!" Both riders spurred their horses toward the platform and the rhythm of the hooves thudding against the ground continued.

They'd already ridden halfway across the vast lake bed when the ground began quaking underneath them. From the streaming swaths of shadowed sand flowing down the front face of the great dune ahead, a dark shape emerged. Its features hung still, gargantuan and ominous yet, from this distance, its composition appeared to roil as if covered in moving parts, and there was shouting and screaming.

"*Hyah! Hyah!*" the highwayman called out. The horses charged steadfast and determined.

The mouth of the colossal visage protruding from the dune tore open and the pits for eyes shined an emerald light, beaming out over the lake bed and the surrounding desert. A booming horn rang out, echoing into the night, and the figure at the base of the black monument fell, scooting backward and away from the platform.

The highwayman's eyes narrowed once more, the wind shear whipping at his jacket as he rode. Something moved on the platform. The glare from the infernal projection up in the sand illuminated a small shape rising into the air, a tiny body suspended by jagged legs. Rags that had wrapped it fell away as it rose. It moved to face the man on the ground before it. The crystalline glow from the visage strobed slowly—dark, light, dark, light. In one of the moments of light, the infant creature appeared to be descending from the platform. Its black legs moved with stilt-like rigidity. Darkness fell again, then the bright emerald gleam reappeared and revealed the creature on top of the cowering man, one of its sharp legs sunken through his skull.

The smooth sound of iron escaping holster barely preluded a *crack* as loud as thunder, with a flash of blue fire erupting from the barrel of the revolver the highwayman now held out in front of him. The bullet zinged through the air, obliterating the creature's front leg at the joint. The man's body crumpled to the sand below as the putrid thing stumbled back. Its infant legs and arms dangled like dead weight and then it turned its head toward the riders.

Emerald light from the dune above strobed faster—dark, light, dark, light.

The creature quivered violently. A curdled shriek boiled out from somewhere within its grotesquery. The skin of its stomach tore open in a mist of blood, exposing a cavity of jagged little ribs that glistened in the viridian radiance. The sides of the stomach snapped together, open and closed, like an eager jaw chomping at the air. The remaining black legs speared into the ground and the beast scrambled toward the riders, dripping innards from its newly formed mouth like drool to the dirt beneath it.

Both riders dismounted, their boots scraping into the dry ground as they skidded to a stop. The pale rider's long rifle slid out from its holster once more and was immediately fired. Blue muzzle fire spewed into the distance ahead of them and another of the creature's legs was vaporized. The two continued to fire with learned marksmanship, blue flashes interspersed with the scintillating emerald light from the facade overlooking the clash. The decrepit infant appeared to move in stop-motion, blinking closer to them with each flash of color, like some spectre or phantom. Singing bullets whizzed through the air and shattered the other legs. As it came just within lethal proximity, the thing fell to the crusted dirt below, reduced to a wriggling immobile mass.

The highwayman approached the infant's shredded corpse. The pale rider followed close behind. The thing's chitinous legs were only stumps now, save for one which lay against the ground, writhing back and forth in the dirt. The husks jutting out from the spine oozed a dull pale fluid that crawled to the ground beneath it. The highwayman reached into a rough leather pouch dangling from the front of his belt and pulled out a handful of fine powder. The stuff shimmered in the flickering light as his fingers fluttered, sprinkling the dust over the gurgling creature. It made an unholy sound from its deformed throat as its flesh burned and boiled.

The riders turned to the platform and moved toward it, the horses held in tow. Their spurs jingled in unison with each step. The old man's body was lying lifeless on the ground with one of the creature's legs still impaled through his forehead. The highwayman pulled another handful out and sprinkled it over the old man's disfigurement. The necromantic essence of whatever events transpired here had to be cleansed.

The emerald light stopped flashing to beam steadily out of the great mouth and eyes above. A chorus of screams erupted from the hundreds of entities hidden amidst the visage. Under the glowing runic horns below, the slab of black stone still glistened with the fluids of the infant's mutation. The rags it had worn lay tattered in the dirt.

The highwayman stared up at the dark simulacrum, at those screaming ghoulish faces, while the pale rider reached into a saddle pack of her horse. She returned with a four-stack of dusty dynamite and a crusted stone that, even in the demonic light, glowed a ghostly blue.

The shouting voices fell silent.

The highwayman pulled out a rolled tobacco cigarette, wrinkled and bent from his pocket, and set it between his lips. His fingers reached once more into the pouch at his hip and returned with just a pinch of the powder. He held it in front of his face, whispered a quiet incantation and snapped his fingers. A small wisp of blue fire seemed to float just above his fingertips and, as he cupped his other hand around it, he leaned in to light his cigarette with it, blowing the flame out afterward with a quick exhale.

The pale rider knelt at the base of the monolith. She placed the dynamite into the corner divot where the black horns met the platform and shoved the ghostly stone in next to the explosives, then stepped back. Her thin pale fingers drew the long spiraled wick out across the ground and she looked to the highwayman once more.

The highwayman glanced toward her, then nodded at the tome in the dirt next to the platform. "Don't forget the book." He picked up the end of the wick and took an extra-long drag of the cigarette. He set the glowing end to the wick. Sparks spattered as it began to burn and he tossed it to the dirt. Both riders turned back and the screams from the collective mouths rang out once more. As the wick grew shorter, the woes and curses became more violent in anticipation of the explosive inevitability. The riders moved with the horses and passed the infant creature's body, now a puddle of putrid goop that steamed and hissed from the burns. The emerald light shimmered off of the freshly mutilated flesh. The old man's corpse was still limp with death, the head dissolving quickly.

The two mounted their horses and spurred them. In the growing distance behind, the shouting of the rotted collective simmered. The wick burned down to almost nothing when the many mouths joined into a voice of legion, a singular unhallowed intent, and together spoke as one:

Rider.

The highwayman looked back over his shoulder as the dynamite erupted. The explosion obliterated the monument in a cloud of fire and smoke. Dust and pebbles rained down, pelting the dry ground and spreading bits of glowing blue stone over the area. The boom echoed off the surrounding dunes for leagues.

Near the other end of the lake bed, the pale rider looked back toward their work in the growing distance. The dune appeared dark and undisturbed, with no sign of what had protruded from it so menacingly. A plume of smoke rose from the rubble of the monument to the sky above.

They made their way back through the thin sand-walled

pathway of the river bed. After some time, as the trail reached the border of the *Red Scar* and the expanse ahead, they slowed the horses to a stop. The highwayman looked out into the night over the endless salt flats, lit by the stars and quiet as Death. The pale rider forsook her silence to use her natural voice. It sounded like rocks grinding, coming from under the cloth over her mouth:

We can't stay here.

He didn't look back. After a moment's pause, he said, "I know", then pulled another rolled cigarette from his jacket and put it between his lips. He pinched some more powder from the pouch at his hip, chanted and snapped his fingers to produce another blue flame to light it with.

They sat on their horses, side-by-side, staring into the far off distance. The night sky was cloudless and thousands of distant points of light floated in the infinite above.

"I'm not sure how much longer I can do this, Una," the highwayman said in a low voice. He exhaled a lungful of smoke. His face was stalwart, emotionless, but his free hand was shaking and so he clenched his fist. His eyes shifted toward the ground, to the horse licking at one of the hexagons of salt crust. A light breeze had picked up, blowing from the distant West, cooling the trails of sweat that ran down his jaw and neck.

After a long moment, the pale rider nodded. This time, she spoke to him with her mind:

There's only one left and then we're done. Then we'll both get the rest we've been waiting for.

The moment passed and the highwayman reached his hand out and locked his fingers with hers. They were thin and cold in his palm.

"Alright."

He took one last long drag of the cigarette then threw it to the dirt below, the remnants of which produced a thin trail of smoke rising back up at him. Exhaling the last drag from his lungs, he glanced up to the sky once more and pulled the pale rider's fingers to his lips and kissed them. He let her hand go and then whipped the reins.

"*Hyah!*"

They rode hard into the night, headed west by northwest. The glowing cluster of the God's Milk galaxy lay unfathomable and immense overhead. A hundred leagues of open desert lay between them and the icy snow-covered crags of the mountains of Aton. The thudding of the horses beneath them drummed the songs of a rhythmic determination. Salt-dust rose into spiraling plumes in their wake, illuminated under the light of the moon coming up over the dunes far behind them.

Angelic Tendencies

There was a small hole in Abigail's favorite blanket towards the end that she kept at her feet most nights. It was near the side with the worn paper tag and she often woke up in the mornings with one of her toes poking through. It was still night however and, as her big toe wiggled in and out of the tattered hole, she stared out into the clear midnight sky through the window above her bed.

Uncle Reed was going to visit again tonight like he had every night since Aunt Cheryl had gone. She left on some trip for work a week ago. Abigail remembered her aunt telling her that they were going to go together to the elementary school in town to register for third grade when she got back. Abigail couldn't recall exactly how long Aunt Cheryl was supposed to be gone but she had stopped hoping for her return after the last few horrific nights.

The first night he had come to her, she'd awoken to him sitting on her bed. His face had been shrouded in darkness while he stroked her cheek with his calloused fingers. They were rough but he was family and she assumed it was meant to comfort her. And it did, at first. When his hand had moved down to her chest and stomach, she did not think ill of his touch. But then his fingers were inside of her and that's when the pain had started.

Even now, as she stared out the window to the backyard and the forest behind the fence, her insides were sore from what he had done to her last night, and the night before, and twice the night before that. She slept lightly for she had grown to expect the creaking of the hardwood floorboards outside of the bedroom they'd given her. It wasn't *her* room, no matter how many times her uncle said it was. She never felt safe within the confines of its walls and, when that sound would eek out from the hallway just beyond the door, that's when Uncle Reed would come and that's when she would feel that silver tension. Sometimes, he wouldn't come into the room. Sometimes, Abigail would hear the old wood floor groan and time would stop. Fear and dismay coiled themselves around her gut while she waited for him to open the door. Sometimes, it didn't open but Abigail would find herself wide awake for hours, waiting and listening and imagining what he was going to do to her, until exhaustion would finally catch up to her, sending her off into a whimpering sleep.

Abigail had lost count of the days since Mom and Dad had gone to Heaven. She wasn't even sure what Heaven meant, where it was, *what* it was. In her mind, bits and pieces of descriptions from her parents, and how the old people at church talked about it, painted out a picture she still couldn't will into focus. She remembered sitting in the car, listening to her parents murmuring back and forth to each other from the front seats. Dad's hand was crawling across the center console toward Mom's legs, and Mom batted his hand away and laughed a special laugh Abigail only heard when Dad was around and Mom thought no one else was listening. Abigail remembered giggling and Mom's face turning back to smile at her before saying...

Her memories go dark in that moment, no matter how many hours in the middle of the night she spent trying to remember what her mother had been saying. It became almost more important than having them back. Abigail needed to know what her mother had said, as if in those final words of her mother's life, some phrase or word could exist that might've helped prepare her for the events soon to follow their deaths, for the experiences she was fated to live through once they were gone. She awoke in a hospital, covered in tubes and sticky wires with machines all around her that beeped and whirred and blinked multi-colored lights. There was a device that made an intermittent hissing noise and it sounded like a snake the first time she'd heard it, scaring her enough to cry out for someone. When the nurse walked into the room, Abigail explained the noise and the nurse reassured her of the machine that was making it. It was not a snake but had something to do with *blood pressure*. Abigail hadn't been sure what that meant, so instead she asked where her parents were. The nurse's face went pale and, instead of answering Abigail, said, "Let me get the doctor for you," and quickly walked out of the room.

The doctor was a man, tall and broad, and Abigail thought he looked like a giant. The color of the papery clothing under his white coat was the same color as her favorite crayon from daycare, Sea Foam Green. He snapped the stretchy gloves off of his hands and tossed them into the trash bin near the door as he entered. A barely visible residue of powder floated in the air above the garbage afterward. He wore one of those heart-listening things that plugged into the ears, which was draped around his neck like the doctors on TV. *Hello, Abigail*, he had said, grabbing the chair from the desk in the corner of the room and rolling it over to the side of her bed. She remembered the croaking sound it made as he sat his full weight into it, and that he had thick black hair on the backs of his hands, but she couldn't remember much of what he had said. *There's been an accident* was one thing, and that something had happened *on impact*. She remembered him standing and clearing his throat, then saying *You're lucky to be alive* before walking out of the room. Her mind had only been able to hold onto a few pieces of what he told her before he left seemingly as quickly as he'd come.

Several days later, Aunt Cheryl had told Abigail that, "Your mom and dad are in Heaven, now." There was that word again, that *place*, Heaven, but it didn't fit… The story didn't *fit* and Abigail's mind couldn't process what she had been told. What good was Heaven if she couldn't be there with Mom and Dad? Why was she lucky to be alive if they weren't here with her? She just wanted them to come home and take her away from Uncle Reed, who, when he had come to pick her up from the hospital with Aunt Cheryl, had told her that *everything was going to be alright*. He told Abigail that he loved her, especially when doing those things to her at night when they were alone, but she didn't believe him. He said that he loved her, like Mom and Dad used to, yet he would cause pain in areas that had never been touched before, both physically and emotionally, and she could feel a numbness growing over her heart.

Life felt heavier with each cycle of the distant moon, the moon that glared down at Abigail in those nights with its cold indifferent illumination.

She had little concept of God or of the cosmic, but she had heard of this place called Heaven one other time before. At the daycare she had attended, before the accident, before everything changed, a boy named Shane once told her that angels were nice people from Heaven and that they had big bright wings that protected him from *bad guys*, or so Shane's mother had told him.

Abigail hoped with every ounce of her being that the angels were listening now. She hoped that they wouldn't be so busy with protecting Shane from the bad guys that they couldn't hear her plea. She missed her mom. She missed her dad. She didn't want to feel the pain of her Uncle Reed's visits anymore. The looks on his face when he touched her were monstrous, and he said things to her, whispered things that sounded hollow yet hungering, like she was Little Red Riding Hood and he was the big bad wolf. She no longer felt whole and every time he touched her, it was as if a piece of her broke off and fell into the emptiness that grew inside of her soul.

Tears streamed down her cheeks as she lay staring into the distant sky outside her window. Thousands of tiny lights twinkled in the above and, through her watery eyes, she saw a shooting star, soaring across the endless backdrop of the galaxy. She raised her hand to the window and pointed at the moving light, trailing its trajectory across the dewy glass with her fingertip. After the light continued past the halfway point to the horizon, it stopped dead in the sky. It sat there for a moment, flickering multiple colors—red, purple, green, gold—then zipped back the opposite direction.

Abigail sniffed and sat up quickly in her bed, wiping the tears away. She watched with astonishment as the light stopped once more in the sky, then moved in a circle, twice, and stopped again. She pointed her finger at the light and then pressed her hand to the glass, which felt cool against her palm. Could it see her, staring up at it from the little window?

It could.

An angel finally visited Abigail that night. In fact, many angels visited her. They didn't talk using mouths. Instead, they used their thoughts, connecting with her in a way she never imagined possible. There was something frightening about the mental intrusion at first but, after hearing their voices resonate within her mind, the fear melted away and Abigail felt nothing but gratitude for them. She welcomed the soothing sounds of their communication which, in her head, sounded like a mixture of buzzing electricity and the playful clinking of wind-chimes in a gentle breeze. They did not reveal themselves but, instead, channeled into her mind from the tenebrous forest beyond the backyard fence.

Using her own mental will to communicate, Abigail stared back through the glass into the dark woods and told them everything about her parents—what her dad looked like and how he used to laugh, about her mother and how aged yet purposeful her hands were, as well as how beautiful her eyes had been. Abigail even told them about the doctor with the hairy hands and her excitement for third grade, about Shane from daycare... And she told them about the car accident. She was grateful that they could see her thoughts as she hadn't been able to find the words or imagination to describe what little fragments of memories she remembered from that day. Somehow, she knew they could see it all, even if she couldn't.

Then she told them about Uncle Reed.

Memory after memory let loose, draining from Abigail's mind like water from a tub. The angels analyzed every single one of them, turning each of her recollections over and around like specimens under bizarre examination. When she had finished, Abigail realized she'd been crying again. The angels collectively spoke into her mind, promising that they would make Uncle Reed's visits stop. She was afraid of clinging onto that promise but the angels reassured her and told her their plan for making everything better. All she had to do was listen to their instructions and follow their wind-chime voices into the night.

*

She'd been as quiet as she knew how to be after the angels told her to get her shoes on, to grab her blanket and to meet them out in the woods. It hadn't taken long for Abigail to slip into the white sundress she wore the day prior, to buckle the straps on her matching white sandals, then to wad up her blanket and slip out of the open window above her bed. Her coat was on the rack out next to the front door in the living room. She would go without it for fear of alerting her uncle.

As her sandals touched down onto the beauty-bark below, pieces of it pricked at her toes, and then she heard the creaking of the wood floor inside, just beyond the bedroom door.

Uncle Reed was coming for her again.

The growing night air was cool in Abigail's lungs. A faint breeze whispered through the grass around her ankles. Adrenaline pumped through her tired veins as she left the window and made her way out of the beauty bark and onto the lumpy lawn. She headed toward the gate in the back fence that led to the forest beyond. The cold fear grew inside of her the further from her window she got but she held onto the promise from the angels. They said they would make this better.

When she was halfway across the lawn, Abigail heard the faint creak of the bedroom door hinge opening through the window behind her. She knew that it was only moments before her uncle would see the open window and look out to her, to see where she was going. She imagined his face, distorted by the shadows of night, his eyes burning into her back upon seeing her fleeing form. She shuddered and ran toward the fence.

Though she'd anticipated its arrival, she still jumped when her uncle's voice called out in a harsh whisper through the window.

"Abigail, what the *hell* are you doing? Get back here!" he shrieked.

As she closed in on the fence and the forest beyond, the grass grew damp with dew and it licked at her toes as she ran. She almost lost her balance, the slick bottoms of her sandals doing her no favors, but caught her balance after slamming into the gate. The doorway to the forest was carved wood with frayed splinters at the top and it was much taller than she was but, standing on her tiptoes, her longest reach was able to undo the lock and pull the latch back. She stepped swiftly through the precipice into the dark of the woods and looked back once more toward the house.

Rolling black clouds hovered in the distant northern skyline, beyond the house and the city, but the rest of the sky was clear above. The full moon still rested low in the east, rotten yellow and glowing with a warped light that shone down on the roof of the house and grass like an old lamp. The sky and backyard appeared like a strange painting. The house stood dark and ominous.

Just inside the sliding back door, Uncle Reed was standing, *watching* her through the glass. The lights in the house were still off, yet his carnivorous gaze appeared strangely illuminated in some unnatural way, enough for her to discern it in the darkness.

He looked like a monster.

As she closed the heavy wooden gate behind her and the latch clicked into place, Abigail heard the back sliding glass door of the house roll open and close. Heavy footsteps thudded across the lawn immediately following. Her heart beat rapidly, matching the rhythm of the pursuing footfalls.

He was coming for her.

The forest ahead was black as coal, barely lit by the moonlight through the holes in the thick canopy above. Abigail stepped quickly, moving down a thin trail that snaked between the dark evergreens ahead. A dozen steps in, she broke off to her left, away from the trail, and hid under the massive exposed root of a particularly gnarled pine. Her hand lay on the rigid bark of the sentinel and her eyes followed it up though she couldn't see the night sky, blocked by countless intertwining branches of needles.

The angels said they would meet her out here in the forest, out in the dark. Abigail believed in them, to find her before *he* did. She waited silently, her face buried into her blanket. It smelled like her old bedroom, where she used to live with her parents. It smelled like her real home. She wanted it to consume her, wrap around her and float her off to her old bed, far away from here, far away from her uncle.

The hinge on the fence gate let out a gross sound as it opened, screeching into the night. A moment passed, then a similar sound marked the gate's closing. Damp twigs and fallen branches cracked under heavy steps that moved slowly into the forest. Though it was cold and her legs were prickled with goosebumps, Abigail's blood was on fire. The anticipation and fear grew in her chest and she sobbed as quietly into her blanket as she could.

"Aaaaabigail."

The man's voice sung through the cold air of the woods. It quavered with a type of intensity Abigail had come to know over the course of the last handful of nights. It sounded like he was about to scream or maybe cry. It was something he didn't show around other people, only around her, only in those elongated moments of pain and fright. During the day, he acted as normal as an uncle would be expected to. In the dark hours of night, however, he transformed into something that looked like Uncle Reed but smelled musky and acted differently. This other being fed off of Abigail's suffering.

Fresh tears streamed down her cheeks. A small whimper crept from her lips, faint but audible in the silence of the woods.

The boots stopped. There were no sounds of nocturnal animals, no hoots of owls or skittering of mice. There was only silence. Abigail could feel her uncle's gaze peering into every shrub in the quiet dark, crawling up every tree trunk and rock like some decrepit snake. She held her breath and pushed her face further into her blanket, hoping against everything that he wouldn't see her, that his searching pupils would pass right over her and that he'd leave.

And then the boots were moving again.

The stomping got louder as it closed in on the root she was under.

Abigail lifted her eyes. A yelp erupted from her mouth as her uncle's face appeared in front of her, shadowed by the night but still visible. The saliva on the wretched teeth of his smile gleamed in the distant sick moonlight, as did his eyes, which remained fixated on her in a violent stare.

She buried her face in her blanket again and crouched. Her shoulders rocked as she sobbed. They promised to save her. They promised they wouldn't let Uncle Reed hurt her or put things inside of her again.

But they weren't here.

"Aw, Abigail," Uncle Reed said. "Sh-sh-sh-ssshhh."

Abigail's body flinched as his large hands gripped her shoulders, pulling her up to her feet. She still held her face in the wadded up blanket, willing herself to stay in that warm embrace of wool and tears, away from the dark world unraveling in front of her. Even with her eyes covered, she could feel her uncle's mass crouched in front of her. The warm breath of whiskey and cigarettes poured over her with each of his tense exhales, that *stench* of the predator.

"Why would you run from me, sweetie?" he said. "Huh?"

The cold of the forest was beginning to creep up through Abigail's legs and her uncle's hands provided no comfort. They were tense and rough, exuding only a malicious energy she found no warmth in. They were compassionless and feeling his fingers wrap around her arms sent her thoughts tumbling through the memories of the previous few nights.

"Abigail."

She lifted her teary eyes from the blanket.

He wasn't smiling anymore, only watching. Sweat glistened on his neck from a beam of rotten moonlight. His eyes appeared as black pools of violence, staring directly into hers. The dark is where this thing that once was her uncle came from, where it hunted. Or, perhaps her uncle *always* been this creature. It didn't matter now. The thing had Abigail in its grasp and, out here in the dark, this was its territory.

The man's grip tightened around her arms and her body shook. "What," he started in a low tone, "the *fuck* makes you think you could drag me all the way out here at this time of the night?"

She cried from the pain of his grip when he squeezed to emphasize the words he spoke. She tried to bury her face back into the blanket once more but he stopped it at halfway. She clung to the cloth but he ripped it from her little hands, tossing it behind him into the shadowy woods. Abigail's fingers throbbed from the yanking force. She tried to scream but only a whimper escaped.

"Ah, sweetheart," he said. He softened his grasp, then let go of her arms. "Abigail, sweetheart... Sweetheart." He sighed and looked at the ground, glancing at her sandals, then slithering his eyes up the rest of her. "You know I just want to take care of you, right?"

She didn't believe him. As he stood up, she wanted to run. In some instinctual corner of her young mind, in the dark recesses of genetic fight-or-flight, she knew she *needed* to run. Her feet felt like they were made of thick tree trunks, though, like the ones surrounding them, with knobby roots burrowing into the ground below, preventing her from moving.

She looked again to the dark pine needle canopy above.

Why aren't the angels here? Did I do something wrong?

Her uncle reached a tense hand up to her shoulder and traced down the flesh of her bare arm, the callous on his index finger scraping her skin as he did. Abigail's eyes were watery and blurred her vision, but in the dark blurriness, she could see his other hand fidgeting with the zipper of his pants, shaking with a savage impatience.

She had been here before. She knew what was going to happen next. The angels weren't coming for her this time, just as they had never been there any other time. They had tricked her and now Uncle Reed was angry beyond measure. She could sense it in his tone and she was terrified.

The zipper of his pants was undone now and he reached behind her. His sweaty palm slid to the center of her back, then snaked down further and lifted her dress, reaching into her underwear.

Abigail closed her eyes and sobbed into her hands in anticipation of what her uncle was about to do. He was going to put things inside of her again, things that scratched and stretched and tore at her insides.

Heat washed over her as he crouched down in front of her, his sweaty face creeping close to her ear. A grizzly cooing leaked from his lips like grease. "Oh, Abigail. You shouldn't have run off like that." His nose brushed against her cheek. "You wouldn't want Uncle Reed to tell Aunt Cheryl about how you've been a bad girl, would you?" He sniffed her neck, then licked his tongue across the trails of tears on her cheek. She could hear him suck his tongue back into his mouth. A guttural growl billowed out of his throat.

And then he stood up. A large hand grabbed Abigail's hair to the scalp and she cried out as he pulled her up against him.

"Now you listen to me and you listen good, Abigail." Venomous words oozed from his mouth above her. "Don't you *ever* fucking run like that again, or I'll make you wish you died with your parents. You understand me?" His grip on her hair tightened and he leaned down to her ear. "This could've been much easier. *You* are the reason this is happening! This is *your* fault!"

He threw her to the ground then and she landed below the large root she he had hidden under before. Her elbow scraped against the damp dirt, soon accompanied by stinging pain that shot up her arm. Behind her, Uncle Reed's belt clinked and rattled as it was being undone. She heard him spit, followed by a repeated slick sound. She had grown to despise and become very afraid of that sound as it was always followed by him putting something painful inside of her.

They were supposed to be here.

The angels were supposed to save her.

In that moment, she wanted to be back in the car with her parents. This was a nightmare from which there was no escape... What was the point in living if her life had been reduced to a constant suffering at the hands of someone who supposedly loved her? She had nowhere else to go.

Abigail lay on the ground, her face pressed into her bare arms. The scraping of one of her uncle's rough hands moved from the calf of her left leg up to behind her knee, then up the back of her thigh. She felt the mass of her uncle's body hovering over her, and when he began to reach once more into her underwear—

Crack.

In the distance behind them, a branch snapped somewhere near the forest floor. Abigail heard her uncle's movement freeze with a sharp intake of his breath. His hand slowly slid out from under her dress but she could still feel him hovering over her back.

Mmmmmrrrrrrrrrr...

A bizarre sound, like a moan of some kind, crept out of the dark of the woods. Abigail felt the mass above her move back and her soft sobbing went silent. It was a long moment that she lay there, unmoving and seeing only the void behind her eyes, listening and waiting. Eventually, the moment slid by and she glanced up from her arms.

Her uncle was scanning the woods behind him like an owl in the night, quietly stuffing something back into the front of his pants. His hands quickly zipped up his jeans and he cleared his throat.

"Who's there?!" he called out.

There was no answer. The silence seemed to last an eternity. Then there was a shuffling in the bushes to their right, on the other side of the small trail that led back to the gate.

Her uncle's eyes snapped toward that direction.

In the deep recesses of her mind, Abigail felt an echo of some kind, a small static tickle beyond the perception of her normal senses. There was an airy presence all around her, next to her or inside of her. She wasn't sure where it was coming from. And then she heard a voice deep in her consciousness, a gentle communication of a sort.

Don't be afraid. Let's go up, okay?

It was the angels. She had heard their collective speaking earlier, when they had visited her bedroom window. She hadn't been able to see them before but could only hear their voice, a chorus of barely audible wind-chimes singing together. They didn't speak the language her parents had taught her but she understood them nonetheless. There was a feeling to it that she picked up on as easy as picking up on a catchy show tune or a new board game. And now they were speaking to her again, not bound to this reality by her sense of sight but seeming to exist through every other sense of hers. They were all around and through the dark world she lay in.

With the damp ground soaking her dress, and with her uncle standing just a few feet away distracted by the sounds in forest, Abigail nodded her head, unsure of whether the angels could see her doing so.

And then she was staring down from above.

Abigail's feet were dangling. The cool night air caressed them through her sandals. She glanced to either side, feeling bark under her hands and legs, and realized she was sitting on a branch, high above where she was just a moment before. Her stomach lurched with a rapid vertigo from the transition. She tried to remain calm, even as a few more anxious tears leaked from her eyes.

To the right, on the branch next to her, was a black amorphous mass. Abigail couldn't make out much of the details in the dark but, against the dismal moon beams coming through the needled shroud above, she saw its form gyrate and manipulate and bend in each moment, constantly moving in waves of contractions and protrusions. One such protrusion slowly extended out, like an arm or appendage of some kind, and rested gently against her back.

We won't let you fall. Don't worry.

Another slight nudge rested on the left side of her back and she turned toward a second formless entity sitting on the branch to her other side. Somehow she knew they spoke the truth. It was a recognition by some deep-seated connection she couldn't describe, as if she'd met them before, maybe in her dreams. Everything in her blood told her that she could count on them to keep her safe. They had no wings, nor did they appear like people, but Abigail knew she had found the angels. The more this realization came to be, the more a sense of relief began to flourish within her.

There was more scurrying in the bushes at the base of one of the trees below and Abigail's attention returned to her uncle. He was standing still, his head moving in long motions as he scanned the dark ahead of him. There was a breeze picking up from further off in the forest that sounded like it was growing closer, rustling thousands of distant needles against each other in a strange whispery song.

"Who's there?" he questioned the dark again.

There was no response. Abigail watched in silence as her uncle turned back toward the tree root that he'd thrown her under.

"Abigail?!" he called out in a harsh whisper. "*Fuck!*"

He took a step toward the trail that led back to the house, crunching twigs under his boot. Abigail noticed that the few moonbeams that served as the only light through the thick canopy went dark, blotted out from the sky above. She felt it in her skin that something massive, some type of weight, hovered now over the scene from beyond.

There was a small nudge from the protrusion resting on her back.

Can you close your eyes for a moment, Abigail?

The wind-chimes were beautiful and Abigail nodded, closing her eyes. At the exact moment her lids shut, an instance of light cracked beyond them as if someone had just snapped a picture with the flash on. The smell in the air turned immediately from pine needles to something like smoke or electricity, an unearthly musk that assaulted her senses.

A cackled moan came from the forest floor. Abigail's eyelids slowly parted to see that her uncle had fallen to his knees, grasping at his own face and eyes.

"Oh, god. My eyes... My eyes!" he cried. "Oh fuck, oh *fuck*!"

Her uncle sat back on his calves, weeping like a child. His hands shook uncontrollably and there was desperation in his movements. "Abigail!"

In the dark below, Abigail could barely see shapes, not unlike the angels that sat next to her now, materializing from the black depths of the flora surrounding her uncle. She counted seven of them and they formed a circle around him. The darkness made them appear to shape-shift, roiling in place like animate globs of oil.

Uncle Reed's whimpering had stopped and he was blinking rapidly, his eyes scanning frantically over the forest and the ground underneath him. Abigail wasn't sure if he could yet see again but, as one of the formless shapes pooled through a small bush to complete the circle, her uncle stopped and squinted out into the darkness toward the noise.

"Wh-who's there? Abigail, is that you?"

A buzz resonated in from the corners of reality then, laying low on the spectrum of sound, barely audible. Then there was a light from above. It appeared like a spotlight having just been turned on, already directed toward her uncle as if he was the star of some circus show and she was sitting up in the dark cheap-seats. The angels below stood just beyond the precipice of illumination and were all but invisible in contrast to the lit forest floor surrounding her uncle. The bright circle of light lay on him, stretching a dozen yards in all directions with him in its center. He was looking up now, squinting between the fingers of his raised hand. Abigail glanced up as well, toward the source of the spotlight.

An orb or circular aperture hung perfectly still, floating in the indeterminate above. The glaring beam emitted an intense yellow-gold and, beyond it, Abigail could see nothing but darkness through the canopy. She wasn't sure how she knew but this strange glaring bulb was attached to the weight she had experienced earlier, whatever it was that was blocking the moonlight, hovering just above the trees.

Uncle Reed rose to his feet, murmuring something as he looked back to the ground. He placed a careful step toward the trail that led out of the spotlight and back toward the fence gate. The knees of his pants were soaked and dirty and he snagged his shoe on a twisted fallen branch, stumbling but managing to stay on his feet. "Just… Just head back… Just head back," he kept mumbling. His gait was rigid and his hands still shook. Abigail wasn't sure who her uncle was talking to or whether he could see the angels now like she could.

The light shrunk in that moment, collapsing to a smaller circle around Uncle Reed. His steps ceased. The beam focused directly on him, shrouding the rest of the surrounding forest back into darkness. He turned to look up toward the source of light again. His face wore an expression of desperation and cold visible fear.

A second source of light flashed. Abigail smelled the electricity again and watched her uncle fall onto his back, face up. His chest rose and fell rapidly. A wheeze of desperation rode each breath he took. The beam of light pulsed and wavered and grew in its intensity.

There was a mechanical grinding from above and the spotlight expanded back to its original circumference. Standing in a circle around Uncle Reed were the angels.

Now that the light exposed them, Abigail saw that they were no longer black amorphous shapes. Instead, they appeared as bulbous brown sacks, skin like wrinkled dark leather, with no facial features. They were in the shape of upside-down tear drops, each of them a large orb coming down to a point at the forest floor, almost floating like sagging lumpy balloons. Beneath their wrinkled exteriors, things moved and churned like bones and muscles, rolling just under the flesh. Even up here, she could hear the sounds like knuckles cracking and liquids gurgling from the ones sitting next to her on the branch.

Something pinched the back of Abigail's neck then and she recoiled. When she reached her hand back, she barely felt something burrowing into her nape before it disappeared under her skin. Tears welled up again in her eyes as she glanced toward the angel to her right.

We're sorry, Abigail. You have nothing to be afraid of. It's just so we can find you again later.

And then she was back down on the forest floor, before she could react, back under the root she had hidden under before, as if she'd never left it to begin with. The transition was instantaneous and jarring, so much so that she lost her balance and fell clumsily back onto her behind. She was just outside of the light that her uncle was lying in, surrounded by the other angels. Her head swam.

Uncle Reed managed to shout out of his paralyzed mouth. "Oh,

God!" It shook Abigail from her daze when she heard it. She looked to the circle of light and saw that the angels were now moving. Each one of them swayed side to side, their wrinkled brown skin coiling and undulating. Up above, from the source of the light, whatever *thing* it was attached to, the hum beyond the canopy grew louder and the distant breeze closed in, rustling needles and branches in the surrounding trees.

mmmmmmmmmmmmmMMMMMMMMMMMMMMMMMM.

The angels below all danced in unison. The wind's whisper morphed to a howl with the leaves of the nearby shrubs rattling. Uncle Reed was still lying on his back on the forest floor. His arms were outstretched in such a way that he appeared restrained by an invisible force, one that Abigail could not see. His eyes darted from angel to angel and he sobbed heavily, shaking his head back and forth.

"Oh, god. What the fuck!" His teeth were gritted and saliva squeezed from between. "What the *fuck*! No, no, no!"

MMMMMMMMMMMMMMMMMMMMMMMMMMMMMMM

.

The hum grew louder. Abigail could feel the vibration in her stomach and a mixture of fear and adrenaline tightened her breaths. Then, as if some great switch was flipped, there was a loud mechanical *click* and the light from above turned to a deep red. Uncle Reed, the dancing angels and the forest floor were lit by the burning glare. Abigail could see the tears streaming down her uncle's face. A mammalian fear contorted his features. The angels had gone perfectly still, floating on the wrinkled tips of their tear-drop shapes. Their masses were ominous and silent in the red light.

And then the light went purple, accompanied by another loud chunky mechanical sound. The damp leaves of the forest floor made visible by the light glistened with a beautifully harrowing glow.

Click! And then green.

Click! And then blue.

Red.

Purple.

Green.

Blue.

Red. Purple. Green. Blue.

The kaleidoscopic strobe pulsed and the colors changed in succession one after another, over and over. The loud clicking sound was happening faster and faster. The hum in the background reverberated, pulsing in sync with the shifting colors.

MMMMMmmmmMMMMMMmmmMMMMMMmmmMMMMM.

Red. Purple. Green. Blue. Red. Purple. Green. Blue.

And then Uncle Reed was standing, or hanging, as if being held up by an invisible rope attached to an unseen anchor in the center of his chest. His feet rested limply against the ground. His arms were shaking at his sides and his face was toward the lights above. The rolling colors reflected in his frightened eyes. His body was tense, the veins bulging on the sides of his neck as he resisted the unknown pull. Abigail could only imagine what weird miracle or magic was causing her uncle to float like that.

And then the lights stopped. The mechanical *clicks* and loud humming from above ceased and, once again, her uncle, the angels and the forest floor were bathed in a deep creepy red.

Only the gentle breeze could be heard. The angels floated still and menacingly. From where Abigail sat, there were two angels in front of her but, in between them and across the circle of light, she could see one of them directly on. Abigail watched from the darkness just as something was beginning to happen on the other side of her uncle.

A slit appeared in the skin of the angel directly across the circle of light from her. The slit extended from the very top of its bulb to the base of the wrinkled point below it, as if some invisible knife had carved down the front of the strange flesh. From the center of the cut, things wriggled. Glistening digits wormed their way out of the sack, pulling the wound open.

Abigail's breath heaved.

The folds of exposed pink flesh flayed back. Rising out of the mound of gore was a hideous creature, donning two large black eyes, like puddles of oil, sat in a crested skull of bone, with a hollowed nasal cavity and rows upon rows of brown needle-like teeth, protruding from the small but chittering mandible. A slimy layer of effluence covered the entirety of the creature, the same substance that coated the inner walls of the pod, slick in the red light from above. Thin boney arms unfurled out of the wet heap, fingered with black burnt appendages. They splayed out in the air above the creature, like some sort of signal, and then began to sway back and forth.

Slits appeared on the other angels and each one of them unraveled themselves in their birthing processes. The brown sacks were not their bodies. Rather, they were vessels of some kind, like the stroller Abigail's mother used to roll her around in when she was younger. All of the angels in the circle had unfurled themselves from their sheaths of wrinkled skin. Each one of them had raised their dripping skeletal arms and joined in a synchronous dance once more. Abigail watched in horror as they swayed silently in the burning luminescence. That specific moment stretched forever, an image she would never forget.

The loud humming burst forth once again, shattering the silence.

MMMMMMMMMMMMMMMMMMMM-

The leaves and branches of the flora were windswept once again and then her uncle was floating off of the ground. The limp toes of his shoes left the earth. There were no strings or rope, no platform raising him. A force Abigail could not see carried Uncle Reed up into the source of the red light. His mouth was open the entire time but she could not hear if he was screaming. The heat of the beam grew scorching. The warmth rolled against Abigail's skin in waves from where she stood as she watched her uncle's eyes turn a blood red. She could see the skin of his face and neck begin to smoke under the direct glare.

Over the roaring hum, another grinding mechanical sound screeched from above. As Uncle Reed got closer to the light, a hole opened up in the center of the orb of red, an orifice of some kind. Abigail was reminded of an eye, the red light around the black center hole, as she watched her uncle's head disappear into its pupil, smothering his unheard screams even further. His shoulders were sucked in, then his arms, hands, legs and finally his feet. All of him disappeared into the horrible aperture.

The world was darkness for Abigail except for that red eye in the black above, staring after its meal.

Accompanied by yet another metallic grinding, the contrasting center of the orb shrunk, condensing into a dot before finally disappearing. Solid red glared down, whole once again.

Abigail cried into her hands. Only for a moment had she buried her face in her palms before the humming stopped. She sobbed heavy breaths as the sounds of the forest faded into nothingness. The horror manifested as a sick battery-tasting feeling in her throat, not only for what she'd seen but the sounds she'd heard her uncle make, the screams and shouts of someone who'd lost complete control.

When she lifted her eyes again, the red spotlight was gone. The wind had stopped. The angels were nowhere in sight. The electrical smell was fading and the forest was not as dark as it had been. Shards of moonlight speared through the canopy once again and only the rustling of the very tops of the evergreens could be heard. High above Abigail, a massive weight faded into the sky beyond.

*

The sliding glass door rolled to a close. Abigail locked it behind her. She made her way back into the living room, then into the dark hallway towards the spare room where she slept.

All of the lights were off. The house was silent.

She reached the door to the spare room and the floor beneath her step creaked. For the first time in what had seemed like a hellish eternity, the sound didn't scare her. It rolled right through her and she was left without the anxiety of the impending abuse from her uncle. Images of him floating in the red beam of light flashed in the dark of her mind. She could still hear his screaming.

Abigail shut the door behind her, tossing the damp blanket onto the bed. She slipped out of her sundress and shook the sandals off of her feet, scooting them underneath before laying down. As she draped the blanket over herself, she pulled the fabric up to her chin and turned to face the window. Her big toe nudged around under the sheet to once more find the hole at the end of the thing.

Outside, the black trees of the woods beyond the fence appeared like jagged rips in the speckled night sky. The moon wasn't so sour anymore. The distant stars behind it blinked at her in the great depths. Abigail's eyes closed. On the nape of her neck, her fingers glided over the bump in her skin. It was sensitive to the touch.

It's just so we can find you again later.

In her mind's eye, she still saw the nightmarish faces of the angels and, in her heart, she could still hear their voices, gentle wind-chimes tinkling against the other side the glass, the only thing separating her from the darkness beyond.

Warmth in the Winter

The small sliding viewport embedded into the cabin's front door was a window to the cold outside. An old set of eyes peered out at the evening and the snow falling. The short day was dying and the blanket of clouds above had turned a forlorn grey, getting darker as the rest of the light was strangled out of the sky. The flakes tumbled down in clumsy curtains to the frigid ground, quiet as Death. The forest had dimmed with the shade of coming night, but even the weakening light still maintained the visibility of the surrounding scenery. White snow lay powdered on every surface. The snowscape amplified the last bit of the sun's distant glow and kept the shadows at bay for a just bit longer.

It wouldn't last. Old Jack knew that as well as anyone. The cold lapped at his wrinkled face through the open viewport as he stared out into the forest. The last few days had been overcast, as it always was in the winters, especially the closer the weeks got toward the very heart of the season and the coldest nights of the year. The majority of the forest was a sea of towering pines covered in snow, full and drooping under the weight. The intermittent deciduous trees were bare, with their branches turning frostbitten and rigid like arthritic fingers. There hadn't been much wind but the air was still freezing, enough to keep icicles lining the roof of the small cabin like teeth and to freeze the pond that sat thirty feet to the west of its entrance.

Twenty years, he'd been here. Twenty years and the solitude

had become a part of him. There was no human contact for months at a time, the closest neighboring home being six miles away, only occupied for a couple weeks out of the year by a man named Jamison. Old Jack had no cable television, no phone line or running water, no malls or gas stations or police nearby. Some folks believed there were no laws out here in the deep woods, that the idea of authority didn't exist so far outside the walls of perceived human civilization, but Old Jack knew better than that. Out here, where technology was scarce and man's effect on the earth around him was a lot less noticeable, there was a natural authority that was birthed out of the very roots that ran through the ground and from the animals that padded along the crust of the forest floor. Out here, where one could argue man was no longer meant to be, nature was the authority. Even attempting to categorize or classify *it*, the all-encompassing will for the natural process of things, as "nature," like something humans could easily put into an understandable package, was a deep misstep, he knew.

Old Jack slid the viewport shut. He grabbed the coat hanging on the crude post jutting out of the wall, then swung the door open and moved out onto the deck and into the chilled evening. There were two rabbit snares that needed to be checked before he called it a night, the first of which was to the northwest on the other side of the frozen pond, just inside the tree line. He judged from the grey glow of the skies that he'd have another thirty minutes before his sight would start to fail him out in these woods without a torch.

Night came quick and ruthless in these parts.

The solitude provided reflection, both as a gift and as the cost of living alone. It manifested as an endless examination of the machinations of life and of death, of old memories and of lost experiences and the paths that led to the present. A man accepted a price when uprooting from what he'd known his entire life, what he thought defined him as a human entity, no matter what tragedy may have sent him packing in the first place. When a man had lost everything, though, one could argue that he'd been *forcibly* uprooted, that there'd been nothing to *accept* to begin with. When everything was taken from him and his soul burned like a slow cigarette, he may simply wait like dust for the winds of change to float him off to some place different, one that might not remind him so much of the empty hole at the core of his being. For that, perhaps a man couldn't be blamed. When all was lost, a will was hard to find and apathy was always there to catch whatever remained. Old Jack wasn't sure the wind had ever come for him and the ashes of his former life. No process or god had taken over for his weary bones. He may have moved from the home in which he'd built his family to this remote place in the middle of nowhere but he still remained a being of loss and dust, with only inner reflection for company.

Old Jack hadn't been too sure of how conscious his decision was to buy this place out here but, then again, he'd been numb in the beginning, devoid of feeling or awareness, moving through the present in a type of sleepwalk, no matter what he did. He'd had the heart ripped from his chest, the meaning torn from his soul in a single night, a single moment of a driver's drunk negligence. *Daniel Stratton* was the guy's name and it was burned into the retina of Old Jack's third eye, branded into the musculature of his heart. Stratton died on impact, along with Lenora and Jackie-boy, and Old Jack had seen that night how unfair the world was to let the man die so quickly for everything he'd ruined. Old Jack had cursed Stratton's name over and over again. He'd read aloud from ancient texts, recited incantations he truly did not understand, all in an effort to bind the bastard's soul somehow, to bring back something he could strangle with his bare hands. Back then, he'd been willing to try anything to exact vengeance on a dead man.

It wasn't until the sixth or seventh year out here, alone in the forest, that he'd begun to feel some sort of willful awareness again, even if its foundation was planted on the scarred surface of painfully endless recollection. At that time, it had been over a year since he'd last cried over them, since his soul had last been left gaping from hours of silent sobbing in the night. For years, he'd kept himself buried in the hollow day's work of cutting wood, setting traps, fishing, gutting and cleaning of food, repairs on the cabin, gathering of supplies, cleaning tools and equipment, ad infinitum. He'd worn his loss like a shell, hidden himself and his desires underneath it and his work like an insect under a rock, for fear of losing what memories he still had of the things he'd loved most in this world, for fear of losing his sanity in the sorrow that continued to push his consciousness further into the dead parts of his animus.

Along the game trail that ran the west side of the pond, the first of the two traps was snared. A bundle of fur hung asphyxiated from the makeshift noose. Its feet rested limply in the snow underneath it. Old Jack hardly made a sound as he stepped through the thick snowfall toward the game, glancing over his shoulder to the frozen water of the pond and the cabin on the other side. He grabbed the animal from the trap and undid the twine around its neck, then held it up to examine it in the dying light.

He'd answered Death's cruel jests with alcohol and dabbling into dark arts and occult texts to find some sort of retribution, an answer or relief from the pain via the mode of revenge. When those didn't work, he thought of suicide. Yet, even in the darkest times of his suffering, when he'd been dragged to the very edge of sanity through prying into forces unknown and suicide seemed a welcome respite from the chaos he'd brought upon himself, he couldn't do it. He *wanted* to die. He wrestled for a long time as to whether Death would be better than living with the knowledge of what he'd lost. He even remembered the way the barrel of his father's old revolver tasted, sitting on the toilet in the house he once shared with his family, shortly after they'd been killed. In these times, he always saw the face of his son. Jack was afraid when he thought of what his son's reaction would be, if he knew his father had killed himself because of the pain. He would see his wife's eyes as she lay in the hotel bed next to him on their honeymoon night, whispering *I love you, Jackson* and when he said it back to her, the memories would fade, leaving him alone. The agony Old Jack had been thrown into had glassed over many aspects of his life for years. The days had blurred into autonomous actions followed by more autonomous actions, interspersed with tasteless meals and restless nights. Loneliness had crept invisibly into his reality. Whether it had been the thought of trying to find another lover while the only woman he'd ever truly felt connected with sat rotting in the ground or, simply, the weight of the titanic sorrow scarring his soul and squelching his libido, he hadn't felt the urges of sexual desire since before Lenora's death. His desire for anyone other than his wife had left him completely, except that he had found a new lover, one that gave him all of her whether he liked it or not, and her name was Misery.

Ultimately, though he dreamed often of pulling the trigger, of tying the noose tight and jumping off the tree branch, he simply kept going. Each day was a continuation of the one previous. Of course he wanted to be dead if it meant reuniting with his family, the core of his being, on some level but neither him nor anyone else knew the truth of what was beyond reality, what consequences existed for those who took their own lives. Maybe some type of Limbo waited beyond for those who had taken fate upon themselves. Perhaps there, one spent eternity in darkness and confusion. It was all unknown. Lenora had been aware of that just as well as he'd been and it was one of the reasons he'd loved her so much. He remembered the way her hair smelled and her voice sounded when they'd lay in bed having deep conversations about life and death and the possibilities of what it meant to live and move on. Any fear of the unknown seemed to only bring them closer, both physically and emotionally...

And then she died and he didn't.

Back toward the cabin and directly north of it was the well, sticking out of the crusted ground about fifty feet into the forest. The second trap was set in a small game trail just beyond that, running parallel to the worn tire tracks that led north away from the property, the only way in or out of this place without moving further into the forest. Old Jack passed the tracks and then the well, moving toward the trap set twenty feet further ahead. He could see the makeshift device cinched with another small animal and slowed as he got within a few feet of it. Even in the shade of evening, he could see something was off with the animal’s fur. It was slick, its fur matted by some dark substance. He crouched down in front of the thing and his old knees cracked as he reached out to the trap. Caring not to touch the corpse directly, he pulled a twig out from the snow and used it to shift the animal's form around, seeing what to make of it. In the uncertain light, it wasn't clear whether it was blood or some kind of sap soaking its fur. It couldn't have been fresh blood, seeing as there wasn't any dripping to the snow below the critter. He thought perhaps it was already injured when it had been caught but the closer he looked, the more the stuff appeared black in the growing night, more viscous than blood. It was gelatinous, spattered all over the animal, some kind of grease or coagulate. Old Jack grabbed the twine and lifted the corpse up toward his nose. It smelled of rot and he knew that he would need to bury it before he shut in for the long night or risk attracting the winter's scavengers. He sure as hell wasn't going to be eating the damned thing. He buried the sick smelling rabbit in a foot deep hole, away from the pond and over toward the old tracks leading out to the road. By the time he returned to the cabin, the sky had blackened with only the faintest glow of sunset still visible in the shrouded west.

The snow had been cleared in a cone shape leading out from the cabin's door. More than usual had fallen last night, leaving a fresh thick layer over the scene. In the darkness of the earlier morning, the old man had shoveled the stuff off toward the shore of the pond, clearing a working area around the cutting log sitting off to the right of the entrance to the cabin, just beyond the short entrance deck. His old hatchet, the one he'd been using for over a decade now, was sunken into the short scarred log with its handle sticking up into the air.

The inside of the cabin was warm and dark. The glowing coals in the fireplace barely illuminated the floor in front of it. Old Jack walked through the darkness toward the stacks of wood in the corner, every inch of the place hardened into his memories like a map. He grabbed two off the top and moved to the fireplace, setting the logs onto the dim bed of coals. A few sparks floated up the chimney out of sight. He sat back into the worn old chair next to the table in the middle of the cabin room, the only chair he owned, and watched as the flames returned to life.

A few quiet moments passed, interrupted only by the occasional *crack* of the burning logs. Old Jack glanced to the singular window embedded into the west wall of the cabin, overlooking the south end of the pond. In contrast to the growing flames of the fire, the world outside had turned to ink, drowned in the smothering night. Not a single form or shape could be seen from beyond the glass.

Twenty years and he still remembered the conversation he had with the man who sold him the cabin. The man, a Mr. Rutger, had owned the place since his father had left it to him twenty years prior to Old Jack's interest in it. Rutger had said that he *never was much of a country man* and Old Jack hadn't thought there was any problem with that. Sure, he'd spent most of his adult life on a farm before moving out here, but living in the wilderness came with a very different set of challenges compared to living with running water and livestock. The price was a bargain for the amount of land and solitude that came with it. Rutger said the price was so low *because of the market* and even offered the chance to spend a few nights out here before making a decision. At the time, all Jack cared about was getting away from the ruins of the life he'd left behind, getting as far away as possible from the horror. His intention in the beginning wasn't entirely self-preserving, either. He was going to stay out here, whether he could survive or not. If he couldn't, he was going to die alone in the snow and he didn't need a few trial nights spent out here to figure that out.

When they were finalizing the paperwork, standing out on the small deck, Old Jack remembered how the skies had begun to snow, then. He remembered looking out into the forest and could still picture the falling flakes, thick as tufts of cotton, in stark contrast to the deep green of the pines. Normally, it would've been a scene that both he and Lenora would've taken in and appreciated together. Yet, at the time, he'd felt nothing. At that time, his reality was tunneled by loss. He'd thought of that scene, that memory, many times since then. It seemed he was only able to appreciate it after years had passed by, after he'd been pushed further away from those heavy moments in time.

Jack, who wasn't so old then, had been reading through the last sheet of paperwork, complete with a Post-It note attached to the corner of the page, when Rutger cleared his throat and Jack looked up at him. *You look nervous*, he'd said in a probably hung-over voice. *Am I giving away my soul, here, or what?* Old Jack's lips mouthed the words as he stared into the glowing fireplace, remembering the conversation these decades later. *Oh, no*, Rutger had replied apologetically. He'd cleared his throat once more and then said *Some people just can't handle living in these conditions and some people can. I, myself, don't think I could handle it. That's all. Sure, I've been out here a few times for a weekend or two, but it's just sitting here now. What this forest... is, what it offers a man... I just want someone here who can truly grasp the responsibilities as well as the rewards of it all.*

After Jack had signed the final page, Rutger flipped through the heavy packet of paper, double-checking each signature line before slipping it all into his suitcase. *You know, the natives have a name for something around here. I don't know the actual phrase but its translation is 'the dark week.' There's about a week, six or seven days in the dead of winter, in which the sun doesn't come out for hardly more than a few moments in a day. It's usually within the first week of January. Just... keep your head low and stay inside during those days. Trust me.* After Rutger shook Jack's hand and had begun to walk back to the Mercedes Benz parked off to the side of the cabin, he called out over his shoulder: *Better yet, just don't be here in the first week of January. Trust me*, he said again.

Old Jack supposed that he could've chased the man down for information on what exactly he'd meant by all that, but he figured what's done is done and, truth be told, he didn't care much at the time. It had been four months that he'd been moving from motel to motel after leaving the farm, trying to find a place within his measly price range while his funds dwindled by the day. Whatever information the guy hadn't divulged didn't matter much so long as it didn't affect the deed Jack had in his hand. This place would become his new home, the only place he could call his own after everything that had happened. Whatever new challenges arose out here, he would simply deal with. He'd cursed God and run from the broken foundations of his life. The only thing he'd hoped at the time was that the events of the past wouldn't follow him, like a dark predator, out into these woods.

Tonight marked the midnight of January 6th and the tail end of the twentieth deep winter Old Jack had spent out here on his own, surrounded by the endless evergreens and the biting cold that swept through them most nights. He'd never taken Rutger's nebulous advice to leave during the first week of January, not this year nor any other before it. Hell, there was nowhere else to go. He had no family, no friends. It didn't matter. To live and provide for oneself in a setting such as this, and to run from the socialization of other humans for the solitude of the pines, required something a bit peculiar in a man, perhaps something broken or misshapen inside of him. Old Jack had pondered this thought quite a bit over the years. He had pondered how a man could allow years to pass him by in a haze and how loss and fear seemed to mold itself over time into something else... especially after what happened during the first 'dark week' he'd spent out in these woods.

In the deep winter of that first year, something else was in the forest with him, something that he believed had followed him from the farm, had been brought forth by his misguided rituals. It was some horrendous manifestation of his fear and anger and sorrow that had burrowed itself into every cell of his body, orchestrating its own birth into his already-ruined reality to make itself known.

Out in these woods, a man had all the time in the world to think and being around the same location for so long never ceased to give Old Jack's memories a vivid playback in his moments of meditation. A tree here or the smell of a plant there only solidified the terrible images from that first winter that still held sanctuary deep in his mind, the familiar forest playing off of his memories like an instrument.

That first night of that first January, among many other events around that time in his life, had pushed itself into Jack's world and, no matter how traumatized he may have been, was something that he wasn't ever able to shed.

*

The screams were the worst part of that night but the gurgling dark liquid pouring over the white landscape, covering the ground between the pines in black, was what Jack first gazed upon when peering through the viewport.

It had all turned black.

A blanket of darkness enveloped the earth around the cabin. Huge swaths of the viscous fluid poured down from further up the mountain. There were forms in the muck, animal-like protrusions of the corpulent stuff, moving and shapeshifting down the slope. There were bubbles that inflated and popped into dark mists and other shapes that appeared to be mixtures of woodland animals and creatures, deformed raccoons and fawns, infernal chimaeras of a world consumed by the goop. It rolled down the terrain toward the frozen pond, pooling out over the ice.

Not more than a few feet from the stunted deck outside the viewport, a different kind of shape manifested in the oil, closer in proximity to the cabin and more vivid than the rest...

It was the shape of a human. Upon this realization, Jack's eyes went wide as two white orbs opened from the thing's face like eyes of its own.

Jack clapped the viewport shut, leaning his back heavily against the bolted door and breathed raggedly. Adrenaline pumped through his body as his fists shook. That shape, forming and mutating to imitate his own species, reappeared over and over in his mind. It wasn't human, yet through the door, he felt its presence creeping closer. In his chest and in his lungs, he felt its decrepit intent inching toward the other side of the wood through a sensation of awareness he had never experienced prior to that moment. It was an unwanted connection with not just the thing outside the door but the entire event, the gross waves of oil, the forest's devouring, caving in on him all at once in an avalanche of psychic stimuli.

And then the screaming began. He heard what had sounded like a child's shrieking, deathly afraid and in some sort of mortal struggle. It coughed and choked and cried out. Jack wasn't sure if time had warped the memory of the sounds the child had made, audibly low and drawn out, inhuman even, or if he was remembering it true.

Whether it was the underlying moroseness of the taking of his family or the things he had witnessed through the viewport those nights, madness seemed to take hold of him in that first dark week. Jack had spent the next eight days in a blur, eating the rations from under the cupboards, never opening the door of the cabin even to relieve his bowels or bladder, instead, using a pot in the corner. His mind had been shredded by the sounds heard shrieking in the darkness. The terror, combined with the recent loss of everything he loved, had broken him while he grew stale in a miasma of his own shit.

For eight days, a fractured husk of a man sat in the shadows of the cabin's interior, wishing that whatever he had seen in the blackness of that first January night would slide its way under the door or through the cracks in the wood and take him away from all that he felt, from all that was dead in him, because his crippling fear had no plans of removing its claws from his psyche. Nightmares plagued what little sleep he could get at the time. They saturated his thoughts, even during the day, with imagery of dark mutations and infusing his blood with a tingling paranoia. He'd been broken through sadness and fear and wished for death at the hands of someone or something, *anything*. If it would've done him that favor, he would've been grateful not to have to do it himself. Suffering created the paradoxical mindset in which he desired to simultaneously survive the horror and be consumed by it, wholly and completely.

Old Jack never again had an experience during the dark week like he had that first winter. Each year, he prepared himself and each year was met with only freezing darkness, no screaming children, no waves of fluid eating the landscape.

Yet there had been, during the terror of that first winter midnight, a type of psychic bridge built between the forest's scourging intent and Jack's intuition. This connection originally manifested itself in the oppressive force that had grown nearer and nearer beyond the door he had leaned against, that *awareness*. He hadn't realized it until years later but the presence in the cold woods goading from just beyond the threshold had activated parts of himself he had never known. Something was unlocked or unattached, deep in his mind. The thing hadn't needed to get into the cabin to manipulate him, to touch his soul in ways he didn't think possible. He could feel it even now, all these years later, that something horrible had bored itself into him that night and, when it fled, had left something else in its place, a marker or beacon of some ill kind.

It had been with him ever since.

*

Old Jack was alone out here, insofar as there were no other humans. His mind, however, was connected to some web that crisscrossed through these woods. It was an intention, a circuit of inhuman presence and energy that he seemed to most connect with when he allowed his body to autonomously go about his work, listening to the chirps and groans of the forest. In these times, he would envision his mind swelling beyond the confines of his skull, reaching out through some extra dimension to the world around to gain a better understanding of it. When this happened, he felt the fingers of his probing intuition move over the contours of the world he saw. He felt them drink of the sounds he heard, the food he tasted and the wind he felt against his skin. Part of him was enthralled by the extra sensory input, like a transcendental happening, yet another part of him was reminded of that which had given this to him, the corruption he'd witnessed. It all felt connected and served as the foundation for this extra vision, darkly gifted to him by the woods and whatever else had existed out here.

He slid the cob pipe off of the table in the middle of the room and packed it with a liberal pinch of dry tobacco from the pouch in his shirt pocket. His thumb and forefinger were brown with the stain of nightly handling of the stuff. The tobacco had grown stale. Unfortunately, he would not be making the trip to the nearest town, over twenty-five miles away, until the winter snows cleared up a bit, until spring had begun to melt the ice on the single highway that led to the small town.

The old stuff would have to do.

He struck a wooden match from the box in his other shirt pocket and placed it to the pipe, inhaling and pulling the flame into the wad of tobacco. The first drag was always the harshest and always the best. Smoking the old stuff was something that seemed to calm the nerves for him. This was either the second-to-last or the last night of this dark week. Nothing had happened to him in nineteen years and, on this twentieth anniversary, it was seeming to amount to the same thing.

Old Jack was just fine with that.

On the table, next to an unlit lamp, was a book, one of six or seven left by the previous owner of the cabin, *A Tale of Two Cities* by Dickens. He slid the book off the table and placed it into his lap while he took another puff from the pipe. The smoke was like liquid, a grey ooze waving through the dark air up to the ceiling, creating its own shadows on the wall in the lapping firelight. Old Jack opened the book and shifted his sitting position to allow the flames to light the words. He didn't like this book, though he'd read it a few times. It was boring, dealt with plot struggles that had no relevance to his life. There was only those six or seven books, however, and for some reason he'd never bought anymore for himself. Beggars can't be choosers, as they say. Considering this novel was the one he'd read least of the group, he simply sought something different, not necessarily interesting.

Flipping through the title and table of contents pages to the start of the first chapter, he took another drag from the pipe, then began to read in his gruff mumbled voice:

"It was the best of times,

it was the worst of times,

it was the age of wisdom,
it was the age of foolishness,
it was the epoch of belief,
it was the epoch of incredulity,
it was the season of Light,
it was the season of Darkness,
it was the spring of hope,
it was the winter of despair..."

It had been a while since he'd spoken aloud. The last phrase sat heavy behind his eyelids, which were already sagging as he read the words. This time of year always messed with his sleep. Even as the years had grown less harrowing and slipped more into apathy and predictability, being holed up in his thoughts under the oppressive darkness during the heart of winter seemed to always leave him feeling exhausted. So much time had passed and the pains in his age and old bones required more rest than they used to.

It didn't take long, only about halfway through the second page, before the fire had warmed the old man's skin enough to allow his eyes to gently close. An owl hooted from the forest outside. Moonlight was beginning to peek around the clouds and through the single window. Sleep and warmth overtook Old Jack and he drifted lazily into a state of unconsciousness.

*

Jackson's eyes slowly opened.

Yellow sunshine beamed through the slatted blinds covering the window just beyond his crib. Motes of dust floated through the light, bouncing this way and that in the warmth of the exterior day.

He rolled his little body onto his side and struggled his way up into a sitting position. His tiny fingers wrapped around the wooden bars that walled the crib and he used all the strength his little arms could muster to pull himself to his wobbly feet. The plastic wrapped mattress underneath him crunched with the weight of his teetering stance.

"Aa-oh!" he exclaimed to the light pouring through the window. "Aa-oh! Aaaaah-oooh!" His speech devolved to a spitty blithering as he made bubbles with the saliva before it dripped down his chubby chin.

Baaaaaaby Jaaaaaaack.

He knew that voice. That was food. That was warmth. That was touch and sensations that were soft and sounded wonderful to his ears. That was the one who held him and pressed her face against his and blew air onto his lips, something that always made him laugh.

That was *Mama*.

"Eee-yah-yah," he said, calling back to her. "Eee-yah-yah-yah!"

Jackson turned away from the window, still holding onto the wooden bar with his right hand, as the bedroom door creaked open.

He saw the shape of her come into his view and he laughed toward her, letting go of the bar and spilling to the bed in front of him. He was still laughing when he felt her lean over him and slip her hands under his arms.

Baaaaaaaby Jaaaaaaaaaack, the voice sang above him. He was slowly pulled up to rest in the crook of his mother's arm and, as he sank into the familiar position, he looked up to her face.

Something was wrong.

The eyes of the face that blew air on him weren't right. The hands that cradled him were different, rough and elongated. Deep in Jackson's core, he felt the presence of an imposter and his eyes began to burn and that familiar feeling crept up his neck and throat as he began to cry. Hot tears streamed down his cheeks and he wailed loudly.

Through the warbled veil of his vision, he watched her face turn a shade of black and cave in on itself. Hot air groaned out of the exposed inner cavity of the skull and rolled over the skin of his naked face and arms. Thick yellow liquid dripped down the thing's neck to the sundress it wore, slicking its cleavage and soaking into the fabric as the stuff oozed down toward him.

Then the hands shifted to hold him under the arms once more and he felt his breath give.

The fingers tightened around his little ribs.

*

"*Nuh*!" Old Jack called out.

His eyes tore open from the dream only to be met by darkness. The interior of the cabin was black. The fireplace held ashes, only a few embers barely glowing toward the center of the heap. Old Jack's mind collected itself from the dream-world as he wiped the drool from his grizzled chin. The images of the thing in the dream were fading from his thoughts quickly but the chills in his flesh remained.

"What the..."

Dreams seemed to be few and far between for Old Jack, but a dream like *that*, a nightmare, hadn't occurred in years.

Baaaaaaby Jaaaaaack.

He could still hear the voice singing that phrase in his mind. It was his mother's voice, even if he hadn't heard it in decades. He knew that for certain. He'd also recognized that room with the sunlight through the blinds but couldn't remember from where.

The wood chair creaked underneath him when he sat up and stuck his chest out, cracking his back. A dull pain throbbed in his neck. He leaned his head back and grimaced, rolling it slowly side-to-side. Old Jack supposed that's what he got for falling asleep in this poor excuse for a chair. He'd grown too old for that stuff, he knew, but hadn't seemed to learn his lesson.

He opened his mouth wide and moved his jaw around until his ears popped, then relaxed back into the chair. His eyes rested their focus on the fireplace.

Baaaaaaaby Jaaaaack.

The old man had spent many nights in this forest listening to the noise of the woods as he drifted off to sleep. Snow had a way of deadening most sound to city-folk but, over time, Old Jack had grown accustomed to the subtle volume of the forest's sighs and lamentations and, along with the crackling of the fireplace, they would sing him to sleep some nights, a lullaby for aged ears. Sometimes tufts of snow would fall from branches and thud to the powder below, sounding like heavy footfalls. Other times, trees would groan while swaying in a high wind or wolves might howl from the distant dark.

Not now, though. There were no sounds, save for the quickening heartbeat in his ears and that demented ethereal voice, the one that sang his name, echoing in his mind. Still sitting in the small worn chair, Old Jack gazed out of the single window on the west wall. The corners of the pane were fogged with creeping frost that appeared to be growing before his eyes.

The silence inside the cabin had grown thick and the weight of it sank down into the old man's flesh. His limbs were tingly and the air felt electrified with something intangible. He had grown familiar with this feeling. The tingling that crept up Old Jack's chest and neck was the feeling he always got as the *other* vision began to open up, the awareness given to him by the interactions of his past and this ancient forest. It was a type of focus that left the barriers of his brain matter and pushed out to the world around him, collecting interdimensional stimulation through a strange indescribable sensory input.

He watched the fog of his breath disappear into the dark ceiling above and his fingers extended and contracted. The night cold had seeped through the walls and into his knuckles and wrists during his sleep. His right knee, the bad one, cracked in the silence as he stood from the chair. His boots thudded roughly against the old wood floor as he moved toward the half cord of firewood stacked in the corner. He could hardly see the logs but his hands had the muscle memory of thousands of fires and grabbed two cuts off of the tops of the stack.

Only a few strides back toward the fireplace, he heard a sound. It stopped him in his tracks, the unsure quality of it, a noise that he didn't recognized. It was so quick to pass, he wasn't sure he'd even heard anything at all. The tendrils of sleep were still releasing their grip from his mind while he stood there, mid-stride, still as stone, listening and waiting, the two pieces of wood still held in his hands. In his memories, the voice from the dream sang again.

Baaaaaaaby Jaaaaaack.

The silence was deafening in the darkness that surrounded him.

And then he heard it again.

Shlup!

This time, it was a little clearer, as in he now knew he had heard *something*, but still couldn't determine what it was. He was certain, however, that it was coming from just outside the cabin.

Old Jack set the two pieces of wood down, leaning them against the pockmarked stones of the fireplace, then turned and stepped quietly toward the door.

The viewport cover screeched as it slid open.

The forest floor was awash with a fresh coating of snow from some time earlier in the night while he'd slept. The area cleared around the cutting log was no longer discernible from the rest, covered heavily by a blanket of the stuff. The hatchet was still buried in the log. The trees were silent and still, their branches drooping with the weight of the powder. The air slipping through the viewport was frigid and unforgiving.

Old Jack fancied that he had a good sense of time but his eyes still felt dry and groggy from the dreams. The short daylight and overcast skies gave him little to work with in discerning where the moon was and how long he'd been out. He guessed early morning by how cold it was inside the cabin and how long it had appeared that the fire had been dead.

And then the sound came out of the darkness once more.

Shlup!

This time, Old Jack heard it clearly. It was a sloshing or slurping, a muddy suctioning of some kind, and it was coming from just outside the field of vision from the viewport, beyond the door and off to the right, over near the old interstate-bound tire tracks. There wasn't a window on the east or north wall of the cabin and the old man was inclined to walk outside and see for himself what was making the noise, as he would most any other night.

He reached out for his jacket on the post, then the door handle. The moment his fingertips grazed the doorknob, however, something stayed his hand, something instinctual nagging in him. So, instead, he slid the viewport open once more and stared out into the snowed pines, waiting for any sort of movement in the night among the shadows. Minutes passed silently as he scanned the trees and the darkness. He still couldn't get those images out of his mind, of that sunken face in his dreams. There was something about that place, that sunlight and the crib...

Old Jack stepped back and slid the viewport closed. At the sound of the small cover clapping shut, the hairs on the old man's nape prickled and a chill ran through his body. The dark in the cabin around him grew foggy and the sounds of his own breathing echoed and reverberated in his ears. The details of the table, door and fireplace smoked over with a mist in his eyes. His hands moved to his face but his limbs felt numb and heavy at the joints.

Baaaaaaaby Jaaaaaaack.

*

Jackson's chubby fingers gripped the wooden bars in front of him. He looked through, beyond the cage he stood in, to the window with the slatted blinds and the sunlight pouring through. Dust motes bounced off each other in the yellow beams and he could feel the warmth emanating into the room.

He wobbled on his baby legs and hung his head just as the door creaked open. *Mama* walked into the room, his comfort, his protector. But even before his little grip failed him, Jackson could feel something was off. The plastic wrapping of the mattress crinkled as he fell into it and then hands were reaching under his arms and pulling him up.

Intruder, his nubile instincts kicked.

Tears were already watering his vision. He'd been here before. He didn't want to go up to this one's face. It scared him and it wasn't Mama. It wasn't his warmth.

When he was sat in the crook of her arm, Jackson stared down at the fingers that stretched across his bare legs and stomach. They were longer than Mama's with cracked scaly calluses on each knuckle and brown nails that appeared diseased. His crying eyes wandered above and saw only dripping pus from the face of the one who held him.

*

Old Jack shouted, stumbling back over the small table. The old man slammed to the floor, his knee bashing into the planks, and he hissed through clenched teeth as the pain shot through his leg up into his torso.

"Son of a *bitch*!" he cursed.

In the dark, in his mind's eye, he saw that face from the dream and it was horrifying, smeared black, carved out, decayed. He saw the gaseous stuff coming out of her head and the curves of her throat and collar bones oiled with the coagulate. His tether to the dream wasn't fully severed. Something in his nerves was still a part of the transmission and connected. His instincts were on fire, screaming of an intruder here in reality as well, not just within the fading dream. The presence of that thing was all around him.

"My god..." he murmured.

The old man's vision was beginning to clear. He could see the interior of the cabin once more, but then an oppressing stillness, sagging in the air, enveloped him. The interior of the cabin was filled with a type of pressure, heavy on his eardrums. He hoisted himself up and stood to his feet, grunting at the pain in his bad knee now made even worse by the fall. His head was woozy from standing and he hardly had time to reflect upon the wretched dream before it hit him and he knew for certain.

Something was definitely here with him.

It was in the dark air. Old Jack sensed it in the space between his breaths, not in the cabin but outside, *just* outside, something bizarre yet familiar. Twenty years he'd been out here and had only ever felt something like this once before, during that first night when he'd seen the human shaped thing emerge from the dark corpulence. A metallic taste floated in the silence, accompanied by an otherworldly static beyond the normal audible spectrums. He could almost *hear* it, like the steady hum of power lines, just through the north wall of the cabin.

Old Jack felt himself moving slowly to the bed, not by his own will but by some other, orchestrated from somewhere in the creeping mana invisible around him. As this played out, his mind became hyperaware. It grew from the tingle in the base of his spine and moved up his sides to the jugular areas on either side of the neck, prickling and shocking. There, the tingling stayed, hovering behind the arteries and tendons in his flesh, reverberating and intensifying with each passing moment. It was an expulsion, some non-physical part of his being reaching out to the area around him, searching for spectral sensation.

The bedsprings screeched as he sat and scooted his back against the inner wall of the cabin. He forced his eyes closed and the strange sense, the *connection*, burned in him. His hands shook in the dark while his soul's tentacles oozed away from him and into the beyond. In his mind's eye, he watched them, watched *through* each of them and all of them at once, like a thousand eyes moving together. They slithered through the cracks between particles and slid outside the earthly world of physics, traveling in the realms beyond mortal life. Though they seemed to have a mind of their own, Old Jack was along for the ride, experiencing the trip through the aether right alongside his soul's seemingly autonomous proboscises.

The spectral feelers crawled up and down the cabin wall on which his back rested, probing underneath every splinter in the wood and every crack in the mortar. In the dark of his mind, he saw them as canyons, wide and vast, and he soared through them like a hawk, gliding across miles of shadowed terrain. It was an entire world, an alien one that existed right under the surface of his life. He'd seen the pictures of microbial in a National Geographic, the ones that were a fraction of a millimeter long but, up close, looked like something out of an alternate dimension of horror. Down here, on this level of perception, this *was* an alternate dimension in which horror thickly permeated its space.

And then the eyes, the tendrils of his consciousness, all at once poured into a particularly deep crevice in the old mortar, burrowing into black nothingness and, almost immediately, Old Jack knew where they were moving. The tendrils of his psyche were being *pulled* through to the other side of the wall. Something outside was sucking at the shreds of his soul and he could feel himself stretching and shrinking all at once, squeezing through the imperceptible tunnels that led to the cold night air beyond.

His ethereal eyes birthed into the freezing temperature on the other side. He saw crystals of frost like diamond landscapes along the external wall of the cabin. The skin on his physical body inside prickled with goosebumps and he shivered, both from the cold his soul felt and the fright of his possession. The strain for balance was futile, with half of his consciousness sat inside on the bed and the other half emerging into the night outside. He sensed both locations using separate modes of input, like two different channels playing on the same radio. He could hardly focus, taking in images and feelings and sense stimuli he both could and could not comprehend. It was almost maddening as he felt the pull, a type of assault he'd never known before, feeling as if his skin was being peeled.

The wispy ends of his consciousness fluttered and bobbed around in the cold, probing and touching the ice particles in the air when, like black lightning crashing through his mind, his outstretched soul detected something horrid, so foul that it seemed to shock the very space around it. Heinous signals were sent back through the aether, through the wall and into the old man's perception. It was the thing he'd felt earlier, the presence that had been waiting just outside the wall. It was the presence that had approached from just beyond the door twenty years ago. The thousand eyes of his non-physical appendages simultaneously directed their sights to the thing that stood dripping grotesquely in the snow.

There was only a brief moment before Old Jack's connection zapped out and, in that moment, that microcosm of time, he saw its face.

Baaaaaaby Jaaaaaack.

*

Jackson was already crying, even before he heard the heavy footsteps slowly coming up the hall leading to his room. His little hands gripped the wooden bars of his crib prison and his knuckles whitened from the tension. Dust motes floated in the yellow light of the sun, beaming through the parted blinds of the window in the far wall. The steps grew closer from out in the hallway. Jackson's cries grew in anticipation of what was sure to follow.

When the steps went quiet and the doorknob *clicked*, the sunlight from the window went red, plunging the room in a deep sinister light. The redness burned against the walls in the shapes of the slatted blinds and these shapes mutated and shifted and changed into things Jackson had never seen before, the uncertainty accentuated by the tears in his eyes.

The hinges creaked as the door opened and he cried harder, holding onto the bars with all his infant might. He didn't want to see what was behind him. It wasn't safety. It wasn't warmth. It wasn't Mama.

It was the Other.

Baaaaaaaby Jaaaaaack.

Its voice was lower this time, a deep purr that was distorted somehow. He didn't want to see it. Everything in him screamed to be away from this imposter. He pressed his chubby face hard against the bars as he cried desperately. The red light from the window grew more intense, brighter, and then he felt quivering elongated fingers coil under his arms and around his chest.

Shhhh-sh-sh, the presence cooed.

The hands pulled him away from the bars. His grip was no match for the strength of the thing and failed almost immediately. He rose in the air and felt hot breath on his back and heard a guttural inhaling. It was smelling him, smelling all over his head and nape. The coppery scent of rotten blood rode the thing's breath. The hands shifted him as he cried and turned him to face it.

*

Old Jack screamed into the dark of the cabin but only a part of him could hear it. He was split between three experiences: the inside of the cabin with his physical body, outside of the cabin with the tatters of his consciousness being held by the thing that stood just on the other side of the north wall, and the rest of his mind stuck in that dream, in the hands of the creature that held his infantile body and stared directly into him.

Inside the dream, the eyes of the Other were horrendous, like orange goat's pupils sat in bulbous black spheres. They were lidless and twitching up and down, side-to-side, seeing and witnessing and analyzing all forms of Jack through the aether. The open maw for a face was an abyss. The eyes seemed to float on thin roots that disappeared into the dark sunken gore.

It was a psychic attack, aggression from the presence he knew from long ago. It was manipulating his memories and dreams into a weapon, cleaving him with the horror. He sat against the inner wall of the cabin in the dark, bound in all dimensions by spiritual subjugation, both within and outside of the nightmare. Old Jack's mind struggled between the multiple streams of experience and, in a moment of synchronistic terror, he saw that the warped intruder in his dream was the same presence that stood outside the cabin. It quivered and gurgled in the darkness and held his mind's eyes close, pulling him further towards its diseased feeding hole. He felt its influence in every part of his being. It blinded him with fear, hardening like ice in his veins and squeezing the air from his lungs.

The hag's eyes stared through the windows in his mind, from outside the cabin and through the sight of little Jackson. Old Jack tried to yell but no sound produced from his clenched teeth except an exhaustive grunt of will. He was terrified, unequivocally, and driven to the edge of sanity, staring into the face of the entity. Pain shot through his body, some kind of separate constriction it was performing against him. It gripped his thoughts with its sadism and wrung him out like a wet rag. Fight-or-flight burned in his cheeks as he struggled to move from the bed, exerting everything in himself, his heart beating tumultuously.

The probing fingers of his soul began to retract, slipping away from both the hag that stood out in the snow and the one that held him in the dream. Outside, her carved out face was still but her orange pupils rattled in the frigid night, watching as the clustered eyes of his consciousness moved themselves as one back through the mortar. He retreated over the long dark valleys in the splintered wood and, just as the last of the tendrils returned to their source and his mind once again existed within the confines of his own skull, he pushed himself forward and rolled off the bed, dropping with a *thud* to the old wood floor. He cursed, not from the pain in his knee but from the shrill ringing in his ears, an aftereffect of the entity's violent hold over him.

Old Jack's nerves were still electrified when he caught a full breath of the thin cool air blowing in from the fireplace and sat himself up against the bed frame. His breathing was quick to match his racing heartbeat but, even as his lungs quivered with shock, he forced himself to inhale slowly and methodically.

A few long moments passed in which he calmed, if only slightly, staring into the void behind his eyelids. He opened them, peering into the darkness of the cabin and, like a moth to the flame, his eyes sought the only bit of light in his field of vision, the small window on the west wall. With the backdrop of a glowing black sky, the shape of a head was staring in through the glass.

Baaaaaaaby Jaaaaaaaack.

Old Jack felt his mind ripped from its home once again, his body pushed back against the bed frame, and the interior of the cabin was replaced with the red light burning deeply through the blinds on the window, beyond the crib in his bedroom. His fingers gripped the wooden bars tightly and his knees trembled underneath him and he was already crying before he heard the thing's voice again.

Baaaaaaaaaby Jaaaaaaack.

The footsteps were thudding loudly in the hallway behind him, vibrating the rungs of his crib.

"Jesus Christ!" Old Jack cried out in a terrorized fury. The gazing eyes from the thing in the window, twitching in the darkness, sent horror shocks throughout his entire body. The pain forced him back down to prone. Through the bombardment, he crawled with every ounce of his strength toward the downed table in the center of the room. Instinct made it clear that he needed to get out of eyeshot of the thing in the window. His hands clawed the wooden floorboards and something like nerve damage boiled behind his eyes as he lowered his head and pushed.

Jackson screamed toward the red window but his cries seemed to die just beyond the threshold of the crib. Old Jack screamed with him. He didn't want to see the face again. He didn't want to feel those hands on him anymore, yet there was nothing to save him. The footsteps in the hallway came to a stop outside the bedroom door. Jackson still held onto the bars as he looked back and saw the doorknob begin to turn. He cried out again, as did Old Jack, and turned back toward the window and the red light that saturated everything. As the door creaked open behind him, the glare pulsed vibrantly.

A deep abominable voice sang as the entity slithered into the room.

Jaaaaaackiee-boy.

The bedroom door clicked shut and Jackson could no longer hear his own screams. He felt the vibration of exertion in his chest and lungs, the involuntary spasms of fear that rolled through his little body, but heard only the thing behind him. It breathed a metallic grating sound that rattled, piercing through the dream veil into all realities.

Old Jack finally made his way into the cover of the downed table, forcing himself not to take another look at the thing peeking in from outside. He, too, yelled in terror but heard nothing except the breathing of the creature in his waking dream.

Jackson pressed his head as hard as he could into the space between two of the wooden bars and cried at the red window. Shaking rigid fingers crept under his arms and around his chest. He felt the hot wheezing breath on the back of his head and in his hair, accompanied by an acrid smell that stung his little nostrils.

Old Jack covered his mouth with a shaking hand and sobbed

through his fingers.

And then the crippled hands pulled him from the bars and they rose him up as his feet hung below him. The blackened nails at the end of grotesque fingers dug into his soft stomach and there was a growling behind him. As it began to turn him around, Jackson shut his eyes.

Open... your eyes.

The thing's voice bubbled like hot grease and Jackson squeezed his eyelids tighter, screaming silently in the face of whatever lay beyond them. The rank breath crawled over him in waves and he could feel the heat from burning red light on his back. The pain behind Old Jack's eyes cracked like glass, shattering in his brain.

OPEN YOUR EYES!

In that moment, something indescribable occurred from the shared experience between Old Jack's reality and the dream of his infant self, a washing away of sorts. The rotten miasma of the creature dissipated, carried off by something he could not sense, replaced instead with an old familiar smell.

Old Jack's heart fluttered in his chest.

Jackson's crying slowed into silence.

It was the smell of a different one. It was the smell of...

Jackson opened his eyes to gaze upon the face of the one Old Jack had loved more than life itself. He gazed up into Lenora's big brown eyes. She stared down at him, her smooth lips smiling and her warmth exuding a love words could never describe. In that moment, Old Jack felt himself fall out of his physical body and his soul pushed itself fully into the dream, reaching out to her in any way it possibly could. It was as if every aspect of the nightmares and the terror and the misery he'd felt in the last twenty years evaporated in a single breath, mystified and floated off to realms outside of this one.

Hey, Jackie-boy. How you doin', my little handsome man?

Old Jack whimpered into the darkness, covering his sobbing face with his hands. He could smell his Lenora in the cool air creeping from the fireplace. His body ached for her, a burning need revitalized after decades of morbidity and stale wanting.

You ready for breakfast?

Her gentle hand floated up to her shirt and tucked the lapel under the breast that flopped out. The nipple was a dark pink circle on her flesh and he felt himself, both in the dream and in reality, reaching out for it. Old Jack's penis hardened in his jeans and, in the dream, the nipple entered his mouth and he closed his eyes and, in reality, he could taste Lenora on his tongue. He remembered the feeling of her in his mouth during their times of intimacy with each other. He had been a reserved lover, shy to come out of his shell, and she had been patient and understanding with just enough pushing to break down the walls he had built over so many years prior. And, like then, the same walls he'd rebuilt in his sorrow and loss were being taken down by the experience, the worship he now participated in. It broke him into a million pieces and his vulnerability let itself go. His carnal desire for the one he had loved before, his one true lover, reanimated within everything he was.

The images in his mind, the dream to which his soul was giving its all, splintered and then melted into a swirling darkness. The room shifted into abstract pieces that gently vibrated. The fireplace shifted out of its position against the wall, floating back and dropping, then floating forward and raising up. The table behind which the old man took refuge extended and condensed, then extended once more.

And then he was on top of her, of his Lenora, in the hotel bed where they had always spent their anniversaries. She was staring up into his eyes while the candlelight flickered in her glistening pupils. She smiled and there were words that she was going to say. He knew this because the dream was a memory, but not just a memory. He was reliving it in his mind and he knew what she was going to say. *I'm pregnant* is what she was going to say, what she had said every time he had remembered this moment in the past. And then she said it, *I'm pregnant, Jack*, but it was so much more vivid than he could've ever imagined.

He could *see* her again.

He felt her words more than any memory had ever offered. They laughed together in the dreamlike sanctuary, held in a naked embrace, and Old Jack laughed into the empty cabin. Then they cried together and the tears streamed down his face in the dark. He felt her sliding his penis into her in his dream, saw her brow furrow up as she moaned and he leaned in to kiss her neck and he smelled that smell that was only hers. Old Jack was transfixed by the potency of the dream and all of himself fell into the memory and into Lenora, leaving only a shred of consciousness behind to dwell in his mortal body. That shred was toying with his mind because his hands reached out into the darkness and he could swear he felt Lenora there with him. He could taste her neck and lips in his mouth, feel himself removing his pants and climbing back onto the bed. He slid himself onto the empty mattress in the same position as in the dream...

And in the moment of synchronicity, the dream and reality joined as one and Jack was making love to his wife again. He felt the vigor of decades shaved off of his age. The passion he experienced was more than he'd been capable of since her could remember, perhaps more than he'd been capable of in his entire life. He felt himself sliding in and out of her, felt the warmth of her body squeezing him, her fingers digging into his back. She moaned into his ear and he inhaled deeply of her hair, a smell that filled his lungs and pushed him further into euphoria. He kissed her lips, breathed her breath , sucked her tongue and swallowed her saliva and, as he felt himself reaching climax, her arms gripped him tightly and pulled him close.

The ejaculate pumped from the old man's body. Tears flowed from his eyes and the sensations covered him completely, as if his very life-force was being drained from him, dragged through his body in a process of pure ecstasy, to be joined with Lenora's.

I love you, Jack, she said to him.

He gasped and let out the breath he'd been holding as the last contractions of his erection diminished. His body went still. A moment passed and he rolled to where the mattress met the wall and laid with his head against it, breathing heavily into the corner. Without any grand exit, Lenora's eyes faded from his thoughts with the rest of the dream and his mind was brought back to reality in the dark cabin. The vigor of his younger self had gone. The aches of his aged body returned to him, like slipping a sore foot back into a tight shoe. He could still smell her on him, as if she were still next to him. The dream had awoken old memories of Lenora's eyes and the sound of her voice, which he thought he'd completely forgotten after so many years. His mind rushed through old moments, just the two of them sitting at the bar in the kitchen of their home, watching old movies on the little black and white tube TV that sat on the counter. He could never get enough of the way her skin smelled or how her lips tasted and felt against his own. Sometimes, when they watched the boring love stories, he'd catch her letting out a sigh as she gazed upon the theatrical love displayed in front of her with disinterest, potentially regretting her movie choice but unable to let her pride take the hit. He would always nudge her then and find ways to maneuver himself behind her to kiss her neck and take her attention away from the TV.

His heart drank these recollections like a long sought sustenance and, along with the lingering smell, they gave him a type of momentary peace he couldn't imagine was possible.

"I love you, too," he mumbled to the darkness he lay within.

The bed shook.

Old Jack's eyes shot open but his body didn't move, motionless as rigor mortis.

A weight shifted behind him on the mattress, then lifted off the side of the bed. Old Jack stared at the wall directly in front of his face. Shock froze him in place and stopped his breathing.

Slow footsteps crossed the room, around the downed table, then toward the door. Old Jack heard the latch for the lock slide along its track before the groan of the door's hinges sang their laments. The oppressing silence inside the cabin was replaced with a wave of sounds rushing in from the outside world. He was driven even further into horror from the strange noises coming from beyond the walls of the cabin. Long groans and countless voices crying, cracking bones and shattering rocks, sloshing and slathering and bubbling fluids of unknown origin...

Old Jack's body broke free of the fearful stasis. He turned back.

The door lay open but the rest of the cabin was empty. The window was clear yet a bizarre glow came from beyond the glass. On the mattress next to him, a dark ooze was slicked across the sheets and puddled in the middle of it. In the dim light, Old Jack saw that he was covered in the same stuff, all over his hands and caked onto the skin around his genitals and thighs and in the fabric of his shirt. He tasted the stuff in his mouth then, felt the grit of it between his teeth, and stumbled off the mattress to retch on the floorboards.

Oil-slicked footprints on the wood led to the open door. They were average in size and humanoid by the looks of them, and Old

Jack's eyes followed them as he spit the rest of the vomit from his mouth. Adrenaline coursed through him though his muscles felt weak and the pain in his knee screamed like a banshee.

He could still smell her, though he couldn't tell if it was Lenora's skin that he tasted on his lips or if it was the stuff still caked onto them behind the sour remnants of puke. His emotions were tortured and his mind walked the razor line between being grateful and being horrified, his own sanity now a worry of the past. He had tasted something beyond the world he thought he knew, the world of *what's dead is dead* and *when they're gone, they're gone*. The fear wasn't the same now. In this new fear, he'd been able to hold his Lenora again, to hear her say that she loved him, to watch her lips as she smiled and kissed the corners of his eyes again.

The otherworldly noises coming from outside continued to grow more eerie but Old Jack found himself beginning to calm. The possibilities of seeing his wife again scratched at his mind. He felt himself almost hopeful in the fantasy. His heart still pounded like a drum but the rate at which it did was slowing, as was his breathing. The stuff caked onto him, the goo still lingering on his tongue...

It was *her*.

Old Jack stood from his vomitus position and stepped toward the open door, still naked from the waist down. The night air chilled him as he approached the doorway, a portal to the woods. The strange sounds rode the freezing midnight breeze into the cabin.

When he stepped around the door and looked outside, his very essence seemed assaulted by he witnessed.

All around were shapes of different things, pushing and protruding out of the black that flowed down the mountain. Bubbles swelled then burst in little spatters of glowing mist, creating the chaotic glow that illuminated the scene. The sparks of weird light were somewhere between grey and green, wavering momentarily in the air before dissipating like gaseous fumes. Stepping off of the deck and walking out into the snow, past the chopping log with the hatchet still sticking out of it, was the shape of a woman made completely of the black goo, the same stuff that was pooled onto his bed and the same stuff as that which poured down the landscape behind her. Her outstretched hand joined that of a smaller shape that approached, a simulacrum of a young child. The figures moved further out together and, upon reaching the slope, stepped into the river of darkness.

The womanly shape looked back at him.

Old Jack lost his breath. The surface of the entity's skin rippled like oil in all areas of its liquid form but the face, the shape of the nose and the eye sockets and the jaw line... It was Lenora. If not, it was a connection *to* Lenora. He felt it as true as any other aspect of reality.

And then the little one looked back, too.

"Jackie-boy?!" Old Jack let out a heavy sob. His feet met the cold snow at the edge of the deck when he stepped toward the strange nightscape, toward the shapes that looked like his wife and son, his family.

The simulacra continued further out into the flowing black and their liquid legs melted into the stuff. The figure of his wife turned as she sank with one last look back to him, then disappeared into the muck.

Old Jack almost followed the forms out into the ooze but stopped after a couple steps into the snow. The forms that had preceded him hadn't left any footprints. When he looked above, the night clouds had rolled back by some force of nature or otherwise and the hole in the sky revealed the starry darkness that waited over him.

The moon sat high, reddened on one side of it. In its dimmed but visible light, something caught Old Jack's attention from up the slope to the northeast. A wave of white poured down the slope, following the dark ooze. Old Jack saw, then, that it wasn't a wave of white but the end of the black goop. The stuff was collecting itself as it rolled down the hill, revealing the immaculate layer of snow underneath it, as if the powder had never been disturbed in the first place. The ooze pooled itself out onto the frozen pond. It roiled and spat and bubbled over the ice as the rest of the crawling liquid mass drained from the woods, siphoning every last drop of itself back into the whole.

When the old man glanced down at his nakedness, he saw that he was no longer slathered in the goop. It had somehow evaporated or crawled off his body and clothing when his attention was elsewhere. The coagulate had gone from his mouth, too, but the taste remained.

He could still taste her.

Strange shapes manifested among the black blob out on the pond, shapes from other worlds, from under the dominion of different gods. They churned and swelled and foamed. Eldritch geometry hardened from the broiling stuff, then broke to pieces and melted back into the rest of it. This process repeated over and over as bizarre forms molded themselves only to dissipate a moment later. In the muck, he saw Lenora again. She manifested like a phantom and disappeared just as quickly into the black, a single frame of a movie reel flashing in the nightscape.

It was then that the fear and hesitation bled almost completely over with curiosity, longing and hope. He was terrified, no doubt about it, but no god or point of resolution had ever produced such tangible offerings in his life, had ever given him something he so desperately needed, the feeling of love again. The reality of the life he had lived in was that his wife and child were dead, plain and simple, but, for whatever this *presence* was, if it was able to allow him to communicate somehow with the only ones he'd ever really loved, who sat on the other side of all of this, what else in the world was left for him to do? There was no guarantee of how many years were left before he, too, followed Death into the void. There was no guarantee he would really be 'reunited' with the dead he so desired once that happened. This could be the only chance he would have to see or feel Lenora again. It could be the only way back to her and Jackie-boy.

Old Jack's heart thumped madly in his chest. The ache of orgasm still lingered in his loins and he stood there, unable to move, and watched. His mind, body and soul was split between the decision to retreat and the decision to pursue. The tight grip of fear still clenched around his lungs but there was something else amidst the chaotic emotions, something like reverie. Whatever it was that waited for Old Jack out on the ice, with its tortures and contrasting pleasures, was beyond the speculation of any Hell of Christianity or otherwise...

Yet *she* waited for him out there, too.

And then there was a shift in the air. Something like static ran along the hairs of Old Jack's legs. The oil out on the pond animated into a singular mass and seemed to leap off the ice, impossible intent from a more impossible sight, transforming itself into a massive geometric shape. The horror and confusion forced Old Jack to take steps back, to blink his eyes to try and see the whole thing. It was a cube, perfectly scaled and balancing itself over a dozen feet in the air. It looked ominous out in the cold and not extant as simply a cube. It had a sentient quality to it, an extra *dimension* about it. Its edges swelled and reverberated, shifting between the physical realm and some other technicolor dreamscape. His eyes burned trying to look at its refraction. His mind couldn't wrap around the figure, which exhibited qualities he'd never known before, interdimensional traits that required some kind of madness for understanding.

The black mass shifted and transformed once again, dropping and flattening itself into a sheet against the ice. It reflected the moon's pale light from the sky above like a liquid mirror. Amidst its oiled surface, a hole dropped out in its center. The pit in the middle of the thing appeared like a black window in the fabric of reality, seeming to drink the moonlight rather than reflect it, like a pupil in an eye. Old Jack's stomach sank at the sight of the unearthly darkness within.

A light burst forth then. The forest was bathed in crystalline sapphire. It radiated off of the snow and the frosted bark of the trees. Beaming out of the hole in the center of the black mass was the source of the colored glow, a shaft of light that impaled the open sky above. The cloud lines had stopped rolling back at a certain point on the near horizon and they hovered in the dark distance, awaiting some unknown command to cover everything in the shroud of winter once more.

He still stood next to the chopping stump, staring into the hypnotic light from the not-so-distant pond, when a wave of heat rolled over his body. It wasn't only heat. It was a comfort of some sort, a gesture from something his body had forgotten the feeling of. The trail of warmth was ahead of him, toward the pond and the light beaming out of the black. It massaged his skin and the old muscles and bones underneath. It lapped at his ears and cheeks and wrapped around his hands and his legs, then tugged at his stomach and caressed his exposed genitals.

Old Jack could smell her again. He could smell Lenora. It came with each wave of warm light, the scents of her hair and her sex, of her breath and her skin. His body ached for her, *suffered* for her. The sapphire light was a beacon in the night, a beacon of hope. Terrifying or not, he had nothing else left in this life to hold onto except surviving and, after the taste of his ultimate desire, the one he would've gone to Hell for if only he'd known how to, there was no going back. Before tonight, he would've ridden out the rest of his days in the gentle cold of the mountains, pondering Death until the day it finally visited him. That was before tonight, however. He was lost in the sensations that now covered his body as he stared into the reverberating brightness.

Then he heard his son's laugh.

Jackie-boy...

Daddy, can we read that one again?

Jackie-boy was standing in the light, or in Old Jack's mind, smiling and holding up his favorite book of the Berenstein Bears. The old man looked upon the form of his son that he'd lost so long ago and it was in that moment that his emotions had reached their singularity, the zenith point in which nothing else mattered, past or future.

Amidst the fear of it all, amidst the years of emotional pain and heartache burning like a fire that never went out, he didn't think he'd ever find the answer, the way in which to lessen the load on his soul. In a cosmic joke, when it seemed that his sanity would be the final cost of his fate, it was in horror that he now found that answer. Tears fell from Old Jack's eyes and he sobbed as his feet took him out onto the ice, closer to the light, closer to his son.

"Oh god, Jackie-boy. I'm here, buddy." In all his life, he'd never cried as hard as he did then. Every step he took, the weight fell off of him, his soul breaking out of the shackles it had dwelt within for so many years. "I'm here, son. I'm here, buddy. I love you so much," he cried.

The beam of sapphire appeared like a portal. His son stood waiting for him in the light and Lenora stood behind their child with her hand on his head. She looked as beautiful as she ever had and Old Jack felt his soul rushing out to her, to them, to the ones that he belonged to, faster than his feet were ambling him forward. This realm, the physical reality, could no longer be home to the old man if they couldn't be here with him. All this time thinking he was "healing" from his loss... The truth was, known in the very core of his being, that it had always been denial. Life did not just go on for him after what happened. Instead, it seemed that time had stopped that painful night so long ago. *He* had stopped but the rest of the world stretched him perpetually ahead, eating and sleeping and shitting and working.

The truth was simple: though he was not in the car with them that night, Jack had died in the accident as well. There was no life without his family.

His steps picked up in pace and, as he moved out toward the middle of the pond, Old Jack's bare feet met the apron of black goop that surrounded the tunnel of light. It oozed over his toes but he paid it no mind. "Lenora," he sobbed, as if saying her name aloud would keep him from floating away from that which was transpiring. "Lenora..."

The heat from the sapphire aura was intensifying and it purified Old Jack to the bone as he closed in on it. He reached the edge of the hole in the ice, his feet covered in the goop, and leaned over it to peer down into the luminous depths.

They waited for him down there, he could see. In the light, the images of his family grew more corporeal, more *real*. The brightness in his son's eyes and the fullness of his wife's expression... They called to him, waving their arms, and the warmth rushed up to bathe him.

He fell to his knees, his fingers reaching for the oozy precipice of the deep light. He gripped onto ice that was beginning to crack and he called out to them with all of his mind and body, funneling his soul into a maelstrom of sadness, rage and relief. He shouted with everything he'd ever been, with everything he ever could be, the many different lifelines he had pondered agonizingly over the years, paths in which he hadn't lost everything, lifetimes that contained companionship rather than soul-crushing heartache.

He cried for all of it and, when the ice gave way and his body slid, Old Jack's soul was freed of its fear and loneliness, from its heartache and its longing. His body plunged into the depths and fell down, further and further into the freezing brightness. *Breathe*, Lenora whispered to him. *Just breathe it in, Jack. Come on, babe*. And he did breathe it in. He breathed in the smells of his Lenora that burned his nose and choked his throat like holy fire. He heard the laughter and sounds and memories of his Jackie-boy that burst his eardrums in the depths of it all and he felt their loving embrace as it unsheathed him of his aged skin. They called to Old Jack, *sang* to him with promises of more than just a taste of what he once had, a mere glimpse of the life he'd lost.

They called to him with the promise of an eternal reunion.

Notes

"The Further We Soar Into Madness" is original to this collection.

"The Tides of Oblivion" was originally published at Fiction Magazine's Under the Bed Magazine in 2015. Its alternate title is "The Weresalmon" and was the product of a ridiculous challenge given to me by my wonderful writers group.

"Sand and Wine" is original to this collection.

"The Gore Hole" was originally published at Fiction on the Web in 2016.

"Burials: The Speaking Dead" was originally published online in a *very* rough draft form under a different title in 2014. It was the first story I'd ever gotten published and it was in horrid shape when I submitted it, a result of my own impatience and inexperience. I learned a very valuable lesson to say the least. The version contained in this collection is much closer to what the story ought to have been.

"Angelic Tendencies" was originally published at Fiction on the Web in 2015.

"Warmth in the Winter" is original to this collection.

About the Author

Jordan writes mostly short horror but occasionally takes a stab at sci-fi and fantasy when he's got the itch. He is determined to actually finish a NaNoWriMo at some point in his life. He hails from the pines of the Pacific Northwest, hates to travel, loves to read and write, and is sincere in his appreciation for the artwork of others as well as really good beer (which he considers to be an art form, in and of itself).

"Terra autem erat inanis et vacua, et tenebrae erant super faciem abyssi..."
Genesis 1:2

Made in the USA
San Bernardino, CA
16 August 2017